THE GOOD NEIGHBOURS

Also by Nina Allan

The Rift
The Race
The Harlequin
Spin
The Silver Wind
Ruby: Stories
Microcosmos: Stories
The Dollmaker

THE GOOD NEIGHBOURS

Nina Allan

riverrun

First published in Great Britain in 2021 by

riverrun

an imprint of

Quercus Editions Limited
Carmelite House
50 Victoria Embankment
London EC4Y 0DZ

An Hachette UK company

A CIP catalogue record for this book is available
from the British Library

Hardback 978 1 52940 517 0
Trade Paperback 978 1 52940 518 7
Ebook 978 1 52940 520 0

10 9 8 7 6 5 4 3 2 1

Typeset by CC Book Production
Printed and bound in Great Britain by Clays Ltd, Elcograf S.p.A.

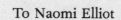

To Naomi Elliot

Come unto these yellow sands,
    And then take hands:
Curtsied when you have, and kiss'd
    The wild waves whist,
Foot it featly here and there;
And, sweet sprites, the burthen bear.
    Hark, hark!
Bow-wow.
    The watch-dogs bark.
Bow-wow.
    Hark, hark! I hear
    The strain of strutting chanticleer
    Cry, Cock-a-diddle-dow.

Full fathom five thy father lies;
    Of his bones are coral made;
Those are pearls that were his eyes:
    Nothing of him that doth fade,
But doth suffer a sea-change
Into something rich and strange.
Sea-nymphs hourly ring his knell:
    Ding-dong.
Hark! now I hear them – Ding-dong, bell.

(From: *The Tempest* by William Shakespeare)

And his work became enormously small, as if the fairies who invaded the most remarkable canvases of his earliest years of solitude were now directing the infinite littleness of the arabesques of the tip of his brush, as if, indeed, he were not painting fancies but, rather, real sitters, from a perfectly material realm of concrete dream.

(From: *Come Unto These Yellow Sands* by Angela Carter)

'ARE YOU SURE YOU'RE still up for going?' Cath said. 'Your dad will go mental.'

'He's on the mainland all day,' said Shirley, 'so he's not going tae find out, is he?'

She pressed her lips together, leaned in towards the glass. Her mirror twin floated to meet her, their mouths almost touching. Shirley had put on lipstick, a deep red, almost purplish colour called Victoria. After the plum, Cath supposed, or maybe Queen Victoria. Wear this and have lips like a queen.

'Try it if you want,' Shirley said. She offered Cath the lipstick in its golden barrel. Cath shook her head. She enjoyed the paraphernalia of cosmetics, the smooth contours of the bright plastic cases, the satiny sheen of powder in an antique compact. She hated the smell though, lipstick especially, and the way she looked with it on, as if her mouth were no longer her own, but a mouth on a poster.

'I'll do my nails instead,' she said. Painting her nails allowed Cath to be daring without feeling uncomfortable. Shirley had dozens of shades, all with different names: Heartsease, which was bright pink, the colour of Bubble Yum chewing gum. Sea Witch, Aerogramme, Shangri-La, Majestic. Cath chose Fairy Dust, a paler pink than Heartsease, and with a glittery sheen. The glitter didn't fully appear until the varnish was set. Cath loved the smell of nail varnish, which reminded her of Tipp-Ex. She flapped her hands back and forth to dry them, watching Shirley as she put in her earrings. The top of Shirley's dressing table was strewn with make-up and items of jewellery: Boots No7 foundation, 10.0.6 skin cleanser, an opened packet of the butterfly hairpins they had on sale in the newsagent's on the High Street.

Cath twisted a silver hair band between her fingers. 'We should get going or we'll miss the ferry.' She could hear Shirley's little brother Eamon downstairs, bashing out 'Three Blind Mice' on his metal xylophone, Shirley's mother Susan singing cheerfully along like Lizzie Dreams on Playdays. Susan could sing in tune but not like Shirley. When Shirley sang at the Golfers folk night back in January, the room had gone so quiet afterwards you could hear voices coming from the TV in the flat upstairs. Shirley had cracked up with laughter suddenly and Norman Bannicroft behind the bar had handed her a beer.

'Not for my daughter. She's only fifteen, or had you forgotten?'

The look on John Craigie's face, as if he meant to thump Norman Bannicroft, old Norman who was stringy as bacon rind and wouldn't hurt a fly. He'd snatched the beer out of Shirley's hand, slammed it down on the bar hard enough to make the windows shake. A thin spit of foam curled over the lip of the bottle and fumed down the side. Little by little the talk had started up again, gathering in momentum until the incident was papered over and safely forgotten.

'Are you OK?' Cath had asked her friend, later.

Shirley gave her a look. 'What are you on about?'

'You know. Your dad.'

'Fuck him,' Shirley said. She sounded pissed off, not so much with her father as with Cath, for making a song and dance out of what had happened. A moment later she was throwing herself into the arms of Tallis Carruthers, who had just come in. Tallis cut Cath dead as a matter of course, shoving her out of existence with a jab of her elbow and a turn of her head. Cath sneaked someone's vodka from where it had been left on a windowsill and added it to the Coke she had bought from the bar. She watched Shirley and Tallis, their narrow outlines in their skimpy T-shirts, the shadows they cast on the wall as they moved towards the door. Going for a smoke, most likely. Cath felt hot and heavy inside. The vodka helped, diluting the anger tensing her limbs to a background hum.

Shirley's father never looked her in the eye. 'Make your friend a cup of tea, why don't you?' His glance slipping past her as if she were invisible, yet she could feel his pent-up energy, like an unexploded bomb.

Cath's own father Colin always brought her a cup of tea when she was doing her homework, his tartan slippers thumping against the carpet as he came upstairs.

JOHN CRAIGIE WAS A carpenter. He had made Shirley's dressing table, the drawers sliding in and out with a rumbling sound as if they ran on rails, the pieces neatly jigsawed together like someone had snipped out the joints with a pair of scissors.

'Dovetails,' Shirley had told her. 'The nubby bits are called dove-tails.'

He also made Shirley's dolls' house, a project he had worked on in the evenings for more than a year. Whenever Cath was round at Shirley's she liked to play with the dolls' house, to swing open the front on its neat brass hinges and examine the perfectly tiny pieces of furniture inside, which John Craigie had also made, to flick the switch beside the front door that turned on the lights. Shirley didn't seem to mind her messing with the dolls' house, though Shirley herself made a point of ignoring it. Almost as if she was pretending it wasn't there.

'I'd like to burn it down, like in a movie,' she once confessed. 'Like when Twelve Oaks goes up in flames in *Gone with the Wind*.'

Cath put down the silver elastic and rolled off the bed. The bed was covered with a quilted counterpane, patchwork hexagons of satin and velvet, sewn together by Shirley's grandmother who lived in Ayr.

'My granny never comes over here because of my dad. She were dead against Mum marrying him,' Shirley had told her, over a year ago, when Cath was still new to the island and safe to talk to. Now Shirley talked mainly about movies and cop shows and *Top of the Pops* and all the things she meant to do once she turned eighteen.

'I'll be able to get away then, leave the island. They couldnae fetch me back neither, it would be kidnapping.'

'How did they meet then, your mum and dad?' Cath had asked.

'My granddad hired Dad to make some bookshelves for his office, for law books and stuff. They'd heard from some neighbour that

4

Dad were first rate, so they paid for him to stay on the mainland while he worked on the job. He was quiet, Mum said. He knew about birds and insects and wood, the things Mum loved. Mum had a boyfriend already though, called Wallace, believe that if you can. Meant he was cruising for a bruising right there if you ask me. Dad had a fight with him in the pub on Christmas Eve. Gave Wallace a black eye and broke his wrist. Mum and Dad were married the following year.'

Shirley's parents slept in the bedroom across the landing. Eamon, who everyone called Sonny, was still in with them. When he was bigger, Shirley said, he would get what was known as the boot room, the L-shaped room that led off the kitchen pantry. There was a third door at the end of the landing that was always closed. Just an airing cupboard, Shirley said. They had to keep it locked or else the door swung open during the night. 'Mum were always banging into it when she went to use the bathroom.'

The bathroom was on the ground floor, off the kitchen passageway. Cold and damp, plagued with spiders and harvestmen. Cath would only use it when she was desperate.

THEY CLATTERED DOWNSTAIRS. SUSAN was still in the living room, playing with Sonny. There were toys scattered about, a plastic bus with smiling animals painted into the windows, the tumbled ramparts of a stickle brick castle. Susan was kneeling on the floor, picking up alphabet blocks. She raised her head briefly as they passed along the hallway then returned to the game. Sonny growled like a cartoon tiger, squealed with delight.

5

Cath's mother, Moira, would have asked them where they were going. Susan not asking gave Cath a hollow feeling, a sense of something being wrong that she could not identify.

'She's OK,' Shirley said, as if Cath had asked her a question, which she hadn't. They started walking down the hill towards the town. Grey clouds, low mist, a faint drizzle. Cath was wearing her fur-trimmed parka, the one Shirley said made her look like an islander and not in a good way. A baggy sea-green cardigan. Doc Martens.

Shirley looked like Shirley, and Cath knew that even after the ferry crossing and the train journey and the endless wind tunnel of Sauchiehall Street the shine would still be on her, she would still look extraordinary. Not like a catalogue model or a stupid pop star but like someone who belonged elsewhere, who was going to show the world.

Your typical golden girl narrative, only with Shirley you would believe it, because you'd feel it was true.

THE BOAT WAS IN. They bought their tickets and went on board and queued up for coffee. John Craigie had forbidden Shirley from going into Glasgow without his permission, which meant basically never. I'm no' having ye wandering the streets making a mischief o' yisself. Whatever that meant. Cath's parents didn't mind her going into the city, so long as she started back before it got dark. Cath had a pass for Glasgow libraries and a subway card, so she could go to the Kelvingrove Museum and the People's Palace. Shirley didn't give a toss about museums. She wanted to trawl Buchanan Street, blag her way into gigs in the basements of pubs on Great Western Road. She used to tell the doormen she was a fashion student. Usually they believed her, or else didn't give enough of a monkey's to throw her out.

'Is that what you want to do?' Cath asked her. 'Become a fashion designer?'

'No way. I want to get on the hotel management course over at Greenock, go and work in Ibiza. Mum says she'll help me. She's got some money put by.'

Cath thought of Shirley behind a bar somewhere, on a beach somewhere, her head thrown back and laughing as she had laughed in the skinny arms of Tallis Carruthers, the image so bright and clear it was like part of the past already, a done deal, a Polaroid snapshot going green around the edges. Shirley wasn't keen on school but she knew how to work hard if she wanted something and of course she was clever. Shirley's father was sharp, but he wasn't clever. Shirley's mother probably had been clever once, but that was over now. Because Susan was scared, Cath realised, knowing the thought was true the moment it popped up. The knowledge made her shiver inside her skin, as if someone had jabbed in a needle and tugged it quickly out again.

It was difficult to understand where Shirley had come from.

Off the ferry and on to the train: Inverkip, then IBM, where Cath's father worked, the ranks of prefabs like an alien village, concrete tentacles invading the hollows of the misty hillside. Shirley plonked both feet on the worn-through plush of the opposite seat.

'Feet on the floor,' said the guard when he came to check their tickets just after Drumfrochar.

'No one's even sitting there,' Shirley said.

'Less of your cheek.' The guard clipped her ticket. 'Feet on the floor.'

Old enough to be their grandfather, hands reddened from cold.

Another half an hour and they had arrived. Out of Central and on to Argyle Street, the rush of Saturday shoppers, the black guy playing bagpipes outside St Enoch's subway. The city grumbled on like they weren't even there, an ancient grandma in a moth-eaten sweater, bottomless handbag stuffed with old receipts and Cadbury's caramels. Glasgow was foul-mouthed but basically sound, so long as you kept to the places you knew and didn't act stupid.

'Come on,' Shirley said, grabbing Cath's arm. 'We've no' got all day.'

In the big branch of Oasis on Buchanan Street, Shirley tried on three dresses and a pair of shoes. The shoes were red patent leather with five-inch heels.

'They're gorgeous,' Shirley said. She strutted in front of the mirror. Couldn't afford to buy them, but that wasn't the point. The point was knowing such shoes existed, finding out how it felt to put them on.

On Sauchiehall Street they were followed by two spotty lads wearing Rangers shirts.

'Great arse.'

'No tits though. Shame.'

'Rack off, youse,' Shirley said, turning abruptly. One of the boys took a step backwards. The other laughed. He and Shirley stood staring at each other, their expressions caught midway between pissed off and randy, seeming so alike they could be brother and sister. The other guy was scraggy as horsemeat, wore a fake leather jacket. He was pretending to look somewhere else, not wanting to catch Cath's eye in case she thought he was interested.

'Who's the ugly one?' Cath could almost hear him sniggering amongst his friends. If he had friends that was, which he had to, somewhere.

A BAR WITH A coloured awning, half pub, half cafe. Downstairs rammed to the rafters, no one cared how old you were.

'Two vodka cranberries,' Shirley yelled, trying to make herself heard above the landslide of noise. The girl behind the bar clanked down the glasses without comment, snatched the ten-pound note Shirley offered, passed her change. Shirley and Cath forced their way back through the crowd, coming to rest in the angled space beneath the stairs.

'This place is so cool,' Shirley said, though Cath could not help noticing how out of place she looked suddenly, how like an islander in her flashy make-up and too-smart dress. The kids in the bar mostly resembled the girl who had served them: shabby jeans and scuffed Doc Martens, like her own. The guy on stage had long blond dreads, steel guitar covered in decals and peeling protest stickers. He sang of the steelworkers on the Clyde, a police shooting that had happened during the Troubles. People joined in with the chorus. They seemed to know the songs by heart already.

'That could be you up there,' Cath said to Shirley between numbers. Shirley either ignored her or didn't hear. She seemed distracted, eyes flickering beneath her lashes as she scanned the room. Like she

9

was looking for someone, or someone she had expected to be there had not turned up.

'Let's have another drink,' she said finally, shouting over the music.

'We can't,' Cath shouted back. 'We don't have time.' It was ten to four. They wouldn't be on the ferry now until five fifteen, which meant they wouldn't be back on the island till almost six.

'Shit,' Shirley said. She sprang to her feet and they shuffled hurriedly through the crowd towards the stairs. Once they were outside on the street they started to run.

'ONE DAY,' SHIRLEY SAID when they were back on board the boat. 'I'll be off the frigging island for good. Drink vodka all night long until I frigging puke.' She leaned backwards, clutching the rail. 'Look at the lights,' she said. She let out a whoop then began digging for something inside her bag. She pulled out what looked like a strip of polythene but was actually a satin camisole with white spaghetti straps, trimmed with lace. Moth-pale in the glow of the harbour, it snagged and flapped in the breeze like a flag of surrender.

'Where d'you get that?'

'Nicked it from Miss Selfridge, didn't I? Easy as shit.'

Cath imagined the hand on the shoulder, the cramped back office, the uniformed officer writing down their names and addresses. All the things that hadn't happened.

'What d'you do that for? What if we'd been caught?'

'It's not like it's designer.' Shirley stuffed the camisole back in her bag. 'You won't tell, will you?'

'Course not,' Cath said. That the fear had even crossed Shirley's mind told her everything about the way things had shifted, these past few weeks. Shirley wouldn't have asked Tallis Carruthers a question like that, even though her dad owned shares in a bank and half a racehorse. Tallis wouldn't tell because Tallis went over to Glasgow to nick stuff every other weekend. She bought far more than she stole – that's what made her so good at it – but the point was that she did steal, just for the thrill of it, just because it was something she enjoyed doing.

'I'd never tell,' Cath said. Her chest felt tight, constricted. What a weird day it had been. She could have gone to the library on her own, but then she'd never have seen Shirley trying on the red stilettos.

'I know you wouldn't. It's just, you know.' Shirley came and stood beside her, their shoulders touching. The ferry came in to dock. It was almost dark. Dad would be putting the supper on. Saturday, so they'd eat in front of the television watching *Midsomer Murders*. Cath had her parents and she had the island. She was happy.

She shivered inside her parka.

'See you Monday then,' Shirley said. Under the street lamps she looked older, a ghost-forward of the woman she would never become.

'Yeah,' Cath said. 'See you.'

She watched as Shirley began her walk home, turning right towards Gallowgate before becoming a stick figure, fair hair shining in the lamplight, too far away to recognise unless you already knew it was her.

Shirley would be home in fifteen minutes, ten if she hurried. With any luck John Craigie wouldn't be in yet. By the time Shirley heard the back door go she'd be sitting upstairs in her bedroom, reading a magazine.

Cath felt a sudden rush of gladness, that Shirley had stolen the camisole. It was only worth a couple of quid anyway and at least it was something. A souvenir to remember the day by. To prove that they had been there, that they'd been together.

CATH HAD READ ABOUT the murder in the *Glasgow Herald*. Once the police tape had been taken down, she took the bus up to Maryhill to photograph the house.

Mary Chant had lived in a cul-de-sac off Rothes Drive, her three-bed semi well kept and nondescript, the same as all the others. Two minutes' walk from Maryhill Park, five from the big Asda. Driveway but no car, curtains closed upstairs and down. The front lawn was bald in places, a yellowish brown. A dry day and peculiarly still, Glasgow's bones creaking from cold as the winter set in. A man in a woollen cap emerged from one of the houses opposite, Jack Russell on a lead, orange trainers. He glanced at Cath briefly then headed off in the direction of the park. Cath found herself wanting to walk up to Mary's front door and peer in through the letterbox. Would there be junk mail on the mat, a stray electricity bill? Were people still posting stuff to the house, as if nothing had happened?

Mary Chant of Maryhill, a college lecturer in her mid-fifties, bludgeoned to death in her own living room. Mary hadn't turned up for work one day. She'd missed an important departmental meeting, which was unlike her. A colleague called her mobile: no response. Mary didn't come in the next day either, which pushed her absence into the realm of the seriously worrying. The police were notified, and Mary's body was discovered face-down on the living-room carpet, the back of her skull staved in by what police officers in detective novels invariably refer to as a blunt instrument. Forensics later concluded it was probably a sledgehammer. There was concrete dust in Mary's hair and caked into the wound.

MARY'S LIVING ROOM, STUFFED with books, a sunburst clock above the fireplace, a fifties classic. A mug of coffee overturned on the rug, Mary's handbag and house keys lying untouched on the kitchen table. The small house as told to the *Daily Record* by a next-door neighbour, the kind of details that persist long after the media attention has died down. The police were still searching for Mary's boyfriend, Ronnie Mackintosh. Ronnie was ten years younger than Mary, the manager of a local betting shop. He'd been AWOL since the body was discovered.

Mary's colleagues at the university described her as pleasant but serious, a bit of a bluestocking. She had been married, to another lecturer, but the two were separated. The idea of her with someone like Ronnie just didn't fit.

Cath took a dozen or so photographs of the front of the house, flattening the perspective, reducing the building and its immediate surroundings to a series of planes. More shots of the wheelie bins, the ruined lawn, a blurred outline on the concrete driveway that could have been part of a footprint but probably wasn't. The police and everyone else seemed convinced that Ronnie Mackintosh was the killer, but no one was saying anything about his motive. What if Ronnie had simply come home from work to find Mary murdered, panicked and gone to ground? As an explanation it sounded tenuous, too convenient, but what if it were true?

Cath turned away from the house and began walking up the road towards the park. Mary must have gone the same route hundreds of times, the thin Glasgow sunshine pale as skimmed milk across the backs of her hands. Sodden drifts of autumn leaves. A swing set, hanging disconsolate above cracked tarmac. In the distance, the man with the orange trainers walking his Jack Russell.

SHORT, DARK-BLOND HAIR FLECKED with grey, glasses, a cherry-red roll-neck sweater. The caption beneath Mary Chant's photo in the *Herald* described her as 'literature professor Mary Chant, 55'. She looked nice. She could have been anyone. There was no photograph of Ronnie Mackintosh, just a shot of the front of the Ladbrokes where he worked. The Ladbrokes had also been cordoned off for a time, while the police conducted a search, though it was open again now. Cath resisted the urge to go inside. She had never been into a betting shop before and didn't want to draw attention to herself. She took a photo of the outside instead, from across the street, trying to recapture the shot in the *Herald* as closely as possible. She was just about to head back to the bus stop when a woman came out. Belted grey overcoat, high heels, bright green scarf. Blond hair, much lighter than Mary's, probably dyed.

Cath waited until the woman was almost at the corner then

raised the Canon again and snapped her picture. The shutter clicked. Narrow back and upright posture. Gone. When Cath went through the images later, at home on her computer, she found that most were disappointing, though there was one shot of the house she was happy with, also the photo of the woman in the green scarf coming out of the betting shop, which had the clean lines and strong composition of a movie still.

The following morning Ronnie Mackintosh was on the news. Cath saw the footage just before she left for work, Ronnie being bundled into a cop car by two uniformed officers. They'd caught up with him in Dumbarton, at the home of a friend. Ronnie was tall and starved-looking and slightly stooped, the hood of his anorak pulled forward to hide his face.

'Do you think he did it?' Norah said, soon after she came in. 'What about the husband, though? He looks well dodgy.' Norah was a fashion student. She worked at Sound of the Suburbs three days a week. Liked Laurie Anderson and Laura Nyro, wore skinny jeans and ballet pumps and half-moon reading glasses. Norah was thoughtful and serious-minded but her friends were try-hard fashionistas who came in en masse to browse the second-hand vinyl. Aside from those rare occasions when one of them wanted to buy something, they all seemed bent on pretending Cath wasn't there. Cath found herself feeling agitated whenever she saw them.

'They'll turn you into an arsehole if you're not careful,' she had warned Norah once. She and Norah were in the pub, after work.

'Don't be ridiculous.' Norah laughed. 'They're insecure, that's all. Most of them will have dropped out by the end of the second year anyway.'

Norah liked to read the tabloids. They revealed the face of anarchy, she said, plus they gave her interesting ideas for her portfolio. She collected found buttons. She talked about resonance and psychogeography and sense of place. She had promised to introduce Cath to Margo Kasabian, visiting lecturer in photography at the University of Glasgow. Nothing had happened so far but Cath wasn't pushing it. She was worried that Margo Kasabian might know Adam. Norah did not know about Cath's affair with Adam Fairlie, who had been a tutor on the residential photography course Cath had attended five years before. She did know about Cath's interest in Mary Chant's murder, and saved her clippings from all the tabloids and colour supplements.

'You could make a brilliant collage out of these,' Norah said.

'I need to keep them intact,' said Cath. 'Thanks, though, they're great.'

Ronnie Mackintosh had to be the murderer, she supposed. Didn't they say that eighty per cent of murderers are known to the victim? Something in that ball park, anyway. Why else would Ronnie have run off to Dumbarton? He'd had his eye on Mary's money from the beginning. Either that or he'd found out she was cheating on him. Both these options were such clichés, though. The brief TV clip of Ronnie getting into the cop car showed a man in despair, the slumped, defeated look of someone who hadn't slept for days. Hardly the scheming killer. But what if he hadn't meant to kill her – wasn't the Ronnie in the TV clip exactly how Ronnie would look when he finally started to realise what he'd done?

*

TWO DAYS LATER, RONNIE was officially charged with Mary's murder. Norah was off. Steve had phoned to say he was stuck in a meeting with his bank manager and wouldn't be coming in until after lunch. Cath put on Bach's Italian Concerto and thought about Mary, wondered how her students were coping with the news of her murder. She thought about the woman in the green scarf coming out of the betting shop. She remembered what Norah had said about Mary's husband looking dodgy and asked herself why everyone seemed so keen to ignore him in favour of Ronnie. The papers were full of Ronnie, yet there was just the one photo of Mary's husband, a blurry headshot that gave him the hooded eyes and receding hairline of a washed-up rock musician.

What if the ex had wanted her back and Mary said no? What if he'd gone round to her place in Maryhill to have it out with her? She'd have let him in, no problem — like eighty per cent of murderers, he was known to the victim.

She supposed Ronnie was in the frame because his face fit. The ex might look like a low-grade mobster but he didn't manage a betting shop, didn't have dodgy friends, didn't shag his way around the neighbourhood or deal cocaine. The ex was a college lecturer who lived off Hyndland Road, exactly the kind of man you'd expect Mary to be with, which was presumably why the police had let him go.

'WHAT MADE YOU DECIDE to photograph them,' Norah had asked her when she started the project. 'These murder houses?'

'I like that they're ordinary — just ordinary houses. They could be in your own street, or one nearby. They're a reminder that crimes like this can happen anywhere.'

'I get it,' Norah said, and Cath believed her. Norah was always on about atmosphere. Norah didn't know about Shirley. Cath didn't talk about Shirley much. She'd never told Adam, for example, because she hated the idea of Shirley's death being used as background, as an explanation for something. What Adam would call context. Wanker. Why did the murder houses have to be any more to do with Shirley than her other projects: the fish and chip shops and seaside hotels, the junk shop cutlery, the snapshot of Norah's found buttons that had been picked up by the *Big Issue*?

An image should stand by itself. It shouldn't need context. All that stuff about core iconography is a load of bollocks.

'I don't trust words,' Cath said to Adam on the first day of the masterclass. 'I'm afraid that having to spell something out will make it less real.'

Three hours later they were in bed together. Cath had wondered plenty of times since if it had been the argument that had turned him on, the way she – just a nothing student – had dared to disagree with Adam Fairlie, prizewinning photographer who'd had a solo feature in *The Sunday Times*.

That was probably bollocks, too. Adam Fairlie was bored and liked the attention. End of story.

CLOSING THE SHUTTER AND fixing the moment, pinning down time. If she'd been pressed to give an explanation for why she took photographs, Cath would have said she liked the way capturing an image granted her the illusion of control, but who cared about wank like that except wankers like Adam?

The woman coming out of the betting shop had reminded her of Shirley, Cath realised. Just for a second. Something about the way she walked in her high heels. The hair too, though Shirley's blond had been natural, the same as the hair of the woman in the old Timotei shampoo ads, only curlier.

THE REP FROM WARNER Atlantic came in. He was excited about the reissue of an album from the 1970s, a recording by the Welsh singer-songwriter Meic Stevens.

'Hasn't been available since it first came out. Rights issues. Did you know Meic Stevens was first discovered by Jimmy Savile?'

'Not exactly the best sales pitch,' Cath said. The rep laughed and Cath put them down for three copies. After he left she put the album on the overheads. The music was percussive and raw: all blasted oaks and haunted mavericks, Celtic warriors and fairy abductions and midnight flits, Chris Taylor playing the flute like a mediaeval minstrel on strong amphetamines. Some people might call that kind of mythic folk old-fashioned but Cath liked those old stories, she found them compelling. Resonant, as Adam might say. By the time Steve turned up she was on her third play-through of the promo disc.

'What the fuck is that?' Steve said.

'Meic Stevens. The Welsh Dylan.'

'That explains it.' He sloped off into the back room to hang up his coat. Cath had been working at Sound of the Suburbs for ten years.

The shop had survived the internet boom partly through Steve's pragmatic insistence on keeping things small and also because, to a large extent, what they sold was knowledge rather than product. They had customers who had been coming in for years, and the shop's proximity to the university ensured a regular supply of new ones. The job was badly paid but it was more interesting than working for Scottish Power and Cath got a staff discount. Steve could be a cunt but he was mostly all right. More importantly, they understood one another. Steve had let her take over the buying for what he called the niche stuff, not just classical but folk and jazz too. All the music Steve wasn't interested in himself.

Cath had first got into folk because of Shirley. Shirley listened to pop and house and R&B like everyone else but she also owned a stack of vinyl records from the sixties and seventies, Incredible String Band and Fairport Convention and Anne Briggs. She used to play them upstairs in her bedroom sometimes, on an old Dansette record player with a built-in speaker.

'Used to be Mum's,' Shirley said. 'Miracle it still works.'

When Cath asked her where the records had come from, Shirley shook her head and said she didn't know, they'd always just been there. 'Anne Briggs played Glasgow once,' she added. 'Dad told me.'

'How would he know?'

Shirley gave her a look. 'Dad can sing, you know. But he only does it when he's out in the van where no one can hear him.'

'What's the point of that?'

Shirley shrugged. 'You know what he's like.'

Cath did know, and yet she knew nothing. When you were a kid things just happened. Friendships happened. Mostly they didn't survive and mostly that was fine. If Shirley were still alive – if she ran into her on the street, say, or down the Chequers – they'd have nothing to say to each other.

THE DAY AFTER RONNIE was charged, Cath told Steve she was planning to take some time off.

'Three months,' she said. 'Once Christmas is out of the way. For this project I'm working on.'

She knew he'd go nuts at first but that he'd have to accept it – they'd known one another too long for him not to and anyway, he'd find it hard to replace her. The thought of having to train someone up would do his head in. Those who'd worked at Sound of the Suburbs before her were mostly students, like Norah. Stayed for a year or two and then moved on. Steve would never admit it, but he was relieved to have someone permanent. Someone who stuck around, someone who knew the business and didn't care how rude he was.

People often thought she and Steve were an item, though they never had been.

'You are joking?' Steve said.

'You can get Norah in to do some extra hours. I've already asked her and she's fine with it. You won't even know I'm gone.'

'What am I supposed to do about all your classical shit?'

'You can email me the new releases. I'll even phone the reps for you if you want.'

He barely spoke to her for the rest of the morning but that was hardly unusual. Then he told her he was going to lunch just as she was about to go herself, came back stinking of beer.

'What dates were you thinking, exactly? Because I need you back before Norah buggers off to Milan or wherever she's going.'

'That's not until September.'

'Exactly.'

Not quite the supportive response she might have hoped for, but Cath was used to that. She and Steve would work things out because they always did.

CATH LEFT THE ISLAND at the age of eighteen, she believed for good. Her parents stayed until 2007, when her father was made redundant from IBM and they moved south again. Cath found it easier to be in touch with them after that, as if the island itself had been responsible for their estrangement. She had missed them, she realised, just the fact of them. The idea of them being gone from her life made her stomach lurch, like when you accidentally stepped into a pothole. Cath still minded about things they had said, things Moira had said especially, but she had learned to keep silent. The repercussions of bringing everything up again were too unsettling.

Moira had hated the island from the start. The draughty house overlooking the bay, which should have been grand but, Moira insisted, always made her think of an old woman huddled inside a shawl. The lack of decent shops, the ghastly weather, the feeling of being nowhere, out on a limb. The three of them, the Naylor family, embedded in the island's gritty substrate like a clump of rusty nails.

Moira: courageous, selfish, complaining, forthright in her thousand and one campaigns against minor injustice. The big stuff she could ignore, at least when it suited her, which was why Cath barely spoke to her from when she left the island until Moira and Colin moved back to Sussex five years later.

If her parents had remained on the island, Cath would probably have stayed away forever. Now, because they had left, she could return. As the ferry came into the harbour she could not help thinking about the day they had first arrived, the three of them, how cold it had been. Unusually cold, their neighbours hastened to reassure them. It's no' normally like this. The scrimshaw of ice on the upstairs windows, the broken boiler, her mother in tears.

'We can't live like this, Colin. The place is derelict.'

A plumber was called, the central heating grumbled noisily into life. Outside, through the large bay window in the living room, the ferries ploughed their ceaseless furrow across the Firth of Clyde. Cath remembered the two postcards she had bought the following morning at the post office, to send to her best friend, Carmen Ramirez, back in Horsham. It's so cooold, she had written, trying to make it sound funny. The house is ancient and there's mould in the bathroom. No ghosts yet (woo woo!) but I'll keep you posted. Cath had never seen Carmen again, though they had written to each other regularly for almost a year. The thought of Carmen out there in the world somewhere was oddly comforting. Carmen might be a doctor, she might have joined the army, she might have three kids. She might sometimes tell them stories of her best friend, Catherine, from secondary school, who went to live on a Scottish island and never came back.

*

CATH HAD FOUND A suitable rental apartment via the internet. The minimum letting period was for six months but the tariff was cheap, less than half of what a similar place would have cost her in Glasgow. The flat was on Argyle Terrace.

'I can take you up there if you wait five minutes. Kevin's out on an appointment but he'll be back any minute.' The estate agent, Jeannie Morris: trim, lively, sixtyish, silk scarf with a design of peacock feathers. She seemed eager to know what had brought Cath to the island.

'I'm a photographer,' Cath said. People tended to be less curious if you were honest. She reckoned the chances of anyone recognising her from before were slim to nil – she had been a child. 'I'm photographing all the places my family have lived. My grandmother used to have a house here. She was from Edinburgh.'

'Is that right?'

'Her name was Margaret Logan.' Distant memories of patterned tiles above an ancient Aga and a ticking clock. A sunburst clock, Cath realised, like Mary Chant's. She took the keys from Jeannie Morris, said there was no need for Jeannie to accompany her, she could find her own way. She hoped she did not sound unfriendly. She did not want to alienate Jeannie Morris, or anyone, but she always found these minor social interactions awkward, close to embarrassing. She envied Steve, who really didn't seem to give a damn what people thought of him one way or the other.

Argyle Terrace was a no-through-road, fifteen minutes' walk from the ferry terminal. Magnificent views of the bay, the advertisement had said, though the apartment itself turned out to be like most rental properties: vaguely down at heel and with a musty smell that suggested it had stood unoccupied for several months. Since the end of last season, probably. Still, it was clean, the living room with its G-Plan table would make a good work space. Cath leaned her wheelie bag against the Dralon-covered sofa and looked about. She was dying for a cup of tea. She decided to go to the Co-op and pick up some groceries, leave unpacking till later.

The Co-op used to be a Somerfield, she remembered, although the internal layout seemed more or less the same. An elderly man pushing a trolley bag saw Cath checking the price of a packet of salami and asked her if she wanted to borrow his glasses.

'You'll strain your eyes, hen, peering like that.'

'It's OK,' Cath said. 'I can't wear glasses.' The old man meant well, people usually did. Too boring and too tiring to explain.

'What's wrong with your eyes?' Shirley had asked, five minutes after they met, just came straight out with it. Cath had been told to sit next to Shirley because there was a desk free.

'They were damaged when I was born,' Cath replied. 'The doctors said my brain was starved of oxygen. My eyes have to keep moving to hold my vision steady. It's called nystagmus.'

'Does it hurt when you try to look at things? Does the picture wobble?'

'Course not. I don't even know they're doing it. I have to look at things up close sometimes, that's all.'

She tried to explain to Shirley how her vision was not blurred, but a matter of missed messages, how the further away something was the less detail her optic nerve transmitted to her brain. Like when she was trying to read what a teacher had written on the blackboard, for example.

'I can see it's writing,' Cath said. 'I just can't see what it says. Not from a distance. It's like it wriggles away from me.' She added that mostly it didn't matter because she was able to memorise what the teacher had written from the shapes of the paragraphs.

Shirley posed some of the usual questions – can you see this, can you see that, how many fingers am I holding up – but the novelty soon seemed to wear off and by the end of her second day at the Academy Cath was just Cath. At her old school in Sussex, hard, pretty girls like Shirley had mostly ignored her, or cut straight to the name-calling stage. What would now be called bullying, though Cath had not thought of it that way at the time. She had thought of it as morons being morons, their problem, not hers. If they thought of her as a freak that suited her fine.

Cath sometimes wondered if she had been drawn to photography in the first place as a way of proving to others that she could see. As a child, she had been taken for annual check-ups at the hospital, where random ophthalmologists – a different one each time – would provide a running commentary on her limitations. The doctors had no idea of how she saw the world, not really, though they continued to marvel at how well Cath was 'managing'. Their insistence on generalities – their findings seemed mostly to be calculated on how far she was able to decipher the letters on an optometrist's eye chart – made their pronouncements invalid and, as Cath grew older, increasingly frustrating. With their standardised, perfect vision, the doctors lacked the capacity to imagine how eye and brain and memory might work together, how seeing was an art that could be learned.

Cath did not blame them for this, especially since she found her condition close on impossible to describe or explain in concrete terms.

In the absence of words, her photographs worked both as explanation and rebuttal. An account of the spaces she actually moved through, in which every detail was a source of potential, even things others discounted as mundane or simply did not notice.

A scrap of purple foil lying in the gutter, a can of pilchards left behind on a windowsill, advertisements for products that no longer existed. Run-down hotels and boarded-up Woolworths stores. The stuff that worked as a marker for the act of remembering. Back at the flat, Cath made herself a cup of tea and a Marmite sandwich then unpacked her wheelie bag. After putting away her clothes she photographed the wardrobe: bow legs and oval mirror, the darkened patina of its varnish, a century old. Inside, the perfume of mothballs and an empty envelope, the characteristic, inimitable jangling of a dozen wire coat hangers. The act of photographing the wardrobe seemed to settle things: she was back on the island. Cath felt both queasy and energised. She was here to photograph a house, the house in which her best friend Shirley Craigie had been murdered. To create a visual map of the events as they had played out, as Adam might have put it. What the shrinks on the TV chat shows would call closure. All the stuff she should have dealt with a million years ago.

Aye, but maybe you weren't ready.

Maybe you're right.

She realised that Adam had no idea where she was, and was surprised by how much pleasure the knowledge gave her.

THE STREET LAMPS HAD come on. Argyle Terrace, heavy with the scent of brine and the cries of herring gulls. Cath walked along the front in the direction of the Winter Gardens. She noticed a toy bus, lying on its side on one of the benches by the pitch and putt. Cath touched its plastic carapace, wished she'd brought her camera, hoped the child who had left it behind would be back to collect it. They'd be missing it by now, would be feeling upset, probably. She crossed the road to the Black Bull pub, looked in through the window. The bar was more or less empty, just two blokes in hoodies drinking Tennent's and scrolling through their phones.

Cath went inside. She asked the woman behind the bar for a whisky. 'Highland Park, please, no ice.'

'You on holiday then, love?'

'Kind of.'

'Cold night, isn't it?'

'Not as cold as Glasgow.'

The woman laughed and rang up her change. Cath took her whisky and went to sit at one of the tables by the window. The Tennent's drinkers ignored her. One had put down his phone and was doing the crossword in the copy of the *TV Times* that someone had left behind on a neighbouring table. Cath sipped her drink, stared out through the glass. The light was almost gone. Cars and lorries were queuing to get on the ferry. Like she'd never been away. She returned to the flat to find an email from Adam, suggesting they meet for coffee 'to talk things over'. Cath thought about not replying then shot off a one-liner: **out of town for a while, maybe when I get back.**

Maybe, maybe not more like.

She congratulated herself on not telling him where she was.

3 ·

THE FACTS OF THE case were straightforward, or at least they appeared to be. At approximately 15:35 on the afternoon of Thursday, 25 August 2001, John Eamon Craigie was driving his pickup along the A844 in the direction of Straad, a hamlet of some two hundred residents on the island's west coast. A mile or so out of town he swerved to avoid an oncoming Ford Granada and lost control of his vehicle. The truck plunged into the ditch that bordered the road, coming violently to rest against a low stone wall. The impact propelled John Craigie through the windscreen. The driver of the Ford Granada, Angus Livingstone, ran to a nearby cottage to phone for an ambulance, afterwards returning quickly to the scene of the crash.

'I wasn't sure what to do,' he explained when the paramedics arrived. 'They tell you not to move them, don't they? He looks pretty bad.'

The ambulance arrived in less than ten minutes. John Craigie, identified from his wallet and driving licence, was pronounced dead at the scene. Two police officers were dispatched to Craigie's home on

Westland Road with the intention of informing his family. They found the kitchen door standing wide open, and a brief search revealed the murdered bodies of John Craigie's wife, Susan, and her two children: three-year-old Eamon, known as Sonny, and Shirley, who was fifteen. All three had died from gunshot wounds. Susan and Sonny were inside the house. The body of Shirley Craigie was discovered in the extensive back garden of the cottage. Scratches on her arms and legs suggested she had tried to escape through the underbrush that served as a boundary between the Craigie property and the neighbouring farm.

There was panic at first, rumours of a murderer on the loose. Householders were advised to be vigilant, to keep their children inside. Such rumours, it seemed, proved to be unfounded. Less than forty-eight hours later, police issued a statement confirming they were not looking for anyone else in connection with the murders, that initial forensic investigations strongly suggested that John Craigie was the killer. A number of local witnesses came forward to give statements describing Craigie's violent temper, his controlling behaviour, his lack of close friends.

The murder weapon – the gun – was never found. Police eventually concluded that the murderer must have thrown it into the Greenan Loch on his way out of town.

'THEY'VE ALL BEEN MURDERED,' Moira was saying. She'd just come in from Somerfield's. 'Shot, apparently. The whole family.'

She dumped her shopping bags on the kitchen table and began to unpack them.

Colin put down his newspaper. 'What do you mean, murdered?'

'Susan, Shirley, the little boy as well. People are saying it could have been the father.' She seemed about to add something else then changed her mind. 'Where's Catherine?' she said instead. Cath appeared in the kitchen doorway. She'd come downstairs to get a 7UP. She still wanted a 7UP. She was thinking about the book she'd been reading, *Sophie's Choice*. The idea that it was Shirley Mum was talking about seemed unpinned from reality, like a news report, a story you listened to or overheard while you were busy with something else.

This is how it happens on TV, Cath remembered thinking. This is where the camera zooms in close, where the person being told looks blank, then shocked, then horrified. Where they reach up to cover their mouth with their hands, maybe. If the programme is really cheesy they might let out a scream.

She could feel the weight in her stomach, what was called the weight of knowledge, she realised later, though she still didn't want to believe it because believing changed everything. What she wanted was to call Shirley, who was most likely not dead or anything like that but sprawled on her bed with her headphones on, or else she was down the yacht club, bumming fags. If she could only speak to Shirley, time would wind back again.

I heard you'd been murdered.

Is that right?

Shirley would laugh the place down. She'd think it was hilarious.

'I can't say I'm surprised,' Moira said. 'I couldn't stand that man. She should have got out years ago. Aisling Carruthers says the place is like a slaughterhouse.'

'Moira,' Colin said. He stood up from his chair. Cath remembered how he'd patted her shoulder, tried to make her sit down.

'I'm going upstairs,' Cath said. She needed to be out of there before she threw up or began to feel faint or started crying. If she started crying Mum would try and hug her, which considering how Moira felt about Shirley might make Cath lose it completely. She could hear a buzzing in her ears and her palms were sweating. Because it was roasting, even inside, and because Shirley didn't feel gone, not at all, not yet. Cath imagined dialling her number, hearing the ring tone, waiting, hoping.

What if the police answered, asked her why she was calling? What would she say?

She could ask to speak to Susan, only hadn't her mother just said that she was dead, too?

There was a photo of Susan in a silver frame on Shirley's dressing table. The Susan in the photo was younger than the Susan of now. She had her hair tied up in a scarf and a baby bump the size of Mount Everest.

'That's me in there,' Shirley had told her. 'A month before I was born. Dad took it.'

Susan was smiling and she was wearing make-up. She looked happy and more importantly she looked alive.

A HOT, HOT DAY, a summer the townspeople would talk about for years afterwards, and in the hours and days following the murders, the island seemed beset by an eerie stillness. The sky looked on, merciless, an unflinching blue eye. People gossiped quietly on street corners and at the butcher's, the baker's, the hardware store there was only one subject – no other subject seemed permissible. The Craigies' names, Cath couldn't help noticing, were barely mentioned. The consensus seemed to be that they were unmentionable, that the Craigies had somehow been complicit in their own destruction. In any case, everyone knew, in that island way, who you were talking about.

The heat made things worse. In weather like this, kids should have been pelting each other with grass clippings, getting eaten by clegs, diving off the pier which was strictly forbidden, watching the tourists in their cardboard sunhats disembarking from the *Waverley*. Instead, there was a candlelit vigil in the town's central square.

'Should we go, do you think?' Colin said. 'Show willing?' A suggestion made mainly for Cath's sake, Cath could tell. She knew already that Colin and Moira were in agreement for once, that such open demonstrations of what Moira called sentiment were not their style.

'You go, if you want to.' Moira's lips tightened. 'I can't stand that kind of display. I don't see the point.'

Cath slipped out quietly after supper, pretending she was going for a walk. When she reached the square she hovered at the edge of the crowd feeling vaguely uncomfortable, as if she'd accidentally gatecrashed a private party. Then someone produced a guitar and started singing. Some people were crying. Cath wondered how many of them had known Shirley, how many of those who had known her had actually liked her. The man with the guitar had his eyes closed. The song he was singing sounded familiar. Cath thought it might even have been at Shirley's that she'd heard it but its name escaped her.

Blackwaterside, you dopehead. Anne Briggs.

Cath felt a lump in her throat.

How did he know?

He didnae frigging know. It's a folk standard. Every bugger sings it.

The crowd stood silently, listening. The song dispersed in the hot mauve air. Like a ghost, Cath thought. Like the last song, ever.

Don't be daft. I wouldnae be seen dead here.

Shut up.

Cath walked quickly away, her eyes on the ground. The late ferry came into the harbour. No one saw Cath leave, or seemed to have noticed she had been there in the first place.

The girls in Shirley's class took to wearing black armbands. By the time the schools went back in September the armbands were gone, but even so the closeness between them lingered like a guilty secret, a peculiar group mentality that set them apart. Cath was not included in the armband craze, or in anything. She felt like a moth trapped under a glass. She could see and hear and think but she could not fly out. The idea that any of these gestures had to do with Shirley seemed like an insult.

Anger rose up to cover her reasoning, like a cloak. She was not used to anger, or not anger like this. The anger she normally went in for was at one remove, the kind that made her excel in school debates, even though there were plenty that resented her for shooting her mouth off. Banging on about nuclear disarmament and never a thought for the thousands of jobs we'd lose. They're never gonnae drop the bomb now anyway so shut your mouth.

This new anger had no words attached, just fury especially at Moira for what she thought of the Craigies. Her mother had as good as said that Susan had it coming. If that was true then why had no

36

one tried to warn her and where did that leave Shirley? Fury at God, for being so hamstrung, that was if God existed, which He probably didn't. What the hell was the point of a hamstrung god?

BEFORE SHIRLEY DIED, CATH had been planning to go to university, to study law, or Russian, or politics, she couldn't decide. A new enthusiasm every week and no sense of the future other than knowing that it would bring an end to the life she had. This knowledge had terrified her even as she pursued it. Cath had always attached herself to places rather than to people: the pub across the road from their old house in Horsham, the patch of wasteland behind the Academy, and of course the ferry terminal, which was really the island, and everything about the island she privately cherished.

After the murders there was only her anger, the satisfaction of rejecting everything that had been expected. What Moira called the deliberate sacrifice of her prospects, and for what?

'You can't bring back the dead,' Moira railed. 'What good is it going to do her, you ruining your future?'

CATH HAD HAD THIS ridiculous idea, that she would leave the island for good and become a cop. She could sit the exams while she was in training, she knew that already, and Cath wanted to be a detective, more than anything. Was there a part of her that believed this was a way of making sense of what happened to Shirley? Maybe, though she didn't dwell on the reasons. Joining the police was what she meant to do.

She didn't even get to the preliminary interview. She didn't meet the medical requirement. Cath should have realised this earlier of course. How stupid can you get? Moira ranting over the phone that she shouldn't have gone running off like that, she should have applied to university, become a lawyer. No eye tests required for becoming a lawyer and what was she going to do now, she'd end up wiping down tables in McDonald's, she should have listened.

Cath worked in cafes for a bit then front of house at the Glasgow Film Theatre. The job was fine but the pay was shit and the only place she could afford to live was a shared house at the wrong end of Sauchiehall Street. She hated the house, not because her room was tiny but because her housemates were all wankers who never put out the bins. She applied for the job with Scottish Power so she could qualify for a mortgage and get her own place.

She stuck it out at SP for three years then left to work for Steve. All that time she was taking photographs, and there were moments when she wished she'd tried to get into art college when she first left the island. She turned instead to books, photography magazines, exhibitions at the Mitchell Library and GoMA. Over time she came to recognise her heroes: Vivian Maier and Daido Moriyama and Stephen Shore.

Cath still secretly thought of herself as a detective. She'd told that to Steve once, when they were both drunk. He'd snorted, said police work was mostly boring – burglaries and car thefts, maybe the odd cannabis farm. The kind of cases you saw on the cop shows came along once in a lifetime, that's if you were lucky.

'You're not a cop, you're a private investigator,' he said. 'Walking the mean streets of Partick.'

They'd both burst out laughing, rolling about in their seats like teenagers. She knew Steve admired her work, though they rarely spoke about it.

Did Steve have a girlfriend or boyfriend? Cath had known him ten years and counting, and still had no idea.

THE CRAIGIE HOUSE ALWAYS had that shabby look, mostly because of John Craigie's ancient pickup on the drive, the rickety car port, the muddy front porch overflowing with Wellington boots, rusted garden implements, logs for the woodburner. More than that though, the sense of ruin had emanated from John Craigie himself. In spite of all Susan's efforts to cheer the place up – the potted geraniums and wallflowers, the beds of nasturtiums and snapdragon beneath the front windows – her husband's presence hung overhead like a thundercloud, even when he was out.

'The man's got a screw loose if you ask me,' Moira insisted. She didn't like going to the Craigies' house, and it was usually Colin who came to collect Cath when she'd been over there. He even stayed for a cup of tea sometimes. Everyone liked Dad, even John Craigie, not that he ever said as much, just grunted and inclined his head, shoved his hands in his pockets. To hide the dirt, most likely, the grime under his nails, the half-healed grazes. Not that Dad would have minded. Dad barely seemed to notice what people looked like. It was their manners he cared about, their way of being.

'She's a nice girl, that Shirley,' he had said once. 'Funny, and kind.'

Moira gave him a look. She thought Shirley was a bad influence, one of those girls who wore make-up to school when the rules forbade it, who sneaked cans of lager out of the bowling club, who would clearly come to nothing. 'I don't like Catherine going there. Not on school nights.'

Not ever, was what she meant. It was awful, how these things came back to you when you thought you'd forgotten.

THE CAR PORT WAS gone. So was the pickup, obviously. In its place stood a small green hatchback, a Yaris, parked on the cracked hardstanding next to a builder's skip. The skip was piled high with assorted detritus: rolls of ripped-up carpet and bits of plasterboard and a set of old dining chairs. The wrought-iron gates, with their leaping hares, were still intact.

Cath walked past the house without stopping. When she came to the crest of the hill she crossed to the opposite pavement and began walking down again. Her stomach churned with nausea, or hunger, or something between the two. It was relief she felt most of all, that the house was still there and still recognisable, relief misplaced yet so intense she could almost smell it. As if someone had told her Shirley was alive after all, that the story about the murders had been a mistake.

'Yeah, that's right, buggered off to Australia. Married a sailor in the Aussie navy, apparently. She's living in Brisbane now, the jammy bitch.'

The scent of damp soil, crushed leaves. Cath imagined ringing the doorbell, hearing footsteps in the hallway. What would she say? She'd read an article in the *Observer* once about people who lived in houses where people had been murdered, how they coped with what the interviewer had referred to as the legacy of violence. Some chose to investigate further, to delve into the facts. Others hadn't seemed bothered at all. 'I leave that stuff to the ghost hunters,' one of them had commented. 'I'll bet every house in Britain is a murder house, if you go back far enough.'

As Cath crossed the road again to the house side the front door of the Craigie house opened and a woman came out. Cath drew in her breath. The woman was tall and skinny, bushy hair caught back in a bandana, dark skin and faded jeans. Hard to make out her features from this distance but that was normal when the person was someone Cath didn't recognise. Once Cath knew someone well enough, her brain would fill in their details for her from even twice this distance, painting in everything she remembered like a 3D imager.

'Hi,' the woman said. 'Are you looking for someone?'

Cath smiled, gave a cursory wave. 'No. Thanks. Sorry to bother you.'

She hurried away, her eyes on the pavement. By the time she was back down by the Co-op she was almost running. She was kicking herself for not saying something more useful, for not asking the woman's name at least. Now that the moment was lost, the ways of playing it differently expanded inside her mind, infinite and easy. Hi, my name's Cath, what's yours? My best friend used to live here. When did you move in?

THE LAST TIME CATH saw Shirley, she had been buying an ice cream in Zavaroni's. She was standing at the counter with her back to her but Cath had no trouble recognising her, even from a distance. With someone she knew well, recognition was less like seeing and more like feeling: the way a person moved or stood, the way they smelled, the shape of their handwriting, the clunk of knowing Cath experienced at the sight of them. An aura, was how Cath usually described it, though that wasn't right either. She supposed it was a kind of synaesthesia.

Yellow T-shirt, cut-off jeans, those strappy white sandals with the three-inch heels Shirley had worn into school once and been made to exchange for a pair of monster plimsolls from the lost property cupboard.

Cath was hurrying to get home, which was why she didn't stop and say hello. That was the excuse she gave herself anyway, later, though there were other reasons.

She'd hesitated for a second, then crossed the road, hoping Shirley wouldn't turn around before she reached the other side.

That was the day before the murders, the Wednesday, hot as the Thursday, pitilessly blue. Cath had been across to the mainland to see Victoria, a girl she'd happened to say hello to two months before at an exhibition that was showing at the Pavilion, a photography showcase on island wildlife. Cath had first noticed Vicky staring at a photo of cormorants. Her hair was in long plaits, right down to her waist. Her dad was something at IBM, like Colin, only higher up. Her mum was half Russian, and a doctor. They lived just over the water, in Colintraive.

Cath wouldn't normally have made the first move like that, but with Vicky things felt different, as if they already knew each other.

'Have you seen the photograph of the moths yet?' Vicky replied. 'Oak eggars. We get them in the garden sometimes.'

Cath said she hadn't seen them and Vicky led her around the

displays to where they were, *Oak Eggars, by Martin Scrimshaw*, the two plump-bodied insects the same bright and tawny orange as a ginger cat. Shirley would have made a joke about the moths, or not been interested. Vicky stared at them quietly for a moment then turned to Cath and asked who her favourite writers were.

Cath was enthralled, by the moths and also by Vicky, who seemed to take it for granted that she and Cath were friends now, that they would turn this chance acquaintanceship into something deeper.

She sees me, Cath thought, the particular choice of words making her blush even though she had not said them to Vicky or even spoken them aloud. She had been to Vicky's house twice and there were plans for Vicky to come over for supper the following week. The visit had never happened though. Vicky's mum wasn't keen, not after the murders. She made it clear she didn't want Vicky going over to the island until the police found out for certain who the killer was. Time had passed and term had started and Vicky made friends with a new girl at her school in Dunoon. They never got round to fixing another date and that was that.

Shirley never knew Vicky existed. If she had, she would have thought she was stuck up, a total nerd. When Cath saw Shirley in Zavaroni's that afternoon, she'd crossed the road to avoid getting into an argument about where she had been and what she'd been doing. Again, that was what she told herself, though it was simpler than that: she'd crossed the road because she didn't want to speak to Shirley at all. Not forever, just for then. She was still thinking about Vicky, about the afternoon in Vicky's back garden talking about where they were going to apply to college and maybe going interrailing the following summer.

'We could go all the way to Moscow,' Vicky had said. She had a grandmother living there, apparently, only Vicky didn't say grandmother, she said babushka, which had both of them laughing their guts out, screeching the Kate Bush song in high-pitched voices.

After Shirley was dead, Cath was left with the feeling that her afternoon in Vicky's garden had been cursed somehow, that she had made it cursed by not stopping to chat with Shirley on her way home. If she had stopped even for five minutes, the future would have been different.

Hiya!

Want an ice cream?

OK but I can't stay long or Mum will go off on one.

They would have sat at one of the tables outside, Shirley gleeful with some random piece of gossip or other bullshit, Cath wondering what the point was and why everything seemed different from last summer and how it must be her fault somehow, the way nothing lasted. But none of that would have mattered anyway because Cath would have said hey, want to go to Loch Fad tomorrow, mess around, take a picnic, whatever? She would have made the suggestion more from guilt than anything else – guilt over Vicky – but Shirley wouldn't have known that, she'd have said yes. She wouldn't have been at the house when the murders happened.

Instead, Cath had crossed the road, and Moira had said of course it wasn't her fault, not just the murders but the way that she and Shirley had been drifting apart.

'This was bound to happen sooner or later, darling, it's inevitable.'

Inevitable that Cath would find other friends, friends she had more in common with, friends like Vicky. Inevitable that Shirley Craigie would wind up being murdered by her appalling father.

A shadow on the ground. A flash of fair hair and a yellow T-shirt. Shirley had needed help, a fact that seemed obvious in retrospect, yet no help had been offered, not by Cath, not by anyone. Unlike Susan, Shirley had run. She had tried, in her final moments, to get away.

MUCH HAD BEEN MADE of the dirty footprint on the Craigies' living-room carpet. The footprint turned out to match the boots John Craigie was wearing when his truck left the road. Big deal, it was his house, he was entitled to leave footprints. Cath wondered if the officers leading the investigation had had similar thoughts, but decided to ignore them. There had been no other footprints for them to consider, after all.

Cath would never have said she was frightened of John Craigie, not exactly, she just didn't like him. She didn't like him because he was moody, and because he didn't like her. She knew he found her arrogant, a little madam. The rubbish she liked to talk about, the way she would always stop speaking when he entered the room. The way she knew she could escape him and his pathetic rules, just by going home at the end of the day.

She didn't like him because he was so different from her own father, mild-mannered Colin Naylor, heading off for work each day on the early ferry, its headlights cutting across the firth in the February dark. Drinking his coffee and reading the newspaper on a Saturday morning, his baggy corduroys and Hush Puppies, the way he would always bring Cath tea and biscuits when she was doing her homework.

His jokes, which were invariably ghastly but every now and then so hilarious you'd almost piss yourself. So different from Moira, who never told jokes because she was afraid of looking foolish, or forgetting the punchline.

'Your mum thinks I'm stupid,' Shirley had said to her once. Cath had told her not to be silly, that was how Moira was, that's all, she was like that with everyone. Brushing Shirley's words aside like they had never been spoken, feeling mortified all the same because she knew they were true.

4 ·

'HI,' THE WOMAN SAID, looking up, her eyes filling more or less instantly with *déjà vu*. She obviously recognised her and Cath felt embarrassed. Cath had managed to convince herself the woman would not remember their earlier exchange and yet here she was, remembering, thinking Cath was some sort of stalker most likely and maybe she was right. Cath had been wondering for days how she might best approach the woman in the Craigie house and in the end she wrote a note, taking care to include her mobile number and email address, saying she used to know a family who lived there a long time ago and would it be all right if she had a look around? She would like to take some photographs, if possible.

She had intended to shove the note through the letterbox and sneak away again. She ended up reciting its contents as if they were a script she'd learned.

The woman smiled. Warily, Cath thought, though she could have imagined that part. The woman had been outside, unpacking shopping from the back of the Yaris, so there was no way Cath could leave without saying something. Without admitting, at least partly, why she was there. 'You can come in now, if you like,' the woman said. 'The place is a bit of a tip, though.'

She should have pretended to be a journalist, Cath thought belatedly, come to the island to do a story about the murders. She could have asked questions then, any questions she wanted, though if the woman did not know about the murders already that could have been awkward.

'I'm Cath,' Cath said. 'Cath Naylor.' The woman slammed the boot, activated the central locking. Her hands were large and beautiful, the nails painted with silver nail polish.

'Alice. Alice Rahman.' She smiled again, and Cath found herself wondering if there was such a thing as just instantly deciding to be in love with someone. Not to do anything about it or even want anything, ever, except to admit the truth of what you felt and be content. If this was, in fact, the finest kind of being in love, because it need never be spoiled.

Sounds wacko Jacko to me. You don't want to go there.

I don't mean her. I mean in general. I was just thinking.

Och aye sure you were.

The leaky porch with its leaded windows, its cracked Victorian tiles, the two steps off the hallway that took you down into the kitchen. The scent of dust and breakfast cereal and old newspapers, and all the time she was looking about herself Cath could not help thinking that the last time she was here, Shirley and Sonny and Susan had still been alive.

'When did they live here?' Alice was saying. 'The people you knew?'

'About twenty years ago.'

To the left of the front door, the living room. Sonny had died in the living room, the papers had said, curled on his side on the carpet as if he had simply fallen asleep in the midst of a game. Cath remembered the carriage clock on the mantelpiece, the picture over the sideboard, a painting of Susan from before she was married.

'Who painted it?' Cath had asked Shirley.

'A friend of Mum's called Melanie. She was one of Mum's bridesmaids.'

Susan in a green dress, holding a red clockwork rooster, painted with blue and yellow swirls. According to Shirley, Susan still had the rooster in a box somewhere. If you turned the key in its chest it made a cock-a-doodle-doo sound.

The living room, where the footprint had been, the footprint that placed John Craigie at the scene of the crime. Craigie had most likely shot the toddler in a panic, the police suggested. To prevent him from saying anything, later.

The cast iron woodburner, the blackened beam over. The sofa was different of course, the sofa was Alice's.

'Take a seat,' Alice said. She gestured towards the sofa, bent to remove her shoes. 'I'll make us some coffee.'

She disappeared into the kitchen. Cath remained in the hallway. The row of brass coat hooks, the telephone table with the barleytwist legs. The table had been Susan's, Shirley had told her, brought over from her parents' house in Ayr. It had not occurred to Cath that there might still be things in the house that had belonged to the Craigies. The wallpaper was the same, too – dark green with a repeating pattern of catkins in an Arts and Crafts style.

She followed Alice into the kitchen. The old range was still there.

New fridge, new washing machine. Still that odd arrangement where you had to go through the pantry to get to the boot room. The room that would have been Sonny's if he hadn't been murdered. A developer would change that in five minutes – rip out the inner hallway, make a larger kitchen-diner, open things up. Create what celebrity architects liked to refer to as an interesting space. Property porn, Norah called those TV home design programmes, though Cath wasn't sure if she meant it as an accusation or simply as a factual description of what she saw.

Two mugs on the countertop, an open milk container. Alice turned to face her as she came down the steps.

'Look,' she said. 'I have to ask you. Is this about the murders?'

It said so much about Alice, Cath realised later, that she'd brought up the subject now, straight away, before either of them started lying about what they knew. Establishing a relationship under false pretences. A lot of people wouldn't have opened up like that. They would have waited to find out what Cath would admit to and what she wanted. They would have chosen, however subconsciously, to retain the advantage.

Alice seemed just to want them not to say anything they might regret at a later stage.

'You know about that?' Cath said. She could feel herself blushing.

'The estate agent told me. Jeannie Morris? She said she thought she should give me the facts before someone else did it for her. So I wouldn't try and pull out of the sale later, I suppose. She said it happened ages ago.'

'In 2001. The whole family was killed. Shirley was my best friend.'

Cath tried to think if she'd ever spoken the facts out loud like that before and thought probably not. Didn't think so, anyway, couldn't remember. The sound of the words in the open air gave them an unreal quality, the news in brief. *Bullet* points, ha ha. 'They were shot,' she added, to clarify. Best to go the whole hog. 'I left the island not long after it happened, when I was eighteen.'

'I'm sorry.'

'I'm sorry too. I should have said something sooner.'

'No, look, it's all right. These things are tricky. Let's go and sit down.'

She said she did not mind knowing, that she would rather know everything, then asked how Cath took her coffee.

'Just black is fine, thanks.'

Alice handed her one of the mugs, added two spoonfuls of sugar to the other with a dash of milk. Her clothes hung on her loosely, as if she had lost weight recently. They went through to the living room.

'How come you're here, anyway?' Cath said. 'On the island, I mean?'

They sat side by side on Alice's sofa, and she was surprised, amazed even, by how normal it felt to be doing that. As if their coming together was natural and to be expected. Like two sailors who had been shipwrecked separately but on the same island. It was bound to happen.

What's with the Robinson Crusoe stuff? That's way out, even for you. Maybe you just like each other.

Shut up.

Alice's sofa was covered with leather, and over that a loosely woven blanket that smelled of sandalwood. Opposite, the pale, oblong outline of where the Craigies' sideboard used to be. The ghost of a ghost.

Alice laughed. 'That's a long story. I'm a financial analyst, or at least I was. I resigned from my job last August, spent every penny I had on this place. Saheed thinks I'm crazy. He's been so supportive about me chucking in work but I know he's hoping I'll get bored and go running back to London.'

'Saheed?'

'My husband. He comes up at weekends. Most weekends, anyway. We met at uni.' She drummed her fingers against the side of her coffee cup. 'I was earning a lot of money. I mean like, a lot. I hated the job though and it was making me ill. Not only the stuff some of Saheed's friends like getting up to but the whole attitude. Saheed says I brooded on things too much but that's what I'm like. It's hard to explain. I'm good at maths, that's all. I don't buy into the lifestyle. That was never what I wanted.'

'What do you want?'

'I guess that's why I came here. To find out.'

'Did you have second thoughts about this place? You know, when Jeannie Morris told you what happened here?'

Alice shook her head. 'I don't believe in ghosts. And it's not like the house hasn't been lived in since. Jeannie says it was rented out. The only reason it came on the market was because the guy who owned it died and his family decided to sell.'

'Did Jeannie say who he was? The guy who owned it?'

'I never asked. The vendors did everything through a solicitor – I never even spoke to them. Their name's on the contract but I don't know if it's the same name as the man who died. Why?'

'I'm curious, that's all. Back when it happened, there was talk of Susan's brother coming over to sort out the house, but Shirley never mentioned having an uncle. None of Susan's relatives ever came here, so far as I know. They didn't approve of Susan marrying John Craigie. That's what Shirley said, anyway.'

'John Craigie was the murderer?'

'Shirley's dad, yes.'

'How long were you living here? On the island?'

'Five years, from when I was thirteen. My parents are back down south now. Mum hated the climate. I think in their own way they wanted to leave as much as I did. We've never really talked about it.'

'Too much baggage?'

'That's one way of putting it. What do you think of the island so far?'

'Wet.'

They both laughed. 'Do you have big plans for the house?'

'Just to strip out all the old carpets and get the floors sanded. That's enough for now, anyway. The range and the stove are both in good nick, thank God, and I've had the chimneys swept. Saheed thinks I should have everything open plan but I quite like all these weird little rooms. I'm going to turn the one at the back of the kitchen into an office – it gets loads of light in there. Do you want to see?'

The boot room, Sonny's room. Cath didn't mention Sonny to Alice. It didn't seem right. Strange to think that if Sonny were still alive he would probably have left home by now anyway, escaped to the mainland like everyone else. Fireman, care worker, hairdresser, tinker, tailor, soldier, spy. He wouldn't give a damn what happened to his old room, or the stuff that was in there, the football posters and *Doctor Who* figures, the pop idols or porn stars or whatever else he turned out to be into. Anything to get away from that father of his who favoured him over Shirley, everyone knew it, but who still clipped him round the ear every second moment right from around the time he learned to answer back.

Or maybe not, maybe Sonny would have grown up to be just like him. Wasn't that what normally happened – like father, like son? Alice led the way through the pantry and into the L-shaped room Susan was permanently in the process of redecorating but that always reverted inexorably to its base state, which was a junk room. There had been a tea trolley in there, one of those that ran on castors, a standard lamp with a yellow shade that reminded Cath of her grandmother's house, not her Edinburgh granny but Granny Foxie, Colin's mother Felicity who was obsessed with the royal family and who they used to visit every other week until they moved north.

In the back room of the Craigie house, the carpet had already been taken up. A concrete floor, patterned tiles around the hearth, the same as the tiles in the porch. Against the back wall, a dust-covered bureau. An octagonal card table with half its baize torn off. Cath thought she recognised the bureau but couldn't be sure. The Craigies' house had been full of such things, all in a state of pre- or partial restoration.

'You never told me what you do,' Alice said. She was looking around the room, as if the things that were in there surprised her with their presence, every time.

'I work in a record shop,' Cath said. 'But I'm a photographer. I'm hoping to go freelance one day. That's why I came back here.'

'To take photos?'

'I'm doing a project. Making images of the places where people have died. I mean, not just died, been killed. I bet you think that's weird.'

'Not weird, interesting. Like those Jack the Ripper walks people go on in Whitechapel.'

'In a way it's like that but I'm more interested in the places no one knows about. Ordinary houses on ordinary streets. The kinds of places you wouldn't notice unless someone told you.'

'And you want to photograph this house?'

'Yes. If that's all right with you.'

'It's fine,' Alice said, and Cath suddenly wondered if that would be it – they'd arrange a time for her to come back with her camera, she'd reel off a couple of dozen shots and then that would be the end of her and Alice. They wouldn't meet again unless they happened to bump into each other in the Co-op. Hi, how are you? Fine thanks, see you around. For a moment it felt like a landslide was happening inside her, then Alice was saying she should come over at the weekend anyway, that she should meet Saheed.

'I know he'd love to hear about your project. Saheed's addicted to true crime shows – *CSI* and *Making a Murderer* and all that. Come for supper on Saturday.'

'I don't want to intrude.'

'Don't be silly. He'll be relieved to know I'm not completely alone here. I know you'll get on.'

'That would be great. Only if you're sure, though.'

You do like her, don't you? I knew it.

Fuck off.

Walking back down the hill, Cath wondered if Alice had already told Saheed about the Craigie murders. She kept going back over what had just happened, the unlikeliness of it, sitting having coffee just yards from where Sonny had been killed. A forensic scientist would probably tell you there were still traces of it — Sonny's blood — ingrained in the living-room floorboards, that you could never be rid of them entirely. Short of burning the house down and maybe not even then.

For more than an hour after arriving back at Argyle Terrace, Cath found she could not get properly warm. She thought of her mother, the way she had hated the island and the north in general. That place, she called it, as if mentioning it by name might bring down a curse. Cath made herself some supper and watched TV, the most recent episode of a police procedural she'd been following about a female murder detective in Naples. A young boy had been kidnapped and there were suspicions of Mafia involvement. At the centre of the episode was a tense, well scripted scene in which Anita Branco was slapped down by her chief inspector for refusing to turn a blind eye to the activities of known criminals.

Branco was tough, though. Her furious, sweary comeback showed up the chief inspector for the dullard he was. The series had been written by a husband and wife, Cath noticed as the credits rolled, which explained a lot.

The catkin-covered wallpaper in Alice's hallway had survived for longer than Susan and Shirley, and now Alice was planning to have the walls stripped that would soon be gone, too. Strange to think that if Cath had never come back to the island, she would never have known the wallpaper was still there. Seeing it before it was taken down seemed important, which sounded ridiculous when you thought about it, though Cath felt certain Anita Branco would understand how she felt.

Being a detective is about taking notice, Branco had said, which accounted at least in part for why Cath admired her so much. For Anita Branco, being a cop was about challenging what people thought they knew, uncovering the secret truths that lay beneath. It was no wonder her bosses didn't like her – most of the time, the higher-ups preferred the official version because it made less trouble, for them most of all.

Perhaps Steve had a point after all, when he said that taking photographs was like detective work. About taking notice and seeking new angles. Drawing attention to things that might otherwise pass unseen.

C ATH HAD ALWAYS FELT no one could get at her when she was
in class. From a young age, she gravitated towards learning as
a source of personal satisfaction. Exams, which she excelled at and
actively enjoyed, became her secret way of sticking up two fingers
to the various arseholes. For Shirley, school was a humiliation and
a mystery. She'd once been so terrified of an upcoming maths exam
she'd seriously considered giving herself a broken arm to avoid it.
Yet outside of the classroom she was imaginative and sharp and
streetwise, nothing got past her. She could think up a hundred ways
of getting one over on her father without him realising, crazy plans
for the future involving swish hotels in Monte Carlo and designer
fashions, TV shows that didn't exist yet but totally should. 'You
should be in TV,' Cath had said to her once. 'You'd be amazing.'

She could make the sternest teacher blush, even Mr McMenemy,
who they all called the Monk. 'You're heading for the high jump,
young lady,' McMenemy said. The Monk taught history but was often
drafted in to supervise detention, mainly because everyone was terrified of him except his favourites, who were never in trouble anyway.

Shirley had dared to contradict him over the name of the executioner who'd chopped the head off Mary, Queen of Scots. The Monk was furious, eyes blazing. Seconds away from striking her, only corporal punishment had been outlawed and in any case, Cath could tell, he admired her spirit.

Everything Shirley said or did appeared to fly in opposition to the life she was supposed to settle for. Shirley Craigie might be a menace but she wasn't afraid of anyone. She wasn't stupid either, and in the eyes of the Monk especially that made her rare.

CATH STILL HAD THE newspaper clippings about the case, all the photos and articles she had collected at the time of the murders. For those weeks when the Craigies were still in the news, Cath was constantly on the lookout for information in the local papers, and for the day or two in which the story made the headlines, the national papers too. She had hidden the clippings in one of the folders she used for storing her homework then slipped the folder under some magazines in the bottom of her chest of drawers. The place you might hide pornography, if you had any. No one would look for it there. No one would look for it anywhere but she needed to be sure.

There were times when Cath felt ashamed, not just that she'd kept the clippings but for still being alive. In the moment of her death, Shirley had lost her autonomy, her right of reply. Cath was now the subject of the narrative, Shirley the object, to be wondered over, *considered*, like one of the bodies in the mortuary storage facility in *Silent Witness*. Slide out the metal drawer and let's take a look.

Cath felt the horror of this, and collected the articles anyway. She told herself she needed those photos, to stop Shirley from slipping away, to keep her story real, and although that was true there was something else too, something like excitement. Something cold as ice cubes and equally hard. Cath thought how beautiful ice cubes always looked in certain advertising photos, impossibly big and impossibly bright, like crystals discovered inside a cave on an alien planet.

The truth of Shirley's absence hit her only fleetingly, and at the most unexpected moments. When the Monk insisted on handing out extra homework, for example. Because the class were behind with their coursework, he said, though the real reason remained unspoken.

Because he's a vindictive prick, you mean. A heartless bastard.

Shirley's voice, with that irrepressible laugh caught in the back of it, derision and mirth combined, a stifled guffaw of triumph, fuck you to the world. Back at home in her room, Cath gazed at the Monk's homework assignment through a screen of tears. Shirley would never have to hand it in. She would never again pull a face at the Monk behind his back.

The Monk missed her too, he missed her comebacks. Cath recognised the truth of this without ever equating it with her own grief. If anything she believed it was probably the underlying explanation for the extra homework.

LOCAL FAMILY SLAIN IN SHOTGUN CARNAGE. The headline appeared in the local paper the week after the murders, above a photograph of the Craigie house on Westland Road, the gates festooned with police tape, a uniformed officer standing guard outside. The house in the photo was slightly out of focus, already part of the past. By the time the paper was printed the police had named John Craigie as the killer. There were more articles, more photographs, more speculation, but in terms of the story itself, time had moved on.

There were several other photos on the inside pages: one of Susan and Sonny taken at the Highland Games the previous summer and a photo of John and Susan Craigie on their wedding day: 20 July 1985, the caption read. The wedding had taken place at St Ninian's Church, which looked out over the firth at the Port end of Shore Road. A fine day, blue and unflinching, like the day of the murders. John Craigie, handsome and unsmiling in a dark, double-breasted suit so stiff-looking and old-fashioned it might have belonged to his father. He was frowning slightly, although that could have been because he had the sun in his eyes. Susan wore ivory silk, held a modest bouquet of lilacs and pink roses. She looked thin and slightly awkward, nervous but happy.

The man standing to the left of John Craigie was taller than him, slimmer, his grey suit more stylish, a blue handkerchief protruding neatly from his top pocket. The best man, Cath supposed. He was glancing sideways at the bride and groom and he was grinning. Most people would judge John Craigie the better-looking, though the other man looked nicer – a bit of a joker, fun to be with, less likely to fly off the handle at a moment's notice.

So easy with hindsight, so tempting to read things into a photograph that simply weren't there. The way the best man was looking at Susan, for example. Might there have been something between them? From the bits and pieces she had gleaned from Shirley, Cath had the impression Susan had stayed living with her parents right up until the wedding. But what about later, after she'd moved to the island, once the reality of life with her new husband had begun to sink in?

Susan's bridesmaids were gathered protectively around her, almost like bodyguards. The one furthest to the right – tanned skin, diamante hair clip – looked older than the others, her expression more reserved. The other two, both blondes, wore wide excited smiles. Cath had three copies of the wedding photo – one from the *Herald* and one from the *Mirror*, one from the local paper. Although the photos were the same they varied slightly in quality. The one in the *Herald* was the clearest, the best-reproduced. The one in the *Mirror* had a dirty grey mark on the front of Susan's dress that looked like a thumbprint. The one in the local paper was slightly fuzzy.

Even at the time, Cath had found the photograph both captivating and sinister, the kind of image that turned up in true crime shows, pinned to an evidence board. Here they were, the key players, both victim and killer. Looking at the photograph now, she wondered about the other people who had been there that day. Had they remained close to the couple at the centre of the photo in the years that followed or had they disappeared back to their lives with no further part to play? The bridesmaids, for instance – she knew from Shirley that one of them had to be Melanie, the friend who had painted the picture of Susan with the clockwork rooster. Which one was she though? The older bridesmaid's name was Abigail – Cath had found this out a fortnight after the murders, when the local paper reprinted the wedding photo alongside an interview with 'Abigail Mercer, right', in which she talked about how Susan had changed after her marriage.

She was such a warm person before. Shy and a bit of a dreamer but highly intelligent. I hardly saw her after she got married. We were both busy living our lives. When we did meet she talked mainly about the children. I had the feeling she wasn't happy but she never said anything definite and I didn't ask. She knew I never liked her husband – maybe that was why she felt she couldn't confide in me. I should have done more to try and find out what was wrong. Susan was my friend. I can't help feeling that I let her down.

The interview concluded by stating that Abigail Mercer was the owner of a successful floristry business and lived in Ayr.

There were a couple of other witness reports – a builder who had been at the tip and swore he'd heard the shots, a nurse at the health centre who had treated Sonny for minor ailments, a neighbour who claimed Susan had turned up on her doorstep ten months previously with the beginnings of a black eye and bruises on her wrist.

I asked her where's the baby and her face went white. I tried to make her sit down, take a drink of water, but she wouldn't stay. I saw her in Somerfield's a day or two later and she walks right by me like nothing ever happened. The little laddie was with her then, all right. Bright as a button, he was.

The following week the murders were gone, not just from the front page but from the entire paper, obliterated in the aftermath of 9/11. The front page was given over to a syndicated photograph of the World Trade Centre, flame and smoke pouring from the north tower, the image so terrible and so familiar it had already become iconic. On the inside front page they ran a story about an island woman whose uncle, a Glasgow businessman, was believed to have been killed in the attacks.

Cath didn't remember the story about the businessman, not at all, though she remembered every detail of how on the afternoon of 11 September they had been made to file out of their classroom and gather in the school assembly hall. Mr Dolan the headmaster explained to them what had happened the best he could, warned them of what they were likely to see on their TV screens when they went home.

'I want to reassure all of you that you and your families are perfectly safe,' he said, 'but if any of you have any questions or anything you feel you need to talk about then you should let your teacher know right away.'

Mr Dolan looked grim and pale, his jaw set in a rigid line. Different from how he'd looked on the first day of term, when he'd made a speech about Shirley in assembly and told them all they should try to remember her the way she was. Then he had seemed exasperated, world-weary, as if Shirley Craigie getting herself murdered was the last straw, one more thing that had been dumped on his desk, at the beginning of term too. And wasn't it just typical of John Craigie, who had waited for him in the school car park the week after spring term break and told him he shouldn't be filling young girls' heads with nonsense the way he had with Shirley.

'Dad were pissed as a frigging hedgehog,' Shirley had told her the following day. 'Not that that makes him less of an eejit. He's so embarrassing. I couldae nailed him one.'

On the evening of 9/11 Cath lay on her bed with the television on, listening to the endlessly repeating speculation and trying not to see what was happening on the screen, which for Cath was easier than it sounded, one of the few times when having restricted vision came in useful. To watch the footage properly she would have had to sit upright on the edge of the bed, close to the TV. When she lay back against the headboard, the images receded to a kind of shorthand, a visual summary of what Cath already knew from the news bulletins but in simple blocks of colour, meaningless without context and shorn of detail. Watching but not seeing, just hearing the sound that stood in for all of it, the thwack and whoompf of the second plane hitting the south tower, twisting itself into her brain like a knife into butter.

Cath pulled the duvet up around her shoulders and thought about how that noise was one more thing Shirley did not know about and never would, how it was OK now to be feeling like shit because everyone else was, realising at the same time it would be even harder to talk about Shirley than it had been before.

She'd called Victoria on the landline, just to hear her voice.

'I'm scared,' Vicky said. She sounded pleased Cath had called. 'What if they're coming for us, too?'

There's no point bombing Glasgow, it's a bomb site already.

Not Cath's words, but Shirley's, the kind of thing Shirley might have come out with if she'd still been alive. 'Don't worry,' Cath said instead. 'The buildings here aren't high enough, not like in America.'

Had the last time she had spoken to Vicky been on 9/11? Cath thought it might have been. The fall of the towers had rewritten the rules, the tragedy so all-consuming it drew a line under everything. Cath wondered now if what happened on 11 September might similarly have led to the closing down of the enquiry into Shirley's murder, to the police not giving themselves the time to consider alternative scenarios. Such as why John Craigie had been driving away from the ferry terminal instead of towards it, or what happened to the gun. How come a nobody like John Craigie would have had a gun in the first place. Craigie was used to threatening teachers, shooting his mouth off in the pub but he was hardly a gangster. Even now, almost twenty years later, the idea was absurd.

It hadn't just been the police though, it was everyone. The world of Sonny and Susan and Shirley had been destroyed along with the World Trade Centre. Things that had happened there no longer seemed as important or even as real as they had the day before.

BUSINESSMAN SPARED, RAN THE local headline a week later. Gavin Murchison from Glasgow had not been killed by terrorists after all, he had lost his phone. He had not picked up the dozens of desperate messages from family and friends. He had not thought of calling anyone to confirm his safety until the following morning.

There was a photo of Gavin Murchison arriving at Glasgow airport, being met by his family. Wide smiles on all the faces, Murchison's arms around his wife and six-year-old daughter, the conquering hero returns. The Craigie murders were not mentioned again until a fortnight after that, when the paper published a report on the Fatal Accident Inquiry at the Sheriff Court in Greenock.

In the case of Susan Christine Craigie, Shirley Denise Craigie and Eamon John Craigie, the sheriff recorded a verdict of murder. In the case of John Eamon Craigie, the verdict was one of accidental death. When asked why he believed John Eamon Craigie had been driving away from the ferry terminal instead of towards it, senior investigating officer Alan Meaney stated that police had come to the conclusion that owing to the traumatic circumstances of his flight from the murder scene, Craigie had not been paying proper attention to where he was headed. John Craigie had no previous convictions, not even a parking ticket. His fatal accident on a quiet stretch of highway had been precisely that – an accident, occasioned while the balance of his mind was severely disturbed.

Susan's bridesmaid Abigail Mercer had been present at the inquiry, the paper said, also Angus Livingstone, the driver of the Ford Granada who had almost collided with John Craigie on the road to Straad. Cath wondered about John Craigie's best man, the tall blond guy in the wedding photograph with the grey suit and the grin, the guy who had seemed so fond of Susan. She imagined him older, hair beginning to thin and his cheeks hollowed out, but he wasn't mentioned. Also not mentioned were Susan's family and so far as Cath was able to make out none of them had been there, not even a stray uncle or cousin. No mention either of the mysterious brother, who was supposed to have inherited the house on Westland Road.

Cath tried to remember where she had heard about the brother in the first place, who had mentioned him, but found she could not. It was at least possible she had invented him herself, unable to believe that Shirley and Susan and Sonny had died without anyone from the mainland coming to claim them. A brief paragraph at the end of the article stated that a funeral and memorial service was to be held for the three murder victims at St Leonard's Church, Ayr. There was no mention of a funeral for John Craigie, though Cath supposed there must have been one. Even Myra Hindley had been given a funeral.

Cath arranged the newspaper clippings in order on the living-room table. They were brittle now, and faded, the way all old newspapers go in the end. Cath had not looked at them in years, yet the folder containing them, similarly softened and dog-eared, had been one of the few possessions she had taken with her when she left the island for Glasgow. She had not wanted to leave it behind for her parents to find, to chuck in the skip with the rest of her stuff when they moved back down south.

Moira had called, exasperated – 'Why are you ignoring my emails?' she said – and asked if Cath wanted to come over and go through her things, see if there was anything at the house she still wanted and not to worry about the transport costs, she and Dad would pay.

Cath told her they could bin the lot. 'I don't need any of it.'

That was how she'd felt at the time, and now only the folder remained, containing the newspaper clippings and a few other odd sundries: an old ferry timetable, a Tennent's beer mat from the Golfers, the postcard Shirley had sent the time she'd been on holiday to Morecambe with Susan. Sonny was just a baby. **It's cold as fuck here – in the Vegas amusements trying to keep warm. Vegas my arse. There's a bloke who works in the cinema Mum fancies. Love ya bitch xxxx back soon.** A painted tin brooch in the shape of the *Waverley*, a velvet zip-up purse with a few loose coins inside and one of the old cardboard Kodak wallets containing half a dozen assorted snapshots. The photos weren't from the same roll of film, not even from the same year, they were just some shots she'd kept. A photo of Colin and Moira on the quayside at Port Bannatyne, the same summer as the murders – you could tell because Moira was wearing short sleeves. Colin was in jeans and a T-shirt and the silly yachting cap that Cath had hated him wearing in public even though actually, she could see now, it suited him.

A photo of Shirley on the walkway at Loch Fad. A grey day, with low cloud, Shirley in trainers and a khaki anorak she hated. She thought it made her look like an islander. The damp atmosphere had made her hair frizz, which she also couldn't stand. There was another photograph of Shirley, taken in the back garden of Westland Road. Shirley was sitting on the grass, playing with Sonny. They had trucks lined up, Sonny's Tonka toys, a red pickup and a yellow bulldozer, the police car with the flashing blue light that came on when you rolled the car along the ground. Also in the photograph was Susan, looking off to one side as if her attention had been caught by something outside the frame. Cath couldn't remember how she came to have the photo, only that she hadn't taken it herself.

It was out of focus, and had an unreal, spooky quality, like one of those family groupings from a *Peter and Jane* book. See Peter play. See Jane run. There was a shadow on the grass, a dark and elongated silhouette of a human form. The photographer, Cath supposed, before realising with a start that it was probably John Craigie.

6.

'THIS MURDER CASE,' SAID Saheed. 'That's why you're here, right? That's why you got in touch with Alice?'

Cath glanced across at Alice, wondering if this was it, the story they were planning to tell about themselves, planning to tell Saheed at any rate, a story that was true as far as it went but that had details missing. The emails, for instance, the half-dozen chatty notes they had exchanged over the past couple of days, notes about nothing in particular, significant only in that they existed, proof that both of them had felt the need to be in touch. Although this was only their second meeting, the relationship felt older, with more weight behind it than could easily be explained away by this simple cover story.

Cath realised that if she'd met Saheed without the context of Alice she would have liked him. He was good-looking and obviously intelligent, with a disparaging and caustic sense of humour that made her think of Steve, although Steve would have most likely dismissed Saheed as a pretentious wanker.

Saheed had brought all the cooking ingredients for their meal with him from London in his rucksack, Alice had told her. 'He thinks you can't get couscous here.' Apart from the comment about the food Alice had not said much. She seemed pent up, tense in a way she had not been when it was just her and Cath, not even when they were talking about the murders. Cath found herself resenting Saheed for being there, for altering the balance of the conversation.

'Well, can you get couscous?' he said, laughing a little. 'Is there even a proper supermarket on this island?'

'The Co-op's fine,' Cath said. She found his comment annoying but laughed along with him anyway, she couldn't help it. At least the man could cook. They stood around in the kitchen while Saheed prepped the vegetables, chopping and dicing with a vicious-looking double-bladed knife Cath would have felt nervous even touching. She felt aware of his eyes on her, not hostile exactly but questioning, as if he suspected an ulterior motive, a reason for her being there other than the one she had divulged.

He doesn't like me, Cath thought, before insisting to herself she was imagining it.

They ate in the living room. Alice had strung fairy lights around the chimney piece and across the curtain poles.

'That's right,' Cath said, when Saheed asked about the murders. 'I knew Shirley from school – she was my best friend. I'm doing a photography project on – I suppose you could call them murder houses? It made sense to include this one. It would have seemed strange not to.'

'Shirley was the girl who was shot?'

'Yes. Her and her mother and brother. They all died here. Well, Shirley died outside, in the garden. Susan and Sonny were killed inside the house.'

Saheed rocked back in his seat, glanced up at the ceiling. He made a whistling noise through his teeth. 'Fuck, Ally, why didn't you tell me this?'

'I did tell you.'

'Yeah, right. When you said there'd been a murder here I thought you meant ages ago, like in Victorian times or whenever. Not something you can look up on the internet.'

'It was ages ago. Almost twenty years.'

'You get a kick out of it, I suppose,' Saheed said to Cath. 'Being back here?'

'Saheed!' Alice said.

'Of course not. Why would you say that?' Cath felt determined not to let Saheed wind her up, for Alice's sake, though he had no right to bring on the sarcasm, he barely knew her. The way he was glaring at her, as if she were an enemy, as if they were grappling together in the air like in one of those Chinese martial arts films, *Crouching Tiger, Hidden Dragon.*

Could she swear that what he said wasn't true though, not even a little bit?

Saheed looked thunderous then perplexed then finally sheepish.

'I'm sorry,' he said. 'I'm just worried about the effect this might be having on Ally. All this stuff about murder and shooting, it's not good for her. She's not been well, did she tell you that? She had a breakdown last year.'

'Saheed, stop,' Alice said. 'I don't want to talk about that, I told you.' She sounded upset. Saheed mumbled something under his breath. Fuck this, it sounded like. There was a strange kind of silence, and Cath wondered if it was her specifically Saheed disliked or if he

72

was like this with anyone who tried to get close to Alice, the kind of jealousy so old and well worn it went beyond reason, the kind of injury only marriage could inflict.

Cath felt disorientated, embarrassed, that feeling you get when you're in someone's house looking for the toilet and blunder into the bedroom by mistake.

'I'm sorry too,' she said. 'If I've done something wrong I apologise. I had no idea.'

'Cath, it's fine, you haven't done anything,' Alice said, and Cath found herself trying to imagine what would happen between her and Saheed once Cath had left, whether they'd scream the place down or bonk their brains out or simply pretend the evening hadn't happened. Blurting out Alice's private business like that though, that was just crass, some kind of weird power trip. What a dick.

She wondered if it was true about the breakdown.

'None of this is right,' Alice said. 'I told you I don't have a problem with what Cath is doing. I find it interesting. If I thought I couldn't handle it I would have said.'

'I'm just not sure it's a good idea to dwell on this stuff. Not after everything you've been through.'

'The guy's dead, Saheed. He's hardly going to come looking for me. End of story.'

'I should go,' Cath said. She didn't want to leave – to leave Alice – but she had clearly overstayed her welcome and that was an understatement. She had lost Alice for good, probably. And the irony was she hadn't taken any photographs yet. She experienced a pang of regret, then felt like laughing. What a mess.

'No,' Alice said. 'I want you to stay. This has all got way out of hand. Saheed's had a tough week at work, that's all. He didn't mean any of it. Let's have some more wine.' She reached reflexively for the bottle, which was almost empty. Saheed leaned forward on his elbows, head in hands. He seemed deflated, miserable. Then with a visible effort he pulled himself out of it.

'Ally's right. I'm sorry. And I'm glad Ally has made a friend here. I guess I'm being overly anxious. She has been very ill.'

'And I'm better now,' Alice said. 'That's official.' They grinned at one another. Saheed grabbed Alice's hand and kissed it, their foreheads resting together for a second. Little by little the evening repaired itself. Things went back to how they had been when Cath first arrived. They opened another bottle of wine and talked about the difficulties of moving from the city to the country. Saheed told a long anecdote about a mate of his who had become lost on a Welsh hillside during an Outward Bound course.

'He actually asked the pub landlord if they still had wolves there.' They all burst out laughing.

'That story gets more ridiculous each time he tells it,' Alice said. She smiled at her husband, who leaned across and kissed her. It was past eleven.

'I really should be going now,' Cath said.

'I'll walk you back if you want,' said Saheed.

'There's no need. Honestly.' Her refusal came out sounding harsher than she had intended, and as she walked back down the hill Cath realised she was still angry with him. So bullying, so presumptuous. The way he had embarrassed Alice, gone on about the island. What a Londoner. She wished she could call Alice, make sure she was really all right, but there was no way she could do that. Not till after he left.

74

'Why do you always feel you have to mend things, like other people's cock-ups are your responsibility?' Steve had once said to her. 'Why can't you see that some situations are too far gone to be worth saving?'

Like you falling in love with Alice, you mean? As far gone as that? When you were thinking about them shagging? You hate the thought of him touching her.

You're being ridiculous. I've told you, I'm not in love with her.

Cath unlocked the door to the flat, edged inside almost on tiptoe, as if she were afraid of waking someone. She thought of Adam, found the idea of him had lost all traction. Arrogant prick. His work wasn't all that, either. She didn't know who was worse, him or Saheed.

The air she drew in tasted light, and faintly sweet. Like laughing gas, she thought.

She felt deliciously free.

THE FOLLOWING DAY, THE Sunday, Cath walked out to Loch Fad. The sky was low and grey, the windscreens and bonnets of passing cars flecked with rain that threatened but refused to fall. The air was thick and soft and chilly as a dampened blanket.

How do you stand the weather, was what most of them said at some point, those people who came to Scotland for its wild expanses and cheap accommodation and found themselves heading south again twelve months later. Steve's mate Collie from Bristol, for example, who was in a semi-famous punk band and now lived in Tucson. A restaurant critic named Melinda Stiles who was a friend of Mildred Marks, who owned the gallery on Byres Road where Cath had staged her fish-and-chip-shop exhibition. Melinda had leased a tenement studio in Battlefield, one enormous room with bathroom and kitchenette, south-west facing. Melinda said when she first saw what they were charging for rent she thought it was a misprint. In spite of all this she'd terminated the lease after six months and gone back to London. She found what she called the constant downpour insuperably depressing.

'I guess I'm stuck with it,' was what Cath always said when people asked her if she ever thought of leaving. She still missed Melinda, who in a strange way had reminded her of Vicky. 'I don't think I'd ever go back down south now. Too expensive.' This at least was a reason that made sense to people, though it wasn't the real one, or only in theory. The reason was that she knew she would miss it, the soggy west coast that bound you to it for life even as you cursed the circuitous set of circumstances that had washed you up there. Adam called it 'the northern aesthetic'. His introductory essay for his last exhibition catalogue went on about 'a landscape of distances, constantly replenishing itself'. Which was what rain did, Cath supposed. Replenished things, cleared the air, made you feel unaccountably happy when it finally stopped.

For Cath it was the light. Like the light of another planet, she thought, if you could imagine such a thing. Those endless, pearlescent evenings of the northwestern summers, never harsh but always clear, so unlike the blockish, clotted light of the southern counties. Her eyes especially seemed to grow less tired here. Then there was the luminous glow the northern light lent to photographs, if you could capture it that was, which was never a given.

She bent to tighten her shoelace and then stood up again. The waters of the loch were still, voluminous, clear and grey as rainwater. Cath remembered her first sight of this place: fresh snow lining the causeway, ice glinting like strips of foil among the reeds. She and Shirley had come here often, winter and summer. They liked the loch because it was quiet – people mostly couldn't be bothered walking all the way out there. Also because it was the one place they could be certain of evading Shirley's father.

According to Shirley, John Craigie believed Loch Fad was haunted.

'The woods around here, anyway. He won't come near the place.'

'Your dad believes in ghosts?' Cath thought Shirley must be winding her up. Shirley nodded then shook her head.

'Not ghosts really. Things in the woods, like kelpies or redcaps or some such. He's funny like that – always has been. He'd kill me if he found out I'd told you but he's never going tae know, is he? The point is, Dad wouldnae come near the loch if you paid him.'

They dangled their feet in the water. On the far side of the loch some lads were diving from one of the landing stages. You weren't supposed to do that because it scared the fish off and stirred up sediment. Most of the time it wasn't an issue because it was too cold to swim in the loch anyway but the summer of the murders the loch's banks were dry and cracked and the waters shimmered like butterflies' wings. Kids bobbing about like porpoises right through July and into August. The men who ran the fishery turned a blind eye.

Cath reached into the water, peeled a fragment of yellow leaf from her half-submerged calf. Shirley's hair, bleached white by the sunlight, tapped against her cheek like twizzles of cloud.

It was three weeks before she died, almost exactly.

'What's he scared of, then?' Cath found she couldn't let go of the subject, even though she could tell Shirley was hoping she'd shut up about it, wished she'd never said anything in the first place. Cath was a pain like that, she knew it herself. Wouldn't let things lie. Moira was always telling her she was like a dog with a bone.

'It's daft,' Shirley said. She glanced at Cath then looked away, out across the water, lashes raised and then lowered to hide her eyes. 'He says his sister was taken by redcaps when she were a bairn, and that we should stay away from the woods in case they take us, too. I told you it was stupid.'

'What are redcaps?'

'You know – fairies, elves. That's why you can't move anything in the house without him losing his rag. He'll think it's redcaps shifting stuff, that they're under the floorboards. What an eejit. I hate him,' Shirley said, so casually Cath found it shocking, even though she hated him too, probably.

'Does your mum know?'

'It were Mum who told me about it. She thinks it's romantic, the way he feels about the woods and stuff, or anyways she used to. Says it shows a different side to him. A frigging mad side, more like. A frigging split personality.'

Shirley swung her feet harder, kicking up a spray, attracting the attention of the bathers over by the fishery. One of the lads whooped like a gibbon, pretended to fall into the water and then actually did fall, heavily and sideways. The loch's surface shattered upward and outward, like a smashing windscreen.

'I hope your balls broke!' Shirley stood up, yelled, cupped both hands around her mouth to make a megaphone. 'Eejits,' she added, quietly. She sat down again, leaning back on her hands. 'Anyways,' she said. 'These woods can be frigging creepy after dark. It's like every noise you hear could literally be anything.'

The subject was closed. Cath knew if she tried to bring it up again Shirley would ignore her, though she still felt fascinated – that a man like John Craigie, seemingly so doltish and so impenetrable could nurture this secret weakness, a weakness that was arguably the most interesting thing about him. Susan Craigie was right – it did show a different side to him. If it was true that was. A grown man who believed in fairies. What was that about?

Cath leaned back on her hands. She thought about diving into the water, like the boys on the jetty, how it would probably be their last chance to do that before the summer ended.

'Wish I'd brought my swimming costume,' she said.

'Go in in your bra and pants. I darest you.'

'Bugger off.' Cath thought about how the light would change, even before the weather turned, she could already imagine it. She was always thinking about things ending, the last this, the last that. It was just the way her mind worked.

THE CANON CAME TO life with a whirring thud. Cath had always found landscape photography difficult, close to impossible. Everything you tried to capture slid towards cliché. Objects and buildings were more accommodating, the uglier the better. Even the most commonplace piece of rubbish – a discarded battery, say – seemed to carry its history implicit within itself. Whether you cared about that history or not, it was ineradicably there.

She snapped off half a dozen shots of the fishery building then retraced her steps to the car parking area. Multiple tyre tracks, some faded, some fresh, the gravel muddy and hard, set deep into runnels. Pairs of footprints leading off in the direction of the fishery then returning like clockwork to their respective vehicles. Cath photographed some of them, leaning in close, the way she'd seen scene-of-crime officers do on TV. She felt no desire to photograph the loch the way it appeared on postcards, a nacreous ellipsis, snug between hills. What she saw was an algae-streaked reservoir, sealed within itself, camouflaged by its drabness. Hardly the landscape of fairy tales. The idea that John Craigie really had believed in fairies seemed if anything more outlandish to her now than it had back then, so incongruous it was disturbing.

He'd pretended to believe, more like, to scare his children. That was much more his style.

Shirley had not mentioned the redcaps again after that day, the day of the loch and the lads and the jetty, which was really the last day they had had together when things were right between them. After that they'd slipped back into autopilot, the pretence that nothing had changed when really everything had, partly because of Vicky but not only.

Their paths had already been diverging, bifurcating. Things would have worked themselves out in due course, one way or another. Either they would have remained friends, or they would not. Shirley's death had altered the natural state of things forever. In a way, Cath supposed, they had both died that day: Shirley for real, and the version of Cath in the future she had been moving towards.

The Cath she had become instead was not the same person.

I turned to stone, she thought, and shivered. The woods stirred in the wind, making her think once again of John Craigie, and a song she had learned in primary school, music hour with Mrs Clough, belting out old folk tunes on the piano like a tyrannical ballet mistress, having a go at anyone who forgot the words.

> *Up the airy mountain,*
> *Down the rushy glen,*
> *We dare not go a-hunting*
> *For fear of little men;*

Cath felt sure the song had mentioned redcaps. When she got back to the flat she googled the poem the song was based on and found she was right.

> *Wee folk, good folk,*
> *Trooping all together;*
> *Green jacket, red cap,*
> *And white owl's feather!*

> *Green jacket, red cap,*
> *And white owl's feather!*

The poem was called 'The Fairies', by William Allingham, a famous Scottish verse of exactly the kind that school kids used to learn by heart. It was easy to believe – logical, really – that John Craigie had encountered the same song when he was a child.

Like many fairy tales, the poem was darker beneath the surface than it first appeared, though Cath didn't remember being frightened by it at the time. She'd more likely been bored, passing notes to Carmen under the desk and sticking her tongue out at Mrs Clough the moment her back was turned.

Cath typed the song title into YouTube, hoping she might find a recording of it, but all that came up was a single by Mud, the seventies glam rock group: purple flares and cool shades, 'Tiger Feet', the school disco. It appeared that at some point before anyone had heard of them, Mud had recorded an ill-advised cover version of 'Up the Airy Mountain', a song that became distinctly weirder the longer you listened to it, pipes and drums and a jangling backbeat, clearly aiming for wacky/eccentric but hitting what were they thinking right in the bull's eye.

They'd been on drugs, probably. Cath dropped Steve a one-line email, asking if he'd heard of the song. His reply came bouncing back in less than five minutes.

1968. Their third single. Complete and utter flop. What the hell are you on?

Nothing. Internet rabbit hole. Thanks!

Steve fired back the brain-bleach emoji. Cath replied with the Vulcan salute and then logged off. She knew Steve would be embarrassed if she asked how he was.

7

THE ISLAND CLUNG TO winter. They were on the A844 a mile out of Straad, a stretch of straight, unblemished road that appeared to hold few distractions and fewer surprises. On a clear day, the mountains of Arran would stand out starkly against the horizon. On the afternoon Alice drove them out to the place where John Craigie had died the firth was swathed in mist, the neighbouring island barely visible. On the right side of the road was Woodside Cottage, where Angus Livingstone, the driver of the Ford Granada, had run to call an ambulance. An army of daffodils was beginning to sprout at the base of the beech hedge that formed the cottage's boundary with the road.

'Not exactly an accident hotspot, is it?' Alice said. She had phoned on the Sunday evening, worried in case Cath was still upset about her run-in with Saheed, though she barely mentioned her husband except to say he had left. 'He caught the five thirty ferry,' she said. 'He'll grab something to eat in Glasgow, then catch the train back to London.' She asked if Cath would like to meet up the following day. 'We could go for a walk or something?'

'That would be great,' Cath said, immediately. She told Alice there was a place she'd like to take a look at, to do with the project, though she did not mention John Craigie's accident until they got there. She had felt nervous about seeing Alice again, concerned in case her not hitting it off with Saheed made them awkward with one another but if anything it was the opposite, as if the strangeness of the situation had brought them closer. They hugged. Alice's heathery hair brushed against Cath's cheek. Cath watched Alice pull on walking boots, a bright green puffer jacket. Once they were in the car, she directed her back towards the centre of town and then out again on to Barone Road, passing the Greenan Loch on their right and then on towards Straad.

'Pull over,' Cath said, as they passed Woodside Cottage. Then she explained to Alice why she'd wanted to come here.

'There was another car,' she said, 'travelling in the opposite direction. The driver said that Craigie almost hit him.'

'I don't see how,' Alice said. Cath bringing up the murders again had not seemed to faze her. 'The only bend is before the cottage. The other guy would have seen him coming a mile off. He must have been distracted, or swerved on purpose.'

'John Craigie, you mean?'

'Yeah. It's like he crashed the truck deliberately. The other guy was lucky. He could have been killed.'

'You think it was suicide, then, like the police said?'

'It's the only explanation that makes sense.'

Angus Livingstone had said the only reason he was able to avoid Craigie's pickup was because the road was clear of other vehicles and there was room for manoeuvre. The biggest shock was seeing John Craigie go into the wall.

'He didn't even seem to brake,' Livingstone had said when he gave his evidence at the FAI. 'If anything, he speeded up. You don't expect to see something like that, not on the island. There was nothing else on the road, no one at all.'

The tense pht pht of the wind snagging the trees, the chilly fields descending in a casual slope towards the sea. 'It's lovely out here,' said Alice. 'I still don't get it.'

She meant the crash, Cath supposed. She didn't get it either. John Craigie behind the wheel of his pickup had always seemed less threatening to her than John Craigie slumped in his armchair, watching TV. He drove with a stolid confidence, eyes chained to the road, practical, stubby fingers gripping the wheel. Like a cowman, Cath thought, all competence, no glamour. Craigie knew how to drive, and anyone who told him different could piss right off.

The idea that he would crash his truck on an empty road seemed actively perverse. The idea occurred to her for the first time, that Craigie had seen something – something that had scared him or surprised him so much he'd lost control of his vehicle.

Like a line of dancing pixies you mean? There's nothing here, nothing. Just fields.

The only other car on the road had been Angus Livingstone's. Had Craigie known Livingstone? At the inquiry, Livingstone had said not. Still, it was a small island, and the name was bugging Cath, for some reason, like she'd come across it before somewhere.

Dr Livingstone, I presume?

Och, bollocks to him.

The suicide theory made more sense. Neat and no nonsense. While the balance of his mind was severely disturbed.

'It still wasn't the smartest move, though,' Alice added. 'As a way of killing yourself, I mean. He could have ended up paralysed, or in a coma or brain-damaged. If this Craigie guy had a gun, why didn't he just shoot himself?'

They walked along the edge of the tarmac into Straad. The village, on the island's west coast, was not on a bus route. Cath had been to Straad with her parents many times. They used to drive out there on Sundays if the weather was good, walk down past the scattered cottages, along the rough spit of pebbled strand that formed St Ninian's Point. There was a ruined chapel, coves of translucent water striped with kelp, russet sea anemones, tiny little green-shelled crabs. Sheep wandered everywhere, cropping the tussocks of grass between the fallen slabs of granite. Looking out across the water from the chapel, Cath could just make out the white building blocks of houses on the opposite shore.

Her father had loved the western shoreline. He had talked occasionally of selling the house on Mountstuart Road and buying a cottage in Straad instead, only Moira had vetoed the idea.

'Imagine it in winter, stuck out in the middle of nowhere. Catherine would feel marooned here, for a start.'

If Cath had been safe to ride a bike even, things might have been different. Winter nights, the gales that swept in across the Irish Sea, woofing and thrashing like wolfhounds as they shook themselves dry. The foreshore at dawn, that sacred silver light. A walled triangle of scrubby pasture. Goats. None of these things appealed to Moira. Cath was just a convenient reason to turn them down.

Cath felt no firm allegiance to either party, though the isolation of the place had appealed to her in spite of the difficulties it presented.

She imagined a life, a different life in which she saw no one outside of school, spent her weekends picking along the strand line in all weathers like Perdita in Nina Bawden's *The Witch's Daughter*. Their first summer on the island, Cath had walked to Straad one Saturday without telling anyone, just to see if she could get there by herself. Places she had to be driven to in somebody's car did not feel real to her. For a place to acquire texture and meaning she needed to be able to reach it independently, by walking, or by travelling on public transport. Not every time, but in principle. It had always felt important for Cath to know that her desire to be in a place or leave it lay within her own choosing. Above all, that she should not be dependent on others for where she could or could not go. As with most things that had to do with her vision, Cath found this difficult to speak of, hard to explain.

She still thought about that day sometimes, her sense of achievement as the signpost marking the village came in sight. Arriving on the shoreline, which appeared so different now, like it belonged to her, as if she could return there whenever she wanted in her imagination. Thinking how stupid she'd been for forgetting to bring anything to eat and then having to start the return leg of the journey with blisters the size of acorns on both her heels. The secret relief she'd felt when her English teacher overtook her in the car just past the Greenan Loch and offered her a lift. Greenan then was simply itself: shallow and soft-bedded, fringed with weed that spawned clouds of midges at the height of summer. After the murders, Greenan darkened inside her mind, a theoretical repository for a murder weapon.

'You need to be careful on these roads,' said Mrs Mackenzie as Cath climbed into the passenger seat. 'Drivers don't always look where they're going, you know. The speed some of them go at, you'd think the devil was after them.'

'THEY NEVER FOUND THE gun though,' Cath said. She found she was shouting a little, trying to make her voice heard above the wind. 'Did I tell you that?'

'Can't remember. You might have. But it still doesn't prove anything, does it? Just because the police didn't find a gun doesn't mean he didn't have one. Who else could have done it? Most murders aren't random.'

'I don't think it was random. It's a loose end, that's all. The cops think he threw the gun in the loch, the one we just drove past.'

'They'd have dragged it though, surely?'

'That's another loose end.'

Alice stopped walking suddenly, turned to face her. 'You don't think he did it, do you? I can tell.'

'I don't know,' Cath said. She hesitated. 'It's always seemed strange to me, that John Craigie was driving away from the town, away from the ferry terminal. I want to know why. The police didn't seem to care – they said he'd gone crazy and left it at that. I hated that man. I've spent years not thinking about him because every time I do I realise I don't know the truth, not for certain. Shirley's murderer might still be out there and I feel I'm letting her down by not trying to find out what happened. It's ridiculous I know, but it's how I feel.'

'It's not ridiculous. Not at all.' Alice paused. 'When I was a kid there was this mate of my uncle's who got himself arrested for distributing porn films. Really awful stuff, apparently. He went down for five years. The thing is, everyone liked Richie. Most of his friends didn't have a clue what he was mixed up in. He was round our house a lot when I was a kid. He gave me a Rubik's Cube for my tenth birthday because he knew I liked maths. My dad kind of cut him off after he came out of jail so we didn't see him as much but I still think about him. Richie, I mean. I can't reconcile the Richie who gave me that Rubik's Cube with the Richie who thought it was OK to go round selling images of abused children. Saheed says I shouldn't try, that we can never know anyone, not deep down. If that's true it's terrifying. Why would this John Craigie have killed his family? Was it money? Usually when a man does something like that it's about money.'

'The Craigies didn't have much money. But John Craigie always had plenty of work. I can't think it was that.'

'Something else, then – something must have triggered him. Was his wife having an affair, do you think?'

'I have no idea. I would have said no, no way, but it's like you said – I was fifteen. Susan was just my friend's mother. I didn't know anything about her. Not really.'

'Is there anyone you could ask? She must have had friends.'

'She never went out much. She was always at home. At least while I was there. Looking after Sonny.' Cath thought of the story in the local paper about Susan turning up at a neighbour's with a black eye, then two days later pretending everything was fine. 'There was her bridesmaid.'

'Bridesmaid?'

'A woman named Abigail Mercer. She was at school with Susan,

I think. There was a photo of her, in the paper, after it happened. She runs a flower shop in Ayr, or at least she did.'

'There you are, then. She might still be in town. You should give her a call.'

'Do you think she'd talk to me?' Cath thought how interesting it would be, to photograph Abigail twenty years on. More like forty years on, if you were going by the wedding photo. Cath didn't normally do portraits but Abigail was different. She was as much a part of this story as the Craigie house.

'It's worth a try, surely? If you really do want to know what was going on with Susan.'

'I think I have to. I came back here thinking I wouldn't care any more but if anything it's the opposite.'

Alice laughed. 'You sound like Sarah Lund. You know, in that TV show *The Killing*.'

They sat down on one of the benches along the foreshore. **In memory of Lucinda Glenister, who loved this place.** 'I did think of joining the police, believe it or not. I wanted to be a detective. But there was no way I'd have passed the medical.'

'You're not sick, though?'

'I've got restricted vision. That's why I can't drive. Mostly I don't think about it, except when I'm rushing to catch a train and the departure boards are too high up for me to read. They're the most annoying thing on the planet, overhead departure boards. Them, and the general shortage of Twiglets north of the border.'

Alice smiled and touched her hand. 'Seriously though, you're OK?'

'There are always other ways of doing what you want to do.

Steve – he's the guy who owns the record shop I work at – says my photographs are all about detection, about looking beneath the surface of things.'

'I've not seen any of your work yet. You have to show me.' She drew her feet up off the ground, crossed her ankles in midair. 'I wanted to go to the States, to study on the postgraduate mathematics program at Stanford. Saheed was set on going into finance, though. He said that was where the money was and he's right, I guess. For a while I thought we could make it work – me going to America, him staying put in London then applying for jobs in the US once I'd got my doctorate. I got scared, I think, scared things would fall apart if we were separated for so long. I'd never met anyone like Saheed – someone who saw who I was and still didn't freak out. Then I messed up my finals and Stanford withdrew their offer. I cried for a week. My tutor said he'd speak to the admissions board, that we could apply for a retake, but I couldn't face it. I landed the job at Clearwater on my first interview and for a while I was excited, looking forward to the life we could have in London, feeling relieved at the way everything had worked out. I only realised how bad things had got when I found myself not going back in after lunch one day. It was like I just flipped.'

'That was when you had the breakdown?'

Alice nodded. 'I'm kind of on hold at the moment. Part of me wants to turn the clock back, to be back living in college and winning prizes, being one of the nerds. I know it's too late, though. I could always go into teaching but I think I'd be bored.'

'What about Saheed?'

'I know I love him and he loves me. When we're by ourselves

he's the gentlest man. I couldn't have got through the last year without him. But I loathe his friends, the whole banking scene. I can't go back to that. Last summer when I was really bad Saheed said he'd give up the job, he'd do anything it took, but I know that wouldn't work either. Saheed loves the job. He loves being in the thick of it, all the high-octane stuff, the money even. And he's got no time for what he calls being a mathematician – he says he'd rather coach boxing. It's my own fault for signing up with Clearwater in the first place. Sometimes I think it would be better for both of us if I left.'

'But you did leave – you came here.'

'Yeah, but Saheed still thinks I'll tough it out for a year then go back to London. And seriously, what am I going to do here, once I've finished dicking about with the house?'

'You could study.'

'Now you see why Saheed thinks you're bad for me.'

'Is that what he said?'

'Not in those exact words. He's still not happy talking about the murders though. He says the house is tainted.'

'Tainted?'

They both started laughing. 'How about you?' Alice said. 'Are you with anyone?'

'Not really, not any more. There was this guy, Adam. A photographer. He's married. He says we have to stop seeing each other.'

'Do you love him?'

'I thought I did. But I'm sick of the whole situation. Him calling things off then phoning me three weeks later, begging me to come back. Me going back because I tell myself it's different this time only of course it never is. Now I'm on the island I can't go back. Not so easily, anyway. I'm beginning to think that's part of the reason I came here.'

'He sounds like a prick.'

'I'm the prick more like, for putting up with him for so long. At least now I want us to be over. I feel like I'm finally getting somewhere with my work too, no thanks to Adam. I should have done this years ago.'

'Come back to the island, you mean?'

'Not just that. So much of my work was bound up with how I felt about Adam. It's only now I'm free of him I feel I can concentrate. It's such a relief, not to have to be thinking about him all the time.'

What? Because you're thinking of her instead? You're heading for the high jump, young lady.

'What if you aren't able to find out what happened to your friend?' Alice tightened her shoelace. 'It was a long time ago. You're probably never going to know for sure. Not everything, anyway.'

'I realise that. But I can still do the project. Let people know Shirley existed. That's the one thing I can do.' Cath hesitated. 'I hope I've not caused any problems between you and Saheed.'

A shadow crossed Alice's face, a look of dismay. 'No, we're fine. He's just a bit tense. He worries about me being alone here, that's all.'

You're trespassing. I wouldn't push things if I were you.

Cath thought about asking when Saheed would next be visiting, but didn't. 'We should be getting back, I suppose,' she said instead. When she asked Alice if she wanted to go for a drink somewhere, Alice shook her head.

'Not this evening. I've got someone coming to pick up some of that old furniture. Later in the week though, yeah? Where shall I drop you?'

Cath said the Co-op car park would be fine, there was stuff she needed, and later, once she'd put away her shopping, she called the number for Sound of the Suburbs. She knew Steve would have probably gone home already – it was well after four by then and the shop would be quiet. In any case, it was Norah she wanted to speak to.

'Sound of the Suburbs?' Norah said.

'Hey,' Cath said. She asked Norah how she was doing and Norah said fine. They bitched about Steve for a couple of minutes, Norah told her about a bursary she was applying for and then Cath asked her about Angus Livingstone.

'I keep thinking I've read about him somewhere, or heard the name,' she said. 'It's driving me crazy.'

'Mary Chant,' Norah said at once. 'He was Mary Chant's husband. Not the betting shop guy, the guy she was married to before.'

'The university lecturer? Are you sure that's the same one?'

'I don't know if it's the same one, obviously, but it's definitely the same name. If you kept the newspaper clippings I gave you you'll see.'

'But this is really weird,' Cath said, then wondered how weird it was in actual fact. People came to the island on holiday, all the year round but especially in summer. The hot weather the week Shirley died had brought them over in boatloads. It was a coincidence though, all the same. 'Have you ever seen him? I mean at the university?'

'He's in History I think, so I wouldn't, would I? What's this about?'

'Nothing, probably. His name cropped up, that's all.'

The town, swelling with crowds of tourists come doon the watter

94

and bunting all along the promenade. That was the island, for a hundred years and more that was the island. People came and people left. Lives touched briefly and moved apart again. That was the island.

'Thanks, though,' Cath added. 'I tell you what – if you hear anything about him could you let me know?'

'Like he's been copping off with students, you mean? Or murdering wives?'

'I mean exactly like that.' They both laughed. Norah asked Cath about a couple of orders she'd placed then they ended the call. Cath spent the next hour scouring the internet for information on Angus Livingstone but there was only his university bio – first class degree in History and Archaeology at Edinburgh, followed by a PhD, which he'd done at St Andrews – and then the photo, the same, slightly blurred head shot that had been in the *Herald*. Looking at him now, he looked less like a gangster and more like a badly photographed history teacher. A nobody. Cath tried to imagine how he might have looked twenty years ago, and found she couldn't.

8.

ABIGAIL MERCER WAS STILL living in Ayr and still in business as a florist. Her shop had a website, Abigail's Flowers, where you could order Flowers for All Occasions, Flowers for that Special Someone, Flowers With Sympathy. A Flash installation rotated a series of images: wedding bouquets and table centrepieces, novelty garlands. The photographs were magazine quality, the colours supersaturated and densely inviting. An interactive map showed the shop's location, just off Ayr High Street and close to the seafront.

When Cath called the number for Abigail's Flowers she was relieved to find it was Abigail Mercer herself who picked up the phone. She'd get to speak to her, at least. She had been worried about trying to explain herself to an assistant.

'I'm hoping you can help me,' Cath said. 'I'm trying to find information about a woman named Susan Craigie. I believe you used to be friends. I was wondering if we could meet?'

'You're not a journalist, are you?' Abigail sounded defensive, which was to be expected, although strangely, Cath thought later, she didn't sound entirely surprised.

Like she was waiting for this day to come, you mean, that kind of bollocks?

Something like it, yeah.

That's your story and you're sticking to it, I get it.

'I'm not a journalist. I'm a friend of Susan's daughter Shirley, or was. We were at school together – I'm here on the island at the moment, doing some research. I found your photo in the paper, the one from when you were Susan's bridesmaid. I'd really like to talk to you about what happened.'

'I'm not coming out there. To the island.'

'I can easily come to you, you wouldn't have to.'

'I can do next Monday. Not at the shop, though.' She named a coffee bar, gave vague directions. Cath found it later on Google Maps, noted the street address. She felt elated.

Like you're flipping Sherlock Holmes now all of a sudden? Give me a break.

'You were lucky to catch me,' Abigail added. 'I'm not normally in the shop on Thursdays. Karolina was sick, so I said I'd cover. I've never talked to anyone about Susan, not since she died. It's almost – I don't know—'

Like you were meant to find her.

'I HATED SCHOOL,' ABIGAIL said. 'It didn't help with it being a girls' school. I had two brothers, I knew my brothers' friends. The idea of a girls' school seemed like an insult, like being kept in a zoo. My father was set on me going there though, so that was that. I didn't really know Susie until we were all doing our O-Grades. I thought she was stuck up at first, but really she was just shy. I started going round to her place mainly so I could get away from my brother Charlie. Constantly at each other's throats we were, used to drive our mother mad. Pretty soon I discovered I just liked being there. Susie read books and she actually got on with her parents. She was clever, too – could have done really well if she'd put herself forward more. As for boys, Susie had barely spoken to any, let alone kissed one. When Johnny came along she thought she'd found her Prince Charming. She didn't have a clue.'

'Shirley told me Susan had another boyfriend before that, someone called Wallace?'

'Oh yes, Wally. He was at the university, in Edinburgh, studying Law. He came to do work experience at Susie's father's practice. Maurice took a shine to him – saw him as the perfect son-in-law, I expect. Wally used to board with the family, have dinner with them, everything. A nice enough laddie I'm sure but he was never going to set the world on fire. Johnny was a working man already and he was good-looking, I'll give him that. Susie was head over heels. I was even pleased at first, thought it would be good for her to have a bit of fun for a change. When I realised things were getting serious I told her I thought she was making a mistake. Johnny always had a temper on him – the way he beat up Wally in The Criterion that time. Men like that become worse with time, not better. Johnny gave me the willies if I'm honest. I know it's easy to say so now but I really did try to warn Susan off him. Of course she was too far gone by then, too smitten. The more I said she should stop seeing him the more she dug her heels in. I still feel guilty, I suppose. I keep thinking if only I'd tried harder, Susie might still be alive now. It's silly looking back all the time, I know, but you can't help how you feel.'

They were in the coffee shop. Abigail looked older of course: heavier, cropped grey hair and spectacles, well-cut trouser suit. You could see it was her though, immediately. She was wearing the same diamante hair clip as in the wedding photo, or at least one like it. Cath had to keep reminding herself that this was Abigail's first sight of her. She had lost count of the times she had brought Abigail's image up on the screen, had studied it, she could admit that now, for clues.

'In the newspaper article you said Susan changed after she got married?'

'She did. She gave up reading, for a start. Even the way she talked was different. When I spoke to her on the phone she'd go on and on about some dress she'd seen in a catalogue, or the price of food in the supermarket. I think now it was fear – she was scared of saying the wrong thing, even when he wasn't in the house. Safer to chat away about nothing instead. It drove me crazy at the time, though – reminded me of that film with Nanette Newman in it, *The Stepford Wives*. I used to feel like shaking her. In the end I stopped calling, or she did. We wrote letters instead.'

'Do you still have them?'

'I knew you'd ask me that. I got rid of them after the inquiry. It was after my friend Melanie died, actually. She was very ill with cancer at the time Susie was killed. I don't know if she ever heard about what happened and I wasn't about to tell her. She passed away not long afterwards – just into the new year, it was. I think that's why I got rid of the letters – what with Mellie and everything it seemed like too much to cope with. Anyway, they're gone.'

'Melanie was one of Susan's bridesmaids too, wasn't she?'

'That's right – Tiziana was the third. We stayed close after school, Mellie and I. I'd go over to Edinburgh for birthdays or for Christmas shopping and we'd have a whale of a time. Tizz was Mellie's friend more than mine. We lost touch after Mellie died. She's living in Hong Kong now, or at least she was. I've not spoken to her in years.'

'Susan had one of Melanie's paintings, did you know that?'

'The one with the rooster? Mellie gave it to her as a wedding present. She was so talented. I have three of hers – one she gave me from her graduation show and two others I bought later. They're quite valuable now but I'd never part with them. You can look her up on the internet – Melanie Brody. Mellie loved Susie. In some ways they had more in common than Mellie and I did. She and Susie fell out of contact after the wedding. Neither of them would tell me why. Look, I brought some photographs.'

She reached into her handbag. 'Here we all are at Christmas – the year before our Highers, that was, Susan's dad took it. And here's one of us at the summer fair – Tizz took that one, that's why she's not in it. This is Susan with Shirley.'

They are in the Winter Gardens, you can tell by the flower beds. Shirley is a toddler, no more than three, blond hair fine and fair as dandelion fluff, pink Bermudas and a *Barbapapa* T-shirt. Susan is skinny, with much longer hair. She is wearing a denim skirt with buttons up the front, a lemon yellow blouse. Cath would not have recognised her in a million years.

The snapshot had the eerie transience of certain holiday snaps, the kind you forget all about and then find again years later, stuffed in the back of a drawer with half a dozen other photographs you can't remember taking. Off centre and slightly out of focus, photos where you'd pressed the shutter by mistake or someone had moved. Again that moment of glancing sideways, freezing time.

'I only went to the island the once,' Abigail said. 'The first time I'd actually seen Susan since the wedding. I'd looked forward to the visit, but talking to her was like wading through treacle. I cried so much on the ferry home it made my stomach ache. I could see things weren't right, but I had my own life to think about, my own problems. I should have made the effort to see her again, tried to get her to talk to me, but I couldn't face it.'

'Shirley told me Susan's parents never visited – is that true?'

'More or less. I think Susie went home a couple of times – when Shirley was a baby, that would have been – but Maurice and Emily never went to the island. They blamed themselves for everything – if they hadn't hired Johnny then Susan would never have met him, you can imagine. They never came to terms with it, with losing her, Maurice especially. They didn't attend the inquiry, either. I offered to go with them – I was afraid for them, to be honest, afraid of what people might say or think if they weren't there, if the papers got hold of the story, but they wouldn't hear of it. I remember Susie's dad saying he never wanted to hear the name of that scumbag spoken anywhere near him, he just wanted to bring Susie home to rest and let that be the end of it. I remember I was shocked to hear him say that – scumbag. Maurice hated bad language. You hear about people ageing overnight but they really did. Maurice McClellan was dead within a year of Susan. Emily went back to Edinburgh to live with her brother. I never heard from her again.'

*

ABIGAIL AND SUSAN HAD both attended Wellington School, the only private girls' school in Ayrshire. Cath kept thinking about a TV documentary she had seen a number of years before, about the police hunt for a serial killer in the American Midwest. The detective in charge of the case kept talking about how no detail is incidental, how everything is connected, how the murderer and the victim are bound to one another from the outset.

'The whole of the victim's life is a crime scene,' she had said. 'Find out who the victim really was and eventually you'll find your killer.' Cath remembered the detective's words because she'd found them intriguing. Whether they rang true she found harder to decide. Life usually had a knottier texture and made less sense. Someone was shagging someone else's wife, someone was filching money from the till, someone happened to walk into the pub just as the Dennis Hopper character was walking out. Chance, in other words. Bad luck. What did it matter where Susan had grown up, where she'd met John Craigie? The point was that she had met him, surely. The background detail was incidental. Nothing to do with Shirley or with the murders.

But then again, maybe the detective had been right after all because Ayr was like its name: solid, busy, prosperous, seen it all before and no need to gossip, thank you very much. Bold straight shoreline, pale sand and marram grass, the squat, functional outline of the ferry terminal. To the north, towards the docks, new developments of luxury apartments fronted the esplanade. To the south, towards the golf course, modern bungalows and old stone tenements stood shoulder to shoulder. Unlike the depleted steel towns of the Clyde estuary, Ayr appeared to be thriving. It had made its fortune through other means and was still doing well. Susan's father, Maurice McClellan, had been a family solicitor, a role so appropriate to his means and background it was almost funny. This was the comfortable world Susan had grown up in, the world she'd been used to. The world John Craigie had entered like a fish out of water. Talk about a stranger come to town. His dark to her light. Opposites attract.

You only have to look at the place. It's got origin story written all over it.

Cath took a series of photos of Abigail standing outside the school, two striking, turreted buildings right on the seafront. Like something out of a gothic novel, Cath thought. Fairy palaces. Difficult to believe such behemoths still existed. Abigail didn't seem to mind being photographed. She told Cath she had a son, Alex, who now lived in Manchester. 'I miss him, but he's doing well, he loves it down there, which is all that matters, really. Me and his dad are still good friends. Ray has another young family now.'

They walked south along the esplanade to where the McClellans had lived, not far from the golf course, on Beaufort Road. The Mercers' house had been just around the corner, on Racecourse View.

'You'd think it would have been the other way round, wouldn't you, what with Maurice being a partner and all?' Abigail said. 'My dad started out as a trucker and ended up managing his own fleet. He always wanted a house on Racecourse View and so that's what we got. Charlie's son, Danny, runs the business now. It's strange, the way things turn out.'

'Do you think there is any possibility that Susan was having an affair?'

Abigail glanced up sharply but kept on walking. 'I did wonder about it, yes. I believe Susie was planning to leave Johnny – once

Shirley had finished school, once Susie knew she'd be able to manage on her own. Susie never said anything outright but there were hints of it in her letters, just little things. Then Sonny came along, which put paid to that plan. Susie adored Sonny but I know that must have been a bad time for her because her letters just stopped. It was over a year before I heard from her again but when I did finally get a letter, something had changed. The old life seemed to have come back to her. She didn't say what had happened and I didn't ask – that bastard could have been reading her mail, for all I knew – but I had the feeling she would tell me on her own when the time was right. Six months later she was dead and now I'll never know.'

'Did she mention anyone – anyone by name?'

Abigail shook her head. 'I just hope she was happy while it lasted. God knows she deserved some joy in her life. I don't see it makes any difference now, who it was. Johnny would have gone berserk if he'd found out and that's for sure.'

'Enough to kill them all?'

'It's the only thing that makes sense, isn't it? Johnny discovers that Susie is seeing someone, shoots her and the children, then dashes off in the van to go and kill the other fellow. You do know he was driving away from the ferry terminal when he crashed? Good job he was killed or there'd have been four dead instead of three. Johnny I don't count. If he did what they say he did he deserves to be in hell. I always knew John Craigie was a scoundrel. I only wish I'd said as much to Susan before she got mixed up with him.'

Scoundrel. A word that was rarely used now, but seemed to fit John Craigie perfectly. If anyone's life was a crime scene waiting to happen, it had been his.

Just before she went to catch her train, Cath asked Abigail Mercer if she could remember the name of John Craigie's best man.

'I noticed him in the wedding photograph. Could he have been interested in Susan, do you think?'

'I don't think so.' Abigail frowned. 'He was called Matt, I think. Matty? He was Johnny's friend though. He wasn't from here, or from the island. I don't think Susie ever laid eyes on him before her wedding day.'

9·

THE FOLLOWING MORNING AN email arrived from Adam. **Where are you?** he wrote. Cath thought that if it was possible for an email to be peevish, this was it. **Let me know when you're back.** Things were bad again with Miranda, in other words. In the past Adam had called Cath clinging, dependent. There was none of that here.

'There is an imbalance in our relationship,' Adam had said to her, the second or maybe the third time they slept together. 'I am in a marriage and you are not. This situation is far more difficult for me than it is for you.'

Cath had listened without batting an eyelid. She had agreed with him even, expressed sympathy for what he must be going through. The idea that she could not live without someone – where had that started? The stark emptiness she had felt, from the first moments of the relationship, at the thought of not seeing Adam, not sleeping with him, not receiving his messages. If she told herself it had begun with Adam she would be lying. Before Adam there had been that guy Ravi from when she was working at the GFT, then that politics student who'd been a vague mate of Steve's. Anyone who showed an interest. Adam had been the worst, though, he'd been like an addiction.

Cath had never done drugs herself, except she had, she realised that now, of course she had, drugs as corrosive and mind-numbing as any chemical. The trembling limbs, the crying, the ecstatic sense of relief when he finally called. As if she could live forever now, everything was all right because she'd had her fix. The terror that began creeping back again almost immediately, that filled up her body and mind like a physical poison. Her constant acquiescence to his demands. Her panicked determination that no one should know.

Now the curse had lifted, like a fever. The urgency of her need, the adrenalin rush of panic was impossible to recall in meaningful detail. She closed Adam's email without answering it. You are in a marriage and I am not, she thought. Enjoy. It was Adam's wife, Miranda, she felt sorry for – she was stuck with him. She found herself thinking of Susan – Susan Craigie, who according to Abigail had been clever but who had never weighed the value of that cleverness, not compared with being loved or just plain fucking, being desired.

Cath opened the window to let in air: the cries of gulls, the parp-parp of the departing ferry, the frothy V-shaped wake of a speeding cruiser. She took out the photo Abigail had given her of Susan and Shirley in the Winter Gardens, Shirley was different from Susan, you could see that at once, so small and yet already resilient, her sense of self apparent in the way she tugged at her mother's hand, demanding to see, to go, to be released.

But what if the Susan Cath had known had been a facade, a simulacrum for the real Susan to hide inside? Who had been murdered, the real Susan or the placeholder? The question was important, because answering it correctly would help define the killer's motive. Compliant, mousy Susan would have been murdered as punishment – for overstepping the mark, for disobeying orders. The real Susan though – intelligent, imaginative, deep-down angry – had she been killed simply for showing herself, or to prevent her from leaving?

Might each of these answers also suggest a different killer? The questions were still circling inside her head when another email came in, this time from Alice.

Come over, it said. **I've found something amazing**. Cath logged off and pulled on her coat, glad to be distracted, energised at the thought of seeing Alice. She arrived at Westland Road to find the porch door open, the front door unlocked. Island habits, rubbing off on Alice already.

'Alice?' Cath called out, not wanting to startle her.

'In the living room.' She sounded excited, turning quickly and smiling as Cath entered the room. Bare feet and skinny jeans, Fair Isle sweater, the island again. Her toenails had been painted an iridescent blue.

Cath drew in her breath. In front of her on the dining table was Shirley's dolls' house.

'Isn't it incredible? There's all this other stuff inside – gorgeous little tables and chairs and beds and things. It weighs a ton. I had to get the guys who've been clearing the garden to bring it downstairs for me.'

'Where did you find it,' Cath said. She did her best to sound casual, though in fact she felt unmoored. If she had thought about it at all, which she had not, she would have assumed the dolls' house had been destroyed or given away, removed by house clearance. The mysterious brother might have taken it even, though Abigail Mercer had not mentioned Susan having a brother, Cath realised belatedly, she had spoken of Susan McClellan as an only child. In any case, the idea that the dolls' house might still be there, inside the Craigie house, was both fantastic and terrible. Cath found herself thinking of a horror film she'd been to see with Steve one time, the awful moment right near the end when the woman with the demon after her realises she's still holding the cursed coat button.

Bloody awesome that was.

Bloody stupid more like.

'In that cupboard at the top of the stairs,' Alice said. 'The one that wouldn't open. It's been bugging me since I moved in. I had to call a locksmith in the end. He cut through the old lock with a hacksaw – it was rusted solid. He said it was strange, because it's normally only outside locks that corrode like that. He's put a new one in now. Anyway, don't you think it's beautiful?' She gazed down at the house. Proudly, Cath thought, as if she'd made it herself, The House that Alice Built. 'I'm almost scared to touch it.'

'That was Shirley's,' Cath said. 'Her dad made it for her. She used to keep it in her bedroom, on an old piano stool. She once told me she wanted to burn it down, like Twelve Oaks.'

'Twelve Oaks?'

'That grand Colonial mansion in *Gone with the Wind.* I can't believe it's still here.'

Cath stepped forward towards the table, hunkered down. The brass catch that kept the front closed was tarnished, but intact. The whole structure smelled faintly mouldy, like dampened hardboard, though there was no sign of any damage, at least not on the outside.

'That's incredible,' Alice said. 'I feel a bit freaked out now, to be honest. Did he make all the furniture, too?'

'He did. Are the dolls still in there?'

The dolls had not belonged to the house, not originally, they had belonged to Susan, a mismatched collection of little people, none of them quite in proportion to any of the others. There had been one doll in particular, called Emmy, that Shirley used to bring to school with her, hidden inside her pencil case. Unlike the house itself, Shirley had been fond of her. Because the dolls had been her mother's? Cath had not thought about it that way at the time, though now it seemed obvious.

The house was haunted by John Craigie. The dolls had been in need of rescue, like Shirley herself.

'I don't think so. I haven't seen any.'

Cath wondered what had happened to Emmy, to all of them, whether they too were still at Westland Road somewhere or adrift in the world. The idea was chilling, saddening, though she'd not thought of Emmy in years until just now.

'What should I do with it?' Alice was saying.

'You bought the main house, so the dolls' house is yours too, you can do what you like with it. You could even sell it, if you wanted to. It's probably worth something.'

'I don't want to sell it.' Alice hesitated. 'I was thinking I might have a shelf built for it, here in the living room. What do you think?'

'Are you asking my permission?'

'No, not really. I just don't want you to think I'm being disrespectful or anything. To your friend, I mean. You don't sound too sure.'

'Shirley would think it was hilarious, having her dolls' house put on show like that. I used to love playing with it. Do the lights still work?'

'I didn't know there were lights.'

'There's a battery under the floor panel. It would be dead by now anyway.'

'I don't think we should tell Saheed about this. Where the dolls' house came from, I mean. If he knew who made it he'd go nuts. He'd want me to get rid of it. I'll say I found it in an antique shop. Are you OK with that?'

'No problem,' Cath said. So now they had a secret, the two of them. A secret from Saheed. No problem at all. 'Was there anything else inside the cupboard, by any chance?'

'Just a box of junk. Christmas decorations. It's up in the spare room if you want to go through it.'

PERSIL AUTOMATIC, THE SLANTED blue capitals faded but still visible, a strip of silver tinsel poking out from between the flaps. Inside, on top of the tinsel, the light-up plastic reindeer that used to stand on the Craigies' living-room windowsill from 1 December until Twelfth Night, walled in between the curtain and the glass so you could see it glowing through the darkness as you came up the path. Glass baubles – green, red, gold – and a paper bag full of old Christmas cards, some of them already cut down to make gift tags – a snow-covered fir tree, a spherical robin. The soft and pliable feeling of old correspondence.

Most of the cards were without envelopes, though the names of the senders would be there on the inside. Maybe the name of the best man – Matt, or Matty? – would be among them. Cath realised with a start that the police had in all likelihood never examined the box or its contents – if they had done they'd have moved it out of the cupboard, taken the cards away as evidence. Maybe they'd tried and failed to get the cupboard open then forgotten all about it. Whatever the sequence of events, it seemed likely that no one had touched the cards or decorations since Susan Craigie had last put them away. Eight months before her death, that would have been. Shirley's last Christmas.

'Do you mind if I take these home?' Cath said. 'There might be more of Shirley's stuff in here. I remember that reindeer, for a start.'

'Be my guest. I was going to take the box to the dump anyway.'

'Seriously?'

'How was I supposed to know who it belonged to? It looked like rubbish to me, something the tenants left behind. Talking of which, I looked up those documents for you, the sales contract from when I bought the house? The vendor's name was Roger Blair. Does that mean anything to you?'

'Was that the person selling the house or the man who died?'

'Selling the house. The dead guy's name was Vernon – Vernon Blair.'

'Susan's maiden name was McClellan – her father was Maurice McClellan. I've never heard of anyone named Blair.'

'Might they have been Susan's mother's family? I mean, technically. John Craigie's family would have inherited the house, because the court agreed that Susan, Shirley and Sonny all died before him – but if he didn't have any relatives left living everything would have gone to Susan's side. All big ifs, I guess, but it's a possibility.'

'I think you could be right. Susan's dad died not long after the murders – I found that out from Abigail. And it was Susan's mother, Emily, who had the brother, not Susan. That could have been Vernon. Maybe Roger was Vernon's son – and Susan's cousin.'

'Or her secret love child.' Alice grinned. 'With the house held in trust for him by his elderly uncle. He'd want to sell, of course, the moment he turned eighteen. He's probably halfway to Australia by now. Only joking,' she added. 'Like I say, I never met him. He could have been eighteen or eighty.'

'The dates would fit though, wouldn't they?'

'Maybe, but if Susan was pregnant back then you'd have noticed, or Shirley would have. Who calls their kid Roger these days, anyway?'

They both started laughing. 'Have you ever heard of anyone believing in fairies?' Cath said suddenly, the words, like greased ball bearings, escaping down the cracks in the floorboards, bouncing away.

Where the fuck did that come from?

Alice stopped laughing. 'Where the fuck did that come from?'

'Just something Shirley said once, about her father being scared to go in the woods because he believed there were fairies there. I thought she was joking when she told me but now I'm not sure, I have an idea she might have been telling me the truth. I'm sure she was, actually. But it doesn't seem to fit with him at all.'

'It depends though, doesn't it? My grandma in Senegal believes in fairies. She even leaves out little meals for them, to stop them coming into the house and messing up her things. The good neighbours, she calls them, or the bakhna rakhna. Me and my brothers used to take the piss out of her all the time when we were children but she didn't care. She used to quote that bit of Shakespeare about there being more things in heaven and Earth than are dreamed of in our philosophies. Grandma loves Shakespeare, she knows tons of him by heart. She worked for the World Health Organisation, she's travelled all over the world. She still takes those old beliefs seriously though. Look after the bakhna rakhna, she once told me, and they'll look after you.'

'You don't believe yourself though?'

'I don't know what to think. Mostly I prefer numbers, though numbers can be scary sometimes, too. When you think there's literally no end to them. There's a school of thought that says numbers are a human invention, that they didn't exist before we thought of them. I think that's rubbish – we didn't invent numbers, we only discovered them. Even when the world ends, there will still be numbers.'

Alice looked tired suddenly, or upset. Like there was a shadow on her, Cath thought. Or maybe the light just changed.

'I should be going,' she said. 'I'm sure there's stuff you need to be getting on with.'

'There are some forms I should fill in, actually. I'm applying for a summer workshop on the history of chess. Saheed found it for me. It's in Toledo.'

'You play chess?'

'Saheed's much better than me but he thought I might enjoy it. Get some sun, meet some new people, that sort of thing.'

People who played chess and understood higher mathematics. The kind of people Saheed wanted Alice to meet. People who weren't Cath.

You're jealous. Admit it.

'That sounds really cool,' Cath said. 'I've never been to Toledo.'

'Let's go for that drink, though, soon – tomorrow evening?' She squeezed Cath's fingers. 'Are you sure you'll be all right lugging that box?'

'It's not heavy,' Cath said. 'Don't worry about it.'

Walking back to Argyle Terrace with the Persil box in her arms, Cath thought of the plastic reindeer inside and felt like crying.

'Ugly bastard,' Shirley had called it. 'Ugly bastard, otherwise known as Boris.'

The both of them screaming with laughter, doubled over. Why Boris? Shirley hadn't said, though of course the name had stuck. Back at the flat, Cath took Boris out of the box and set him upright on the living-room windowsill. She'd expected his bulb to be broken but when she plugged him into the mains he lit up immediately.

Way to go, you ugly bastard. Go Boris.

Cath unpacked the rest of the box's contents on to the table: more tinsel, a packet of red table napkins, a green-and-white checked cotton tablecloth with a lace edging. Small mementoes, pathetic really. Final traces of Susan, trying to make a place of safety and comfort, cobbling things together, hoping not to be noticed.

Beneath the tablecloth was the clockwork rooster from Melanie's painting. Even after all these years, its colours were still lustrous, those blue and yellow swirls, that hot ruby red. Phoenix colours. The tablecloth must have protected it, kept it bright. Cath was knocked sideways by the sight of it, by the little round key in its chest that she didn't dare touch in case she broke something, some fragile piece of clockwork, the spring that connected the present with the past.

She wanted to hug the thing, and squashed in next to the rooster was something else, a spiral-bound notebook with mottled covers, like a school exercise book only smaller. The pages were crammed with writing. Not Shirley's writing, which was wild and chaotic. A dog's breakfast, their form master Mr Sullivan had called it. This handwriting was squarer and more upright, small yet nonetheless bold and somehow serene. Not at all the kind of handwriting Cath would have expected Susan to have and yet who else's could it be? Most of what she'd written seemed to be lists – wildflowers, books, the kings and queens of Scotland and their dates, the buildings of Alexander 'Greek' Thompson with their various locations in Glasgow and across Argyll. Interspersed with the pages of the notebook were a number of loose items: the return half of a train ticket to Glasgow, a printed timetable for a season of talks on local archaeology at the island museum, a folded-over page from what must have been a smaller notebook with the text of a poem written on it. The handwriting was different from the handwriting in the notebook – larger and looser – although the poem itself was familiar.

Yesterday, upon the stair,
I met a man who wasn't there!
He wasn't there again today,
Oh how I wish he'd go away!

When I came home last night at three,
The man was waiting there for me
But when I looked around the hall,
I couldn't see him there at all!
Go away, go away, don't you come back any more!
Go away, go away, and please don't slam the door . . .

Last night I saw upon the stair,
A little man who wasn't there,
He wasn't there again today
Oh, how I wish he'd go away . . .

Like the William Allingham poem about the fairies, it was a piece of text that would be familiar to most people, the kind you learned by heart, that got repeated so many times the words often became confused or even changed entirely.

A little man, Cath thought, uneasily. For fear of little men. She wasn't sure it had been a little man in the version of the poem she remembered, but when she looked up the text online she saw it had been little man, after all. The things you forgot were often stranger than what you remembered. The poem had originally been part of a play, she discovered, and there were a dizzying number of references to it in other, later works of literature and in popular culture. There was even a song. Cath searched for it on YouTube – she had no trouble tracking down recordings of this one, a jaunty, minor key dance tune popularised by Glenn Miller and then covered by numerous lesser-known swing bands in the following years. Cath listened to it several times, quickly memorising the lyric line, whistling along. Like whistling in the dark, she thought. A buoyant, energetic melody to cover the eerie chill of the accompanying words.

Who had copied out the poem for Susan, and why had she kept it? Had Susan shoved these bits and pieces inside the notebook temporarily, for safekeeping, or had they been deliberately hidden?

The care she had taken in concealing the notebook suggested the latter, yet what meaning, if any, could be attached to them? Might the notebook and its contents be a code of some kind? A code at the bottom of a box that no one looked at from one year's end to the next, pushed to the back of a cupboard that wouldn't open.

Why had John Craigie never mended the cupboard lock, in any case? You'd have thought it would have driven him mad, a shoddy piece of workmanship like that.

Chance, blind chance. Either that, or that old adage about it always being the cobbler's children who have to go without shoes. Everything looks like a secret if you stare at it hard enough.

The repeating references to little men, though. Coincidence, obviously, Cath thought, though the explanation was not one she found consoling or even convincing.

QUEEN MAB AND HER
SERVANT, JOHNNY, THEIR
STORY IN THE WILDS

YOU NEED TO GET out of here, Johnny man, before you do
for someone. Don't think I'm joking.

That's what Finn said and Johnny trusted Finn, who still called
him every Friday at six on the dot at the phone box at the top of
the village just as they'd agreed. Best not call the house, Johnny
had warned him. Da'll only go sticking his oar in if you do. Solid
as a rock was Finn. Johnny'd always secretly hoped Finn would
marry Denise, so they'd be brothers for real. Denise had other ideas
though and now she was dead. That cunt she'd been screwing, Iain
Fletcher, had almost pegged out on him, and everyone was saying
it was Johnny's fault that he'd landed himself a holiday in intensive
care, nurses dancing attendance round the clock and more tit on tap
than you could shake your dick at. He should be so lucky.

There's nothing you can do there but harm, Finlay had said,
and I mean to yourself, so best get the fuck out. Finlay was away
to Ardrossan now, working on the ferries. He'd said Johnny was

welcome to stay with him while he got himself sorted, that there was
always work going, That's what mates are for, isnae? And yes, he
and Finlay were friends, had been since before they could walk, the
two of them tight as frogs in the long grass, tumbling and yipping
like fox cubs, jacking off just for the lark of it, to see how far they
could shoot. Wouldae been queer only how could it be queer when
they were frigging brothers. Finlay laughing like a vixen. Yip yip yip.

THOSE ROASTING SUMMER MONTHS before Denise died. Queen
Mab and her glorious retinue stirring in the bushes. Thrashing their
carriages over the flagstones at the bottom of the High Street and
down the auld side path that drowned in mud in autumn, froze solid
in the darkness of January, dry as dust in August but not yet, still
loamy, still sticky as Granny Lin's gingerbread or the sweat between
a girl's thighs as you tore off her jeans.

Like glass she was, his queen, shrieking no! no! no! when the
wind was up, when it whistled between her legs and tickled her
quinny. The little footman who drove her, that mean-faced sprite
in poofter tights and a harlequin hat. Played the flute like a daemon
that one, music that turned into water as if the wee bastard were
actually playing rain. Johnny knew how daft that sounded but
there it was. A sound to turn your mind to gloop if ye listened
too much on it.

His queen, like glass. Johnny swore that if ever she looked at him
full on he'd shrivel like a weed, join the zombie hordes of kingdom
come and be glad to do it. Was it because of Mab that Johnny could
not truly have given a shit about Tassie Hutchens, the girl Finn swore

blind had a fancy for him. Fancy for your cock more like, go for it man, she's gagging.

Violet eyes and her mother's lipstick and was it the eyes that fooled him, just for a second? Tacita, what a frigging poncy name that was, which was why everyone called her Tassie, Johnny supposed.

END OF TERM DISCO and he'd had three cans even before they started with the music because this would be it, Johnny's last time going through those gates and thank fuck he'd survived those endless bleeding years without blinding someone, without getting himself sent to Borstal the way that old punk Mister Harvarden had swore he would. He'd come close though, once or twice, Johnny could think that out loud now he hadnae actually done it and the escape route was clear. Let himself taste the blood the way he knew it wouldae tasted, streaming from his nose and down over his chin. Mister Harvarden or whoever totally out of it, head smashed open on the tarmac and out go the lights. Johnny knew how it wouldae gone down. He wouldnae given a shit about being sent to Borstal either if it weren't for Mab. Mab and the hills. In Borstal, as some wisearse once said, no bugger can hear you scream.

Johnny sighed. They were playing some iffy shit by Kool and the Gang and there finally was Tassie Hutchens in her skintights and a shiny purple top that showed she didnae have a bra on.

Hey Johnny, she goes, like she's been hanging around waiting for him, gagging for it like Finn said, which would be fine but he hated dancing, didn't know where to put hisself, made him feel like an eejit.

Tassie's friends thought he was scum, you could tell, just the way they nudged each other. Fancy going outside? Johnny said and once they were in the open he felt he could breathe. Round the back by where the boys' toilets were he bit her hard on the arm, between the elbow and the shoulder, the meaty bit. He could taste her sweat, like the salt you get left behind at the bottom of a bag of crisps only sweeter, like a poison you wanted to lick and lick and lick until you frigging keeled over.

Hey watch it, Tassie said. She looked down at her bitten arm, the teeth marks set in a semicircle like he'd taken a bite from an apple or a slice of Mother's Pride. Johnny pushed her back against the toilet wall and then they were kissing, his teeth chap-chap against hers, glass beakers clashing. Johnny tasted blood – his lip or hers, he couldnae tell. She pulled back from him a bit or at least she tried to but he wouldnae let her, she didn't mean it. In the hall they'd moved on to ABBA and what the fuck his dick was killing him. Tass, he mumbled, Tass. Grabbed her hand and shoved it in his crotch. Heard her gasp then giggle thought he would die he was so hard. Tugged the zip of her jeans – her jeans then his jeans and by the time he had it in her he was sweating like a fucking pig like a rutting boar and his head was swimming. Going into her like dousing his head in the burn the sweet relief of it. Gripped her shoulders dug in his nails and God the sounds she made, like little sobs and he was coming like a freight train like a fricking omnibus.

Afterwards, through a haze, he saw her purple top was torn from where she'd gone down on the concrete. Ye all right? Johnny said. Tass nodded and edged away, pulled up her jeans. Now it was over he had no idea what he should do. Talk to her, he supposed, only what about?

I think I'll go and see where Jillie's got to, she said. She smiled, or at least sort of, which meant things must be all right. Right you go, Johnny said, shrugged, an awkward wee moment of total silence. Should he say thanks? Didnae sound right to him but then what did you say? He turned away for a moment, his attention caught by some noise, by some wanker flipping catcalling like a frigging maniac and when he switched back again to face her Tassie was gone.

He saw her again the following week, waiting at the bus stop with some mates of hers. That Jillian Murphy who was a right bitch looked at him like he was dirt and all because her da was a flipping parish councillor. Also Miriam Milosz, who everyone fancied and he meant everyone, they'dae been at her like bulldogs only she was going into a nunnery or something. What a waste.

Johnny crossed the road and strode right past them. Tassie glanced round at him then looked at the ground, the other two closing in like she needed protecting. Stupid coo. Like it had been that great. Like he even gave a shit what she and her bitch friends thought of him. Like fuck.

SO MUCH EASIER OUT on the hills and now that school was over he could do as he liked. The hills had always been the saving of him and while Da was away at the construction sites Johnny rambled, ten miles and more on some days. He was used to being out of doors in all weathers although that summer before Denise died was clear and bright and blue as a box of Daz. Hot as a bastard and there were some folk worried about grass fires and the local arsonists. No need to fret with Johnny around. One whisper of anyone trying to set a fire in these parts, they'd have Johnny to deal with. Unlike that ponce who called himself a copper, Johnny had no scruples about using his fists.

The thought of fire in the hills chilled Johnny to his fingernails though he'd never speak of his terror, not to anyone. The movie inside his head that showed him flames ripping through the undergrowth and through the nests of nightingales and plovers, nightjars and lapwings and the famous red grouse, the helpless ground-nesters and Johnny still remembered the time he'd come across the bird-nesters, feckless queers from the city with their fuck-off jackets and skull tattoos. Ten year older than Johnny at least but so frigging what, he'd rattled their cages for them, sent one of them flying, blood uncoiling from his thickshit head like oil from a can.

They'd called him psycho but they were the psychos – they had no right to those eggs and that was that. Johnny had told them so and he'd tell them again, harder, if they were pigshit stupid enough to try coming back.

Lying with his face in the grass, the scents of heather and earth and dried-up rain, salty like Tassie Hutchens, dried in under his nails, greenish and rank. He'd thought about Tassie for days after they did it, replaying it over and over, his shame and his arousal tangled together like grubby sheets at the bottom of the bed. She had fancied him right enough, she'd wanted him inside her. So why did Tassie Hutchens hate him now? Fucked if he knew. The only thing Johnny was certain of was that whatever had existed between them before had been scoured away like mildew from an overflowing drain.

He thought how it would be if he could fuck her again, fuck her in ways you weren't supposed to think about and the pictures inside his head were driving him mad. In the hills his mind felt cooler, sober, even in the blistering heat of Denise's last summer. The music of a burn, the patter of water falling over stones, unseen but still somewhere. A vein in the earth, a secret stash of life, tadpoles turning to frogs and half-wild cattle roaming everywhere, high on freedom and sunshine, the abattoir a cruel mythology, horror stories no one repeated in case the weans heard.

GRANNY LIN IT HAD been who first told him of Mab, his da's ma who'd been a teacher up at the old school before it closed. His father had helped to build the new school, before Johnny were even a glint in the world's eye was the way Granny Lin put it. Granny Lin used words the way Johnny's father Kenny Craigie used bricks and mortar, building something from nothing, like the both of them had a way of seeing what wasn't there before. Granny Lin never had a TV. Never saw the point, she said. Not when there were books to read.

She'd read those books to Johnny, books about birds and beetles and kings and queens, Darwin's voyage aboard the *Beagle* and the Battle of Culloden, the details fermenting inside his mind like parts of one big story. Men lying low in the fields at night, their britches sodden with dew and piss and still they darest not move in case of the soldiers. Dogs barking from a distant farmhouse, the maddening aroma of tatties and mutton stew.

O then, I see Queen Mab hath been with you, read Granny Lin. She is the fairies' midwife, and she comes in shape no bigger than an agate stone on the finger of an alderman. And in this state she gallops night by night through lovers' brains, and then they dream of love. Granny Lin set the book aside, a faraway look as if she too were dreaming. Imagine her, Johnny, she said. With all her glorious retinue, her masters and commanders and jesters and pot boilers and cooks' boys, all the queen's horses and all the queen's men, the good neighbours who ruled this land before us and humans too dull to see them, be they servicemen or lawyers or ladies or plain old labourers. Too set in their thinking, too slow in their ways.

But you can you see her, can't you, Granny Lin?

On Midsummer Eve, perhaps, his grandmother laughed. Keep your eyes peeled, Johnny.

And through the endless afternoons of that endless summer, Johnny lay on his back in the grass and dreamed of how she might come to him, Queen Mab with her violet eyes and limbs like glass. Dark hair tangled from where she'd slept on it, though why should she give a damn what anyone thinks? She's not beautiful like Tassie Hutchens in her purple top, though really wasn't that top like something a slut would wear, a prozzie, which was why everything went wrong after most like, and also why Tassie stank like a can of sardines. She was especially not beautiful like Miriam Milosz, hair like a frigging waterfall and get-lost eyes. Mab was like her name – blunt and vaguely grubby, dirt beneath her fingernails and naked above the waist like the lads on the construction site, not giving a toss that her tits were out and laughing like a hyena at anyone who did.

The inside of her though would be like silk, smooth and clinging as spiderwebs. Johnny'd slip in, go gliding right out of this world and into another, his queen of glass solid beneath him, growling like a dog for the want of a bone. Your faithful servant, he would breathe then, like one of those plays on TV, posh tossers dolled up to look like Henry the randy VIII and his six headless wives. Fling down his coat and off with his britches, straight in hard like iron into mud. Your faithful servant, your faithful servant your faithful fucking service this bitch this cunt this queen like he was going to die and die right afterwards he wished he could die in the grass there and forever with the dirt on his jeans his knees the backs of his sodding thighs right there.

His head spinning like a fairground, like after three drams of Da's Macallan that he'd nipped into once when Da was out and he'd been beaten for it after, yes, but fuck it were worth it. The lilac scent of wind and burning grass. Like Tassie never happened and the world was new.

JOHNNY CRAIGIE WAS GOING to be a carpenter when he grew up. He'd known it from a bairn, from the age of eight, so what was the point of school, all that boredom and agony?

Youse better off with wood, lad, so his da said, Da with three broken fingers permanently crooked from where they'd not set proper and a wrist the same. His left, praise God, still able to take the weight of a block of stone but weren't too clever now nonetheless. No instinct in it, Da said, and Da would know. Fingernails so split they never quite grew back, finger pads callused as crab shells, cuticles brittle as glass when the winter frosts came. Red as meat through the summer and all from the stone, the stone he hauled and the stone he cut, the stone he laid carefully into place like he were doing a jigsaw. His father was like a god, or so it had seemed to Johnny when he was younger. You could read the years in his father's shoulders and in his piggy-bent knees. Stone wore you down, like the climate, like the black roar of time.

*

JOHNNY AT FOUR, SLIPPING on the granite steps outside the village church, opening a gash in his forehead like a knife splitting silk. Blood spilling and spreading like ink across a desktop blotter, his auntie Jennie screaming get the doctor, Johnny blinking not knowing what were afoot, he dinnae feel a thing.

JOHNNY AT EIGHT, TRYING to leap across the burn, catching his varmint heel against a rocky outcrop. Sprawling on his stomach, half in and half out, the pain in his foot red raw enough to make his teeth chatter. His face, pressed hard to the ground, slick with river water and his own muddy tears. Driven to the hospital in someone's pickup, his foot set into plaster like a frigging moon boot. The whole school had signed it, some with obscenities, words they shouldn't have known but flaunted like flags.

JOHNNY CRAIGIE AT UNLUCKY thirteen, messing about on the site with some mates when the men were gone for the day, playing a game on the scaffolding they called Walking the Plank. Johnny hanging by his belt buckle just long enough to find his grip or else it wouldae been over. They'd not known about the foreman, Mental Mickey, holed up in the prefab glugging tea and checking invoices. Seen the whole thing, had Mental – I'll ave youse, hollering like a bull on the rampage, like a flipping stuck pig. Called Johnny's da the following morning, swore he'd go to the management if Craigie couldn't keep his offspring under control. More 'an my job's worth, said Mental. Who'll be liable when he bashes his brains out? Ever think about that?

Da belted Johnny until the blood came. Teeth clenched against the rage against the tears, six parallel lines of welts hardening through the course of the days to puckered scabs. Serves you bleedin right you waste of space. You think I'm losing my job over ye youse got another think coming.

Mam, Johnny wailed. He'd not cried out loud for his mother since the age of three.

You think that bitch is coming tae save you? Scream on, laddie-o.

Another blow, another sheet of fire, spreading havoc through the thickets of his nerves like an undead cigarette igniting the leaves and litter of the forest floor. His young frame creaked and bent, a sapling tested almost to destruction in its first summer storm. His mother Ruth locked herself in the pantry, biting down on a balled-up tea towel like she meant to choke herself.

You bet the fuck youse learned your lesson, his father said. Three days later he let Johnny ride along with him in the pickup running errands for the foreman. At the builders' yard Johnny stayed close to his father, saying nothing.

That's never your lad there, Kenny? Darren Fawcett, one of the truck drivers, his brother Minty still in the nick for picking a fight with his boss and breaking his arm.

Outgrow me yet, so he will, Kenny Craigie replied. Ruffled Johnny's hair and gave him a push. Johnny staggered on his still-sore legs and tried not to smile. The smile would show he was happy and happy was for poofs.

Good lad, his father added, and turned away. On the way back from the yard they stopped at Maisie's Cafe for fish and chips.

*

WOOD WAS WARMER THAN stone and wood was kind. Johnny learned the names of the trees like they were an alphabet: alder, ash, aspen, beech, birch, cedar, chestnut, cypress, Douglas fir, elder, elm. He learned to recognise the shapes of their leaves, from their outlines against the horizon like the silhouettes of gods. In summer when they shimmered with birdsong, in winter when they stood naked, gaunt grey shivering drunks against the sky. Johnny could recognise a tree just from its smell, the scent of the bark when you pressed your face against the trunk, sap rising up through the grain like sweat through pores. Each tree a castle, a stronghold, a bastion, which was Granny Lin's word, and also meant castle.

The whole of Scotland was forest once, Granny Lin had told him. Most of England, too. We had wolves and wildcats and reindeer. We even had bears.

A thousand years ago, lynx had roamed wild through the Borders, down through the Kielder forest and into Northumberland. If humans ever went extinct the forests would grow back again. Like if the Americans dropped the bomb, or wiped everyone out with missiles the way they said in the papers. The wolves would come back too – wolves and snow. And why shouldnae they come back? Johnny asked himself. It was their forest, for Christ's sake.

Johnny sometimes found himself almost weeping with joy at the thought of it, the return of the wolves and beavers, though he didn't know why. Because of the fairies, probably – it were their forest too. No fairy ever trapped a wolf or poisoned a tree.

He thought of Queen Mab in her hazelnut chariot, dashing from treetop to treetop, her footmen whooping and whistling like rodeo riders, tiny maverick daredevils on the black backs of ants. Queen Mab would see all, her pleasure quivering in her violet-painted eyelids. Up the airy mountain, down the rushy glen, we dare not go a-hunting, for fear of little men. Granny Lin had taught him the song when he was small. Johnny could sing, could carry a tune sure as a fiddle though no one knew it. Singing, like smiling and happiness, was for poofters.

JOHNNY KNEW HIS FATHER was watching him, watching as he learned to saw and plane and graft and eventually make things. Not up to much at first though he quickly got better.

He's a marvel with his hands, your lad, Johnny heard someone saying to his da once outside the butcher's. Da nodded, once, said nothing. Johnny ducked his head and crossed the street, hoping his father hadn't realised he was there. For Ken Craigie's next birthday Johnny made him a box to keep his matches in. Cedarwood, with a sliding lid, like the pencil case he'd made already for Denise. The box's sides were neatly dovetailed, the lid slid back and forth with a satisfying clunk.

That's good wood, that, his father said, placing the wooden box at the end of the hearth. So he could reach it from his armchair, Johnny supposed. From wherever you were in the room, you could see the box gleaming.

THE EVENING OF THE day they found Denise's body strung up in the barn, Johnny went round to Iain Fletcher's house and dragged the little eejit out into the street. Everyone yelling and some fat fucker – Hamish McAllister's da, by the heft of him – trying to pull him off of Fletcher like he were a pit bull. Dream on, Granddad, get out of my face. Johnny dug in an elbow, Hamish McAllister tottered and fell away. Cursing like a sailor he were and seriously, talk about beer belly, talk about lardy guts. Molly McLintoch screaming go and get my Davey except they all knew where Constable David McLintoch was, he was down the Whytbank, same as always. Chewing the cud with the rest of the codgers, none of them mentioning Johnny's sister but all of them thinking well if it weren't that Iain Fletcher who got her pregnant then who the hell was it?

Fletcher's little blond curls, that's what did for him, the way they bobbed and jounced against his forehead like tendrils of bracken. Little angel bum boy. Ethereal – Granny Lin's word. P'rhaps if Iain Fletcher had been less ethereal Denise wouldnae ended up swinging from the rafters like a piece o' meat.

The relief of that first blow, like fucking, like the moment he'd first thrust into Tassie and with that same sweet aftertaste. Fletcher's blood, thick as gravy, smeared across his knuckles. The iron-heavy scent of it, like granite after rain, like a bag of wet nails. The urge to lick it, to suck Fletcher's juice from his fingers as if it were chicken grease, the impulse so intense he could barely restrain it.

I'll have youse, he bellowed, or thought he did, though perhaps he'd said nothing. Perhaps the words came from somewhere outside of him perhaps even the devil. Fletcher were trying to raise hisself so what in hell were Johnny to do but hit him again, send him sprawling into the gutter where he belonged?

There was a sound like McKeown the butcher hitting steak with a mallet then Fletcher went limp. Little faker. Johnny kicked him square in the stomach – that ought to shift him – only the kick landed like a boot in cow shit, mulchy and flat. Someone was tugging him by the shoulder, wrenching him back.

Leave him, Johnny', won't yer? Bugger's out cold.

Get the doctor, call an ambulance, someone was screaming. Johnny tugged himself free, twisted around to get a reckoning with whichever twat was trying tae hold him and there was Jimbo, Finn's big brother. Six year older'n Finn and one leg dodgy from where he'd fallen off a tractor but still a man. Had a wean of his own now did Jimbo, wife from Germany or Sweden, one of them places, hair like spindrift. Gave Johnny the willies she did, had the look of a witch on her. Jimbo Matheson was a legend though. If there were anyone on this sorry planet Johnny would listen to, that would be Jimbo.

Johnny, Jimbo said, repeating his name like it were a spell to calm a horse with and it were only then as Johnny noticed no one were looking at him now in any case, they were all dancing the grand fandango around the fuckwit on the ground.

Lad's had it, someone said.

No, no, he's breathing fine, he's just out cold.

Becky Fletcher was sat on the kerb, legs stuck out in front of her like the plastic legs on one of them clothes store dummies, like she'd been dumped there just for the moment because no one knew what to do with her.

You'd best come to ours, Jimbo said, and Johnny went, walking like a zombie, like he wasn't really there. Like he were watching himself on TV, Johnny remembered, and the strangest thing of all was it were still light out. That weird, cardboard-coloured light you only see at the height of summer, like there's no dark left anywhere on Earth and this is all that's going spare.

IS HE DEAD, YOU reckon? Johnny asked once they were back at the farmhouse. Jimbo had made him a cup of tea in his father George's *On the Buses* mug. George was still up and around when they first arrived, nodded to Johnny and then ignored him like it were any other day, like he didn't care who Johnny might or might not have killed so long as he hadnae done it on Matheson land. George had been in the polis, moons ago. Never talked about it much but then you wouldn't, would you? Footsteps overhead in the room above – Finn's mother. Julie, who looked like a film star and always looked at Johnny like he was dirt.

No different from that thug of a father, Johnny had overheard her saying to Finn once, though she had loved Denise, had Julie Matheson, lent her books and all, books that were still on the shelf in Denise's bedroom.

In the end George went upstairs as well and it was just him and Jimbo.

Fletcher'll be sound, Jimbo said. Hit his head on the kerb, that's all. The doctors'll sort him. You need to steady on, though. She was your sister and I know you're angry but you need to steady on. Stay at ours tonight. Cool off, he added, and so Johnny had slept in Finn's room, the room off the first-floor landing where Finlay had slept since he was seven. Still full of Finn's things, that massive UFO poster tacked to the wall with coloured drawing pins, the galleon made out of matchsticks still on the mantelpiece. Took Finn most of a year to build that lopsided monstrosity and it still looked like crap. Finlay Matheson might be his blood brother but he knew sod all about wood and that was final.

He lay on Finn's bed, shoes off but still in his jeans. Jimbo had told him he should clean himself up and so he had, scrubbing himself free of Fletcher's blood at least but getting fully undressed felt too much like surrender. Like he'd be closing the book on the day when he'd lost his sister.

The moon poked spiny fingers through the open curtains. Denise had always been a thorn in his side, her and her fucking books and her countless needling ways of telling him he was a git without saying a word. Pull out a thorn though and the hole that was left behind still hurt like buggery, wouldn't let up from telling you it was there. Johnny wanted to howl and he wanted to kill someone. Each time he closed his eyes he could still hear his mother screaming, Da slapping her across the face and saying leave off will yer, it's finished, there's noot to be done. The two of them staring at each other like strangers, his mother's hair half over her face like in a horror movie.

Denise you stupid bitch. When they were kids they used to spend whole days together, hiking in the hills, exploring the abandoned houses where you could still find all sorts. Coins so thick with tarnish they looked like bat turds, stray pieces of cutlery and china, old photographs in rusted gilt frames. He remembered how Denise had lost a shoe once, came off in the mud somewhere and it should have been easy to dig it out again only neither of them could land it. The two of them laughing like werewolves. Shut up or I'm going to cack my pants.

Everything changed when Granny Lin died, Johnny realised.

What was that about? Like as if the other world rose to claim him, to take him back to her. He could've swore he heard her voice sometimes, out on the hills when the wind was up. Mab and Lin, Lin and Mab, running the river like they were sisters now and most like always had been.

He refused to believe that when he went home in the morning Denise would not be there. That she would never be there, that she was with them now, disappeared into that tumult of darkness that was really a special kind of light. Black light, the light of fairyland. The light of the hole from the thorn in his side that refused to heal.

I O.

CATH WOKE LATE, MUCH later than normal, from a sleep so deep and relentless she had to drag herself awake. She had been dreaming about Alice, she realised, either Alice or Shirley. She felt confused, emptied out in a way that felt familiar from childhood illnesses. She showered and was just about to have breakfast when Steve called.

'Neil Furness has just been in, chasing his order. Where the fuck is it?'

'It's a Japanese import, I've already told him – they can take months to turn up. You can call Meridian if you want but they'll only tell you the same thing. I offered him the NMC recording but he wants Della Armitage playing, so he'll have to wait.'

'How do you remember all this shit?'

'That's what my job is, Steve – remembering shit. It's what you pay me for. I'm glad you called, actually. I need you to send me something.'

'Is it in stock?'

'It was when I left. *In the Faery Hills*, by Arnold Bax. It's on Chandos. Just put it on my account.'

'Fairies again?'

His question startled her for a moment. Then she remembered she'd emailed him before, about the Mud song.

'Long story. Just something I'm working on.'

'It's all this folk shit you listen to. How is island life, anyway? You sound a bit spaced out.'

'I was in the shower. And island life is fine. It feels different from when I lived here before.'

'Different how?'

'Hard to explain. Things I didn't appreciate as a kid, I suppose. I've been taking still lifes, mostly. I found this old notebook – it belonged to my best friend's mother – and I've been trying to photograph that. Not the book itself, the writing inside. Like found text. It's interesting.'

'And fairies fit into this how?'

She took a deep breath. 'There was a murder here – three murders, when I was fifteen. It was in all the papers. I found out the man who was convicted believed in fairies.' *Things in the woods. Kelpies or redcaps or some such.* 'Allegedly, anyway. I've been doing some background research.'

She found herself wishing she'd told Steve more, told him everything. Back when they first started to become friends, when she first started working in the shop even. The potted version felt like an evasion somehow. Not quite the truth.

What's stopping you then? Tell him now.

It would take me all morning. Maybe later.

'Seriously?'

'It looks that way. I've been wondering if it might help to explain what happened — why he did it. Say if he thought he was hearing voices or something. Maybe he was schizophrenic and was never diagnosed.'

'The devil made me do it, that kind of thing?'

'Yes. If someone has those kinds of thoughts — beliefs they feel they can't share with anyone — that would be a terrible pressure, wouldn't it, almost like leading a double life, your inner world against the real world. You'd feel very alone.'

'This bloke — he's not still there on the island, is he?'

'He's dead. Crashed his truck into a wall. The police think it was suicide.'

'The whole business sounds dodgy to me. You should stay out of it.'

Cath laughed. 'I'm taking photos, Steve, not tracking serial killers.'

'Well, if you need help fighting off demons, count me out.'

'Will do.'

Cath ended the call without saying goodbye, the way she would if she knew she'd be seeing him at work the following day. She missed him, she realised. She wondered how he was getting on without her, whether he'd tried to get off with Norah or something equally stupid. The city seemed far away, another country. Could what she'd said to Steve be true, that John Craigie had been mentally ill at the time of the murders? It made sense, in a way: the slow wearing away of a person's sanity, the sudden explosion of violence.

A psychotic break, it's called.

Still doesn't explain the gun, though.

But you'll come to that.

Cath scooped cereal into a bowl and then made coffee. She spent the next hour scrolling through various online articles on fairy mythology, curiously dry treatises on hallowed places and fairy oaks, the most effective way of lifting a curse. Apparently you couldn't, not really, you could only make reparations to the creature you'd offended and hope for the best. There was a lot of horrendous stuff about witch trials, several articles on Bridget Cleary, a woman who had been burned to death by her husband, who believed she was a changeling. Cath vaguely remembered hearing about the case before, in one of the Monk's history lessons. One of the most shocking things about it was that it had happened in 1895 and so almost within living memory.

The husband, Michael Cleary, had served fifteen years in prison. The judge refused to pass a verdict of murder, because in his opinion Cleary had truly believed that Bridget was not Bridget, but a fairy. He had killed his wife, but he had not killed his wife. Had not meant to, at any rate. The verdict was manslaughter.

While searching for more information on Bridget Cleary, Cath stumbled upon an archived newspaper article from the *Cleethorpes Chronicle* about a local man accused of drowning his nine-year-old daughter in a lake. The defendant believed the child was an impostor, an evil supernatural entity sent to spy on him.

The man's doctor claimed – as the judge in the Cleary case had claimed – that the dead girl's father should not be convicted of murder because he fervently believed his daughter was no longer his daughter. The trial took place in 1926. The accused, who had fought in the trenches in World War One, was initially charged with murder and sentenced to death. The capital conviction was overturned on appeal, the sentence commuted to manslaughter and life imprisonment.

The guilty man, whose name was David Coulter, hanged himself in his prison cell a year later.

There had been some cases of women harming children in the belief that they were changelings but they were rare. Mostly it was men – men in debt, men who were bigamists, men whose wives had started new jobs or made new friends they didn't approve of. Men who believed their wives were having affairs.

Through the fourteenth to the seventeenth century, men who killed their wives or daughters often walked free. Say or even hint that a woman was a witch or a fairy and the men who meted out justice would mostly believe you. Come the eighteenth century, such a defence became trickier to get away with. The rise in literacy helped – fewer people believed in witches, for a start. Fewer judges were convinced of fairy abduction as an excuse for murder. Nonetheless there were exceptions, as Bridget Cleary might have testified, had she not been doused with paraffin and set on fire.

According to the doctor from Cleethorpes, David Coulter's delusions were the result of shell shock. Unexplained noises, certain colours, the once-familiar contours of a well-loved face – such things could strike the victim of trauma with a terror the mentally healthy could scarcely imagine. As part of his defence, Coulter's lawyer had cited the case of Richard Dadd, the Victorian painter who had killed his father while believing he was the devil. Dadd was judged criminally insane, confined to Bethlem hospital and later to Broadmoor. His delusions never left him, though his doctors maintained that otherwise he was a model patient.

Cath remembered seeing reproductions of Dadd's most celebrated painting, *The Fairy Feller's Master Stroke*, but otherwise she knew nothing about him. When she looked for more information she discovered that Dadd had been a prodigy, admitted to the Royal Academy at the age of twenty. By all accounts he was also an admirable person – friendly, generous in spirit, open-hearted, adored equally by family and friends. He began suffering psychotic delusions while travelling as an artist in the Middle East. Back at home, his condition worsened, culminating in the murder of his father, whom he had once dearly loved.

So far as the public was concerned, Dadd was most famous for his fairy paintings, though when you examined them more closely, Cath thought, you could see at once how unsettling they were, how perverse, not even remotely like the decorative, idealised world depicted by his colleagues in the Academy. Dadd's colours were often drab, his textures encrusted and stodgy, like cold pease pudding. His good neighbours were prickly, unapproachable, misshapen. These were fairies that fucked and cavorted, they weren't nice people. You definitely would not want to find them at the bottom of your garden.

Modern medicine suggested a diagnosis of schizophrenia.

Dadd, Cath thought, as if his crime had been there in his name from the day he was born.

CATH MADE SANDWICHES, STUFFED them in her daypack with the smaller Canon and walked down into town. She caught the bus for Kilchattan Bay from the stop near the ferry terminal. On those summer days when the temperature lifted into the twenties, the village took on a Mediterranean aspect, the waterfront dusted with sand and swarming with children. In winter, Kilchattan Bay was magisterially bleak, its square-jawed sandstone villas holding hard to the shoreline, gazing stonily out at the water through gritted teeth.

Cath remembered coming here with Shirley one December – Shirley had wanted to buy some marzipan for Susan. 'It's Mum's favourite,' she insisted. She'd heard from Tallis Carruthers that they were selling it in the gift shop next to the post office, the real kind, crumbly and pale and made in Germany. Germans always ate marzipan at Christmas, Tallis had said. It was part of their tradition.

They had bussed down after school, with just enough time to get to the gift shop before it closed. Pitch black already, and the houses along the coast road sparkling with Christmas lights. In Kilchattan Bay the wind came in bitingly cold, buffeting from the east and peppered with ice crystals. The gift shop had fake snow in the window, the interior stuffy with warmth from an ancient convector heater. The marzipan was stacked on a shelf by the till, each bar wrapped in golden foil and tied with a ribbon. They were three pounds each, all the money Shirley had on her, more or less. They spent fifteen minutes or so going through the various knick-knacks that were on display, until Mrs Caister behind the counter told them to hurry and make up their minds, she was wanting to close.

Cath bought a broach for Moira, a silver Scottish terrier with a green glass eye. She knew her mother would probably hate it but at least it was something. They clubbed together their change to buy two hot chocolates, which had the advantage of keeping their hands warm until the bus came.

'I forgot my gloves,' Shirley said. 'It's bloody freezing.' She linked her knuckles tightly together around her Styrofoam cup.

'Have one of mine,' Cath said. 'We can put our other hand in our coat pockets.'

That struck them both as hilarious. This was the Christmas before Cath met Vicky. Sparse lights twinkling from across the bay, the taste of chocolate, over-sweetened and claggy and delicious on the back of her tongue.

John Craigie had been on the mainland all that week, finishing someone's kitchen in Dunoon.

TODAY THE WEATHER WAS kinder, the wind less pressing. The water's surface was smooth and clear, the shoreline gently sloping, a celadon bowl. Cath stood on the jetty, eating her sandwiches and thinking about Alice, staring out across the bay at the island of Great Cumbrae, back curled heavily against the sunshine like a slumbering bear. Once she'd finished eating she began taking photographs, not the view but small things, discarded things. Her water bottle, overturned on its side, the beach pebbles clearly visible through the plastic. A Chinese vase in a half-curtained window, its chipped rim glowing gold against a pale blue background.

Shirley would have loved that vase. She loved anything foreign, anything that offered her proof of life beyond the island. The gift shop where they had bought the marzipan had been closed down, the building converted into flats. Cath watched the bus drive down to the terminus, caught it on its way back from outside the post office. Already the light had changed, had grown denser and less transparent. She thought of Shirley with the single glove on, laughing like buggery. The glove had been black, she thought, or dark navy. Navy with pink stripes.

The memory came to her whole and entire, immutable as a film still. Back at the flat, she decided to have a shower and wash her hair before meeting Alice. While her hair was drying, she returned to studying the online reproductions of *The Fairy Feller's Master Stroke*. The painting depicted a fairy woodsman, surrounded by onlookers, preparing to split a hazelnut, its shell to be used in the construction of a carriage for haughty Queen Mab. A skilful and onerous task, cracking that nut, like cutting a diamond, or splitting the atom, with the ever-present propensity for disaster. The atmosphere of tension in the painting was palpable – you could almost sense the crowd of fidgeting goblins holding their breath. Cath found herself wondering if the onlookers were secretly hoping the fairy feller might fall down on the job, if they were jealous of his status. If the title of the painting was infused with sarcasm.

Dadd had left parts of the canvas unfinished, most notably the fairy feller's axe, the details barely sketched in. As if he could not bear to let his subject go, or, as some of the online commentary suggested, as if his obsession with the painting had acted as a kind of mental buffer against a fuller realisation of the crime he had committed in felling his father.

Before switching off the computer, Cath spent some time examining another painting by Dadd, his portrait of Sir Alexander Morison, who had been Dadd's physician at Bethlem Hospital and had encouraged him to continue with his art. Dadd had painted Morison standing in the grounds of his house at Newhaven, on the Firth of Forth. Behind Morison in the middle distance there were two farmers' wives, robust and unsmiling, talking secretively amongst themselves.

They could almost be fae women, Cath thought, sinister little figures straight out of *The Fairy Feller's Master Stroke*. The colours of the landscape – that clouded green, that pearlescent grey – were the colours of the island, quintessentially Scottish, though Cath read that Dadd, imprisoned in the asylum, had painted the scene entirely from black-and-white photographs.

'I CALLED MY GRANDMA last night,' Alice said. They were in Ghillies bar. 'I asked her about the bakhna rakhna.'

'And? What did she say?'

'She wanted to know why I was interested. I said I had a friend who was into folklore and then she told me to tell my friend she should be careful. I asked her if she was having a laugh but she was deadly serious. She said ancient customs existed for a reason and we shouldn't make a joke of them. She's something else, my grandma. She lived with us in London for a year, when I was still at school. I really miss her.'

'Is she your dad's mum or your mum's?'

'Mum's. Mum came to London to study, like Grandma did, but then she met my dad and decided to stay. She's been in England more than half her life now but I know she still misses Grandma, every day.'

'Is it your mum you get your maths from?'

'Mum's hopeless with numbers. She teaches French. Grandma's always been convinced I take after her.'

'What do your family think about you coming to the island?'

'They think I've lost it, obviously. If I didn't call back to base at least once a week they'd send in a helicopter. I haven't said a thing to Mum about the murders. She'd be totally freaked out.'

'And what about the bakhna rakhna? Did your grandma actually tell you anything?'

'She said they weren't dangerous usually but if you try to get rid of them or damage their hiding places they can turn vicious. Never, ever insult them, she said.' Alice swirled the remains of her beer around the bottom of her glass. 'I realised I'd never spoken with Grandma about her beliefs, not properly, not since I left home. It was like I didn't know who she was suddenly. I called Mum afterwards and asked if Grandma had always thought this way. Mum said it was just how Grandma had been brought up and I shouldn't worry about it. Mum didn't want to talk about it though, I could tell, which was strange. Normally you can't shut her up.'

'People really do believe all kinds of stuff,' Cath said. She told Alice what she'd discovered online, the Bridget Cleary case, David Coulter, Richard Dadd. 'None of this was that long ago. It wasn't just in rural communities, either.'

'Grandma says all fairy mythology comes from the same root, like religion. That it's one big idea that gets pulled in different directions depending on where it ends up and who's telling the story. The central beliefs never change, though. She says there's a pattern at the heart of things, a hidden logic we don't understand yet and maybe never will. It was Grandma who first explained to me about the Fibonacci sequence. She said the golden ratio was the living proof of what we were talking about the other day, that mathematics exist independently from human knowledge, that maths is built into everything, that all life and all matter is ultimately an expression of code – numbers, talking to each other in their own language.'

'Like the way seashells and pinecones are always exactly in proportion?'

Alice nodded. 'That's it – that's the golden ratio. I remember when I was a little girl in Lambeth, rushing outside in my pyjamas to count the spiders' webs. We had a strip of garden out the back, planted with rose bushes. Whoever had lived there before us put them in. Grandma said that if you wanted to see the spiders' webs at their best it had to be first thing in the morning, before the dew dried. I was like, six, and I couldn't believe it, the way they'd just appear in the night like that. The patterns fascinated me. How does the spider know? I kept asking. It was ages before Mum told me that no one has ever been able to answer that question.

'Here, look at this,' Alice said. She took something from her coat pocket and placed it on the table, a small wooden object. When Cath looked more closely she saw it was the tiny mahogany bureau from the first-floor landing of Shirley's dolls' house. The bureau had two drawers, each with tiny brass handles, a sloping front that opened to form a writing desk, rather like the full-sized version in the boot room at Westland Road. The thing and not the thing, Cath thought. So like the genuine article, yet at the same time so perfectly useless it was uncanny.

'If this offends you just say,' Alice said. 'But so far as I'm concerned, anyone who can make something like this must be some sort of genius.'

The idea was shocking to her, Cath realised, probably because she'd never for a moment thought of John Craigie that way. John Craigie had made the desk, as he had made everything inside the dolls' house, yet no one had seemed to think twice about it, about any of the things he made. People would say: he's a good carpenter, or, he's good with his hands, but his work had never been remarked upon as unusual. It was simply what he did, his stock in trade.

'He was always busy,' she said. 'He'd go out to people's houses, make kitchens, fitted wardrobes, new staircases. He could make anything you wanted.'

'This is a work of art.' Alice tapped the little bureau with her index finger. 'It should be in a museum.'

The only time he's not in a mood is when he's working. A complaint Shirley had made on numerous occasions, though Cath remembered one story in particular, an outing John Craigie had ruined, a rare trip to the mainland. Had it been Loch Fyne? He'd been grouchy all day, Shirley told her, then insisted on leaving early, while the family were still in the middle of having their picnic. Typical, Cath had thought at the time, though she realised now that Shirley was right, spot on in fact – John Craigie really had only been happy when he was working.

All that mattered when he was working was the wood. His silences, his inarticulacy meant nothing, there was no one to notice even – who the fuck cared? He didn't even have to think of himself as a person. He was the tool that worked the wood, that best understood it, and that was enough.

'Still no sign of the dolls?' Cath asked.

'Uh-uh.' Alice shook her head. 'I never had dolls when I was a kid. They scared the shit out of me.'

Because they look like us, but aren't us, Cath thought. Like the tiny bureau that looked so like the fully sized article, but was really just a useless ornament, an imitation.

'**H**AS IT CHANGED MUCH?' Moira asked. 'The town, I mean?' 'They closed the old Academy. There's a new joint campus up by the swimming pool. And they're doing up the Pavilion. Mostly it's the same, though.'

'I bet it's still cold.'

Cath laughed. This was the first time she'd called her mother since coming back to the island. Moira knew about the project, the murder houses. Cath had even told her about Mary Chant's house, though as yet neither of them had mentioned Shirley. Moira had seemed more concerned about money, how Cath could afford to take so much time off from Sound of the Suburbs.

'This is my work, Mum,' Cath had replied.

'It would be different if you were being paid for it.'

'I never will be if I don't take the risk.'

The kind of circular conversation that could degenerate into an argument at any moment. Cath knew how depressing it could be if she gave in to the temptation of trying to defend herself, had lived the experience to the full on multiple occasions. A waste of time, so best not to get started. It wasn't as if her parents weren't proud of what she was doing – they had three of her fish and chip shop prints displayed in their hallway, properly lit, too. Splinters of Glasgow, secreted in the centrally heated bosom of Haywards Heath. But it was all 'yes but' with Moira, she couldn't help it. An intrinsic and inalienable portion of her DNA.

She might want to talk about what happened, same as you do, only she's scared in case you go off on one.

Since when have I ever gone off on one?

You've got to be joking. You're the absolute queen of going off on one. Just because you've mastered the art of not losing your shit doesn't mean you aren't a bitch sometimes. Trust me.

Wow. Just wow.

Snidey cow.

Snidey is my middle name, or hadn't you heard?

'Look Mum, that's not why I called. I wanted to ask you some things. Like about how we came to be living on the island in the first place. I know we inherited Gran's house but why did we end up moving here? Was it Dad's idea?'

Moira sniffed, and Cath heard her switch the telephone receiver from one hand to the other. 'Your father had nothing to do with it. The whole thing was my fault. I was bored with my job and I wanted a change. I don't think anyone ever plans on being in medical admin for the rest of their life. I was fed up, especially after Martin Brewster hired that new partner – a right little Hitler, he was. We'd been planning to sell your grandmother's house but then the job came up at IBM. The pay was substantially better than at your dad's old place and I encouraged him to apply. I believed it would be a good opportunity for all of us. I knew more or less straight away that I'd made a mistake. I felt as if I'd been banished to the end of the world.'

'Why did you never tell me you were so unhappy?'

'You were twelve years old. The last thing I wanted was for you to be upset – you had enough problems of your own, fitting into a new school, having to make new friends. I honestly thought things would get better but they never did. My life seemed to come to a standstill and I don't think I realised how angry I was – not with your father, I mean with myself, for making such a mess of everything. There were no jobs on the island, nothing suitable anyway. I could have applied for work in Glasgow but the idea seemed so daunting. Not having any close friends up there – that was the worst thing.'

'You could have made friends.'

'It's not so easy, Catherine. People have their own interests, their own circles. They don't always make time for strangers and I must have stuck out like a sore thumb. That girl, that friend of yours who was murdered – I asked her mother over for coffee once, did you know that?'

'I had no idea. I didn't realise you'd ever spoken to Susan.'

'A couple of times – at the museum and once at the school. She wouldn't come, though. She said she was too busy with the baby but really I think she was afraid of her husband finding out – finding out and making some sort of scene. Just the sight of him made my skin crawl. I'm sure she was scared of him. I couldn't believe no one could see what was happening to her. It made my blood boil.'

'Is that why you didn't like Shirley?'

'Oh Catherine, don't be ridiculous. It wasn't that I didn't like her – it was just that you had nothing in common. Then there was that dreadful house of theirs, that man. I hated you going there. I wanted to put a stop to it but your dad said no, we had to let you make your own friends. He was right I suppose, but I'll never forget the day they were killed. I was in the supermarket when I heard. All I could think was that I had to get out. I was standing in the queue with my trolley and I almost turned round and ran out through the door but I knew if I did people would wonder what was wrong and I couldn't face that so I just hung on and waited to be served. But I was desperate to get home, to make sure you were there with your father and not with them. I don't think I've ever been more terrified in my life. And it was so hot that day. I thought I was going to faint.'

'How come you've never told me any of this?'

'You never asked.'

'Mum, I'm sorry.'

'You're there to photograph that house, aren't you, the Craigies' place?'

Cath hesitated. 'I hope so,' she said. 'I've been to see the house already, actually. There's someone living there now. Her name is Alice.'

'Catherine, be careful.'

A laugh escaped her. 'Careful of what?'

'You'll probably say it's all water under the bridge but those were difficult years. They're not good memories.'

'I'm glad I came back. The island feels different.'

'Why? Because of this Alice person?'

Cath could feel herself blushing. 'This has nothing to do with Alice. I mean I'm enjoying being here. I'm doing good work, I think.'

'I know what you're like, though. You get in too deep and then you get hurt. That's the way it's always been with you and relationships.'

'I'm not getting into anything.'

'Well, I'm just saying. I do worry about you, you know.'

'Thanks.'

'What on Earth for?'

'For telling me what happened, how you felt.'

'Oh, goodness, don't be silly, it's all so long ago,' Moira said, and for the briefest of moments, Cath considered telling her about Boris the plastic reindeer, found in a Persil box, then decided it was probably a bad idea.

'Do you think he did it? John Craigie?' she said instead.

'Of course he did it. Men like him don't need a reason, they poison everything they touch.'

CATH ORDERED A BOUQUET to be sent to Moira from the florist's on Montague Street – pink and yellow fuchsias, **thank you for talking, love Cath.** The florist assured her the flowers would be delivered the following day. Moira would be pleased, and surprised. She would probably end up telling Colin about the phone call. They'd go out for dinner maybe, have one of those conversations about what a shame it was that Cath had ended up in such a dead-end job and what, if anything, could be done about it.

Not long after she'd had her first exhibition at Mildred Marks, Colin had phoned Cath one evening and told her he and Moira had been discussing it and they had decided that if she wanted to give up her job at Sound of the Suburbs and go to art college full-time they'd do their best to support her financially.

'That's a wonderful offer, Dad, but I'm fine,' Cath had said. 'Things will work out.'

She had never regretted turning them down but she did regret not taking up the Scottish Arts grant she'd been offered, two years later, for a half-year residency in Berlin. She had told herself the disruption and uncertainty of moving abroad would be too difficult to cope with, that she would lose more than she'd gain. The truth was she hadn't wanted to take the risk because of Adam, because she was afraid her being away so long might spell the end of their relationship.

When she told Adam she had turned down the residency, it seemed barely to register. He made some throwaway remark about Cath probably feeling out of her depth in that sort of environment.

Cath had not told her parents about the residency. She knew Moira especially would have given her a hard time about not accepting.

'I can't stand them trying to control me,' she remembered saying to Melinda Stiles, the restaurant critic. Cath found Melinda easier to confide in than Mildred. Mildred couldn't stand Adam and made no secret of it.

Melinda had looked at her over the rim of her wine glass, saying nothing. Cath knew what she was thinking though, that it wasn't her parents who were controlling her but Adam, and he wasn't worth it.

There had been one evening in particular when Cath felt almost certain Melinda was coming on to her. Cath pretended not to notice, and the moment passed without incident or consequences. Like the residency in Berlin, this was something Cath had thought about afterwards, and regretted.

AFTER PAYING FOR THE flowers, Cath visited the library, hoping she might find more information about the life of Richard Dadd.

There was nothing shelved under biography, but the art section turned up a generously illustrated book on Victorian fairy painting that had a whole chapter on Dadd, including a detailed account of his journey to the Middle East.

In July 1842, Cath read, Sir Thomas Phillips, a self-made aristocrat, offers Dadd the post of artist-in-residence on his tour of the cultural landmarks of the ancient world. Dadd is to document their journey through sketches and paintings, Sir Thomas explains, to convey the grandeur and strangeness of alien lands. Dadd is already obsessed by the Greeks and the Egyptians. He accepts Sir Thomas's proposal as the chance of a lifetime.

He works, almost literally, like a demon, feverishly sketching, unable to spare himself, unable to capture a hundredth of what he is seeing. He is warned about the sun, its punishing brutality, but barely listens. The sights he sees transfix him. He has never imagined, much less encountered such shocking juxtapositions of beauty and violence. The world as he knows it is void. He embraces the void, he flees the void. The heat is killing, entrancing, and still he cannot stop.

His collapse, when eventually it comes, is seen as a mercy. Sunstroke, his friends insist, he will recover.

Now at last he will rest, lay down his brushes. All we need to do is get him home. Sir Thomas, travelling with Dadd these many months, is not so sanguine. He has seen aspects of his protégé's genius – *a god, he called himself a god* – he does not care to think about. Even so, his friends are right: whatever the depths of his frailty they need to restore Dadd to England as quickly as possible.

At home in Kent though, Dadd's condition worsens. He seems lost in a world of his own, unsure of what is real, repeating odd snatches of Arabic, peculiar ideas. He is the servant of the god Osiris, here on Earth. His friends wonder what the deuce he is on about and his doctor urges his father to have Dadd hospitalised.

Dadd is having none of it: he retires to his rooms, eats nothing but eggs. *Leave me be.*

The murder, when it finally comes, is enacted as ritual: his father Robert, *le diable*, confronted, named, destroyed beneath the noonday sun.

The account was vivid and useful but still full of holes. Cath found herself wondering if Dadd had ever been in love and if so with whom. There were hints that Dadd might have been gay but they were never expanded upon. More disconcerting was the way the doctors at Bethlem and Broadmoor seemed actively to have encouraged Dadd's obsession with fairyland. It keeps his mind off Osiris, they insisted. It's harmless, they said. What is fairy painting if not a harmless diversion, a mode of expression that provides outlet for his genius without preying on his (vulnerable) nerves?

Harmless diversion? Going by what the other artists in the book had painted – diminutive figures in gauzy dresses with shimmering wings, jewel-bright cities bedecked with flowers in dazzling miniature – Cath might have been persuaded to believe them. But Dadd's paintings weren't like that at all. His visions of faerie – twisted, oppressive – were a kind of hell. How come his doctors, respected men of Victorian medicine that they were, seemed not to notice, or to understand the difference?

I 2 .

'I THINK I MIGHT BE pregnant,' Alice said. They were in the kitchen at Westland Road. Alice had called and asked Cath to come over. Cath had arrived to find Alice standing on the doorstep, waiting for her. She seemed agitated, filled with nervous energy. Cath's first thought was that she had told him, that she had left Saheed.

'What do you mean, you think?' Cath said. She felt ridiculous for having misread the situation, although Alice couldn't know that. Alice at that moment seemed barely aware of her as a separate entity.

'I did a test. I ordered it online. I didn't want to buy one at the chemist's in case anyone said anything. Isn't that stupid?' She sounded as she had on the phone: distracted and faintly panicky, as if someone had asked her a question she couldn't answer.

'Have you told Saheed yet?'

'God, no. I've only just done the test. What do you reckon?'

She showed Cath the predictor kit, the clear plastic window with its twin pink lines.

'This looks pretty definite to me,' Cath said. She'd never seen a pregnancy testing kit in reality, she realised. Only in movies – who's-the-daddy relationship dramas, mostly. Cath had once and very briefly thought she was pregnant, one tense and surreal weekend of thinking now something has to happen brought to an end by the start of her period shortly after she went into work on the Monday morning. She remembered crying in the horrible little toilet at the back of the shop, not knowing if she felt relieved or disappointed, ashamed of her feelings whatever, because she realised Adam would be appalled by the idea of her having his child, petrified of the responsibility, that he barely even thought of her as a woman in that way. Babies were for wives, women you flaunted in public and officially gave a damn about, only Miranda couldn't have kids, so in Adam's case at least this portion of the contract didn't apply.

She'd thought of Shirley then, as she had not thought of her in ages. She knew Shirley would have told Adam where he could stick it.

The guy's a fucking eejit, a fucking melt. The kid'll be better off without him, you'll see.

There is no kid, so drop it.

If there was though. No need to bite my head off.

Sorry, but I'm upset.

A dick like that, you're bound to be. Just saying.

'How do you feel?' Cath said to Alice.

'You sound like a tabloid journalist,' Alice said. She gave a tentative laugh. 'I don't know. It's like I'm not here. I came off the pill a year ago because I started getting side effects. Because of the other medication I was taking. We were supposed to be careful. We were careful. I've been freaking out for most of a week now but my periods are often late so I was trying to persuade myself it was a false alarm.

All I keep thinking is can I still go to that chess workshop. Will I be OK to fly, do you think?'

'Of course you will. You'd only be a couple of months gone by then.' Cath hesitated. 'Do you think you're going to keep it?'

The question, so clear and so logical in her mind, sounded different when spoken aloud. Blatant and intrusive, interfering. It was none of Cath's business, after all, and yet Alice had called her, so it must be. In some unexpected, mysterious way, they were together in this.

'I'm having the baby.' Alice nodded, vehemently, kept nodding. 'I'd never thought about it before this week – not seriously anyway, not as in this is something that might be happening now – but as soon as I saw the line come up on the test thing I just knew. I mean, I didn't have any doubts. Does that sound crazy?'

Cath shook her head. 'Not at all.'

'I'll have to – oh God, I don't know.' Alice put her hands up to cover her face. She was crying, Cath realised, or about to.

'It's all right. You're going to be fine.' She put her arms around Alice's shoulders, hugged her close. Alice's whole body was trembling. The thought came to Cath that they could raise the child together, here in this house, that Alice could get back to her maths and Cath could chronicle the minutiae of their island lives in a sequence of photographs. A hundred mornings, she would call it. Things would work out somehow. Why shouldn't they?

Steady on now. Remember what your ma said about getting in too deep?

Since when did you turn all Mother Superior?

I'm thinking you might get hurt, is all. You can be pretty clueless when it comes to stuff like this.

You think Alice will hurt me?

I'm afraid you'll hurt yourself.

'I have to call Saheed,' Alice said. She pulled away, thrust back her hair. 'I really should call him. Do you mind?'

'Why should I mind?' Cath said, though of course she did. The moment was gone, or spoiled. She realised that for Alice, telling Cath had been a trial run, a warm-up. It was Saheed who counted.

'You will stay, though?' Alice said. Her supple spine, the notches of her vertebrae plainly visible beneath her T-shirt, like part of a textbook diagram of the human skeleton. Cath listened as Alice went through to the living room to make her call, the muted assonance of her voice through the half-closed door as the line connected. Hey, Cath heard her say, a familiar intonation rather than a word. She made an effort not to listen to what came after, though the distance between them made it hard to make out in any case. The call didn't last long.

When Alice returned she seemed calmer. 'I didn't tell him,' she said. 'I couldn't, not over the phone. I said I'd decided to come to London for the weekend. I'll tell him then.'

THEY DROVE TO SCALPSIE and walked along the beach. The tide was out, the shoreline deserted. They took off their shoes and walked towards the water, Cath's footprints square and decisive, Alice's elongated and cursive as copperplate script. It was not really warm enough to be walking barefoot but here they were, doing it. Alice walked with her head down, seemingly mesmerised by the movement of her own feet.

'Maybe he's right,' she said. 'Saheed. If I really wanted us to be apart I should have had the guts to say so, not go running off to the other end of the country. This is just – a mess.'

'Is that what you want though? For you and Saheed to be apart?'

'A part of me must do, mustn't it? Why else would I be here? And now I feel like the moment I tell him about the baby, he'll have the perfect excuse to force me to come back to London. He'll say it's not safe for me to be here alone.'

'That's bollocks. And you're not alone, anyway.' She thought of telling Alice what she'd been thinking earlier, about the two of them raising the baby, here on the island.

Go on then, I dare you. See what happens.

'I feel OK here,' Alice said. 'I think I'd like the baby to be born here. On the island. Does that sound insane?'

'Not in any way.'

The sea breathed in and out. 'There was this boy,' Alice said, 'when I was like, fourteen. His name was Ezra. We both used to go to a summer maths camp near Aberystwyth. We spent the mornings working on maths problems and then in the afternoons we'd go and play on the beach. Ezra had a terror of sand. He said he couldn't stop trying to calculate how many grains of sand there were in a single metre of beach. He knew he would never be able to work it out, not accurately, because the true total would depend on depth and not just surface area and he could never know that for sure without digging up the beach. The thing is, in any normal school Ezra would have been bullied half to death for being such a nerd but to us he was normal. We all knew how he felt – it was just that most of us learned to control our obsessions better. Keep them hidden, anyway. I think

I was in love with him. Ezra, I mean. We used to pretend we were twins, so we would never be parted.'

'What happened to him?'

Alice shook her head. 'He kept having problems. I think he was in a mental health facility for a while. Then I went to uni and we lost touch. It's complicated. I was thinking the other day that I don't have any friends now, not really. There were people I met at work, but none of them have been in contact since I moved up here and other than that it's just Saheed's friends, people we know as a couple who were his friends first. I'm not saying I don't like them, but all my real friends – people I knew from uni, friends from maths camp – we've drifted apart and I don't even know how that happened. This started way before I got ill. It's scary, how quickly your life can run away from you.'

'You don't have to tell him, you know. Not straight away. Give yourself some time to work out what you want to do, where you want to be. A week or two won't hurt.'

'I can't just not tell him. We're married. And I've told him I'm coming now. What's he going to think if I suddenly cancel?'

'Don't cancel. Tell him you wanted to save him coming up here for once, that you wanted to do some shopping, felt like a change of scene. There could be loads of reasons.'

'We should get back,' Alice said. She turned her head away, a decisive movement that made it clear the discussion was closed. Whatever she was thinking now, Cath would not be made party to it. 'If I'm going to go I need to get my stuff ready.'

'You will be OK?'

'It's only a couple of days. I'll be back on Monday.'

They walked to the car in silence, drove back into town.

'I'll text you, let you know how it's going,' Alice said. She dropped Cath halfway up Westland Road, close to the cut-through to Academy Road. They hugged, but awkwardly, as if something pivotal had occurred, something neither of them wanted to think about. Back at the flat, Cath realised she had never taken Alice's photograph, not even once. After Alice left, Cath would have no proof of her existence. No image, no London address, no names of parents or friends. Nothing but a few emails. The following morning she woke up wondering if Alice was still on the island. She showered quickly and pulled on her jeans, thinking she would walk down to the ferry terminal on the off chance of catching her before she went. To say goodbye, to check she was all right, to say – what?

She stopped herself just in time. It was a bad idea. The fact that she felt uncertain about it proved it was a bad idea. What was wrong with her?

You're in love with her, that's what. You're obsessing.

How would you know?

It's not how with you, is it though, it's when. When you start worrying about what's normal and what might look weird. When you're scared to call someone in case you say the wrong thing. Or even text them. That's when you know. And it can happen overnight. It can happen when you're sitting on someone's floor drinking tea with them. It's like catching a virus. And what's shit about viruses is that before you even know you've caught them they're already incubating inside you, taking over your body, like in a zombie apocalypse. I know – I looked it up on the NHS website. Basically you're fucked.

Cath put on the radio, made coffee, decided she'd be better off

164

spending the morning at the town museum. Better than hanging around the flat worrying what Alice might be saying to Saheed. Better than obsessing. She remembered her last trip to the museum with the school, some bloke from Glasgow University giving them a lecture about the Viking invasions. The cases of stuffed birds were still there, the Bronze Age beaker, the Roman coins, the collection of postcards and souvenirs celebrating the town in its heyday. The archaeologist had bored Shirley rigid. She'd spent most of the lecture picking at a loose thread in the carpet, winding it round the tip of her little finger, trapping the blood. She had loved the old postcards, though.

'Imagine what the town must have been like,' Shirley had said on the walk back to school. 'Three cinemas we had at one point, and the biggest sprung dance floor in the whole of Scotland. Imagine getting dolled up for a night at the Pav. Better than a piss-up down the Golfers, I'll bet.'

There had been a catch in her voice, a real sense of longing, and Cath thought how well Shirley would have fitted in then, how she'd have rejoiced in the gaiety of the town as it had once been. All those young men and women sailing in from Glasgow with their week's wages in their back pockets. Chasing the good times like maenads then home on the dot of midnight as if nothing had happened.

Like characters from one of those black-and-white films Shirley loved. *The Birds. Double Indemnity. Strangers on a Train.* Those Hitchcock blondes who shone like silver under the streetlights, only to be crushed and thrown away like waste paper as soon as the sun rose.

*

CATH HAD BROUGHT ALONG her printouts almost as an after-thought: the wedding photo taken outside St Ninian's, Susan and the three bridesmaids, John Craigie with his nameless best man. The best man had become crucial in her mind, the most likely candidate for being Susan's lover and John Craigie's intended fourth victim. Abigail Mercer had said the best man was not from the island, that he and Susan would not have met again, but Abigail could not have known that for certain, she could not even remember his name. Cath thought she might ask the museum staff. There was always the chance one of them might recognise him, even if they had no knowledge of the murders.

She progressed slowly around the vitrines, the displays of old photographs. All stuff that meant something to somebody, at least for now. Mementoes needed memories to sustain them, a link with the living. Without memories they became random objects, empty husks. Between one generation and the next, just garbage to be cleared away and chucked in a skip. Cath waited until the museum was empty apart from herself, then approached the woman on the reception desk.

She placed the wedding photograph on the counter in front of her.

'I was wondering if you might recognise any of these people,' she said. 'I'm doing some research,' she added, stiffly. What reason could she give for wanting to know, other than the truth?

'You're the lassie who's interested in the murders then, the pho-tographer?' the woman said at once. 'Jeannie Morris mentioned you were staying here. How've you been getting on?'

'I'm not really sure,' Cath said. She felt blindsided, not because people had been talking about her – she had nothing to hide – but because she hadn't known. Because for Cath that was how things had always been – always the last to know, looking in from the outside, watching. Not so much in the loop as hanging on to a tag end of the loop, hauling herself upwards with difficulty, hand over hand.

Who the fuck cared, though, actually? She'd get there. Getting there was Cath's thing.

'I need to know who this man is,' she said in a rush. She pointed to the best man. That elegant, slate-grey suit, that sun-drenched smile.

'This laddie?' The woman spoke slowly, thoughtfully, as if trawling her memory. Her hand trembled slightly as she touched the printout, pulling it towards her. 'He does look familiar, I must say. I could ask Iris for you if you like – she does our accounts. You don't mind waiting a moment while I fetch her? She's just next door.'

'Not at all,' Cath said. 'Thank you.' The woman disappeared through a door, leaving Cath to examine the pictures on the walls in the foyer: dull-looking men in military uniforms, transport posters from the 1930s advertising paddle steamer trips to the Isle of Arran and the Hydro Spa hotel. The island's game face, a sprightly old lady working overtime to minimise the multitude of ways in which her body was failing.

What are you on about?

Go on, you love it. You are this place.

The museum woman reappeared, emerging through another of the green-painted doors. There was an older woman with her – piled-up silver hair, sharp eyes behind wire-rimmed spectacles. She was beautifully dressed, Cath noticed – paisley-pattern dress in brushed cotton, long-line pearl-grey cardigan, patent leather court shoes. She walked using a cane.

'This is Iris Docherty,' the museum woman said. 'She's lived here on the island most of her life.'

'I knew him, the laddie,' Iris said. She was holding the printout. Her long fingers, the knuckles reddened and swollen from arthritis, glittered with rings. 'His name was Finlay Matheson. He worked on the ferries.'

Abigail Mercer had thought Matt, or Matty – it must have been the surname, Matheson, she was remembering. Cath's first, overwhelming reaction was one of elation – she had found him, finally. A moment later the doubts began to creep in. If this Finlay had still been around, wouldn't Shirley have mentioned him? There had been other friends of her father's she had talked about from time to time.

All of them cunts.

Yes maybe but even so she had known who they were. She should have known who Finlay Matheson was too, him most of all. He'd been her father's best man.

Aye an' I never clapped eyes on him.

Cath was no further forward.

'He wasn't from the island, either,' Iris was saying. 'They were both from Galashiels, I think. Either there or Hawick, somewhere in the Borders. Finlay had a brother who came over after he died. Jimmy, his name was. Older than Finlay but looked just like him. He were a lovely laddie, that Finn. Not like the other one. Fast friends they were though, goodness knows why.'

'After he died? Do you mean John Craigie?'

She's getting confused, Cath thought, swapping Finlay Matheson with John Craigie or the other way around. She wondered if Iris had been working at the museum back when she and Shirley had sat side by side on the parquet floor, listening to the lecturer from Glasgow drone on about pillaging Norsemen. It seemed entirely possible.

Doesn't mean she's doolally though. Listen up.

'Not that Craigie fellow. Finlay Matheson. He drowned. About two, three years after this was taken.' Iris waved the printout. 'A real tragedy. He and some friends were out fishing the Kyles. Finlay was swept overboard and dragged under the propeller. The local paper was full of it. Like I say, his brother came over to arrange for his body to be shipped back home for the funeral. Terrible business. I hope you don't mind my asking, but why are you interested?'

'Shirley Craigie was my friend,' Cath said. There had been defiance in her voice, she realised later. She'd brandished her relationship to Shirley like some sort of pass key. She was angry, she supposed. Angry about all of it, not just what had happened to Shirley but what had happened to her. Not so different from Moira after all. 'I went to school here.'

Iris seemed unsurprised. 'I knew her mother,' she said. 'Susan, wasn't it? To say hello to, anyway. She used to come in here a lot. Said she was interested in history. I liked her. More than I can say for her husband, though.'

The thinness of her wrists, the fragile, almost papery look of the skin around her eyes. Iris Docherty was old, but she remembered everything, she remembered the Craigies. For all Cath knew, Iris remembered her too, had glanced after her in the street almost certainly, Cath looking the other way, not thinking twice.

'This might sound unusual,' Cath said, 'but I would like to talk to you about your memories in more detail. Take some photographs, maybe. Would that be possible?'

'Photographs is it now? You've not got me confused with Helen Mirren?' Iris and the curator exchanged glances, a look that suggested they found Cath amusing but most likely harmless. Cath smiled and even laughed a little, which was the right thing to do, apparently, because Iris smiled back. 'You're welcome to visit, dear, though I'm not sure what use I'll be. Evenings are best – around seven o'clock time. I'm on Shore Road, in the Port. Give me a call and let me know when you'd like to come.'

She placed the photocopy face down on the reception desk and wrote her phone number on the back. A landline, Cath noticed, which of course it would be. 'Nice to meet you, dear. I'll be getting along now, Myra, if that's all right.'

1 3 .

CATH LEFT THE MUSEUM feeling encouraged. Iris Docherty had already confirmed that she knew Susan, that she had spoken to her on numerous occasions. Even if Susan's lover turned out not to be Finlay Matheson, there was a good chance that Iris might hold the key to his identity. Her first instinct was to email Alice, to let her know she had a new lead, but she decided to wait. Alice was probably still on the train. She would have things on her mind. Cath thought she might return to the library, see what they had in the way of local history, but it was closed for lunch. She went to Print Point instead, where she bought a stock of coloured marker pens and Post-it notes and two A1 sheets of white cartridge paper. In the living room of Argyle Terrace, Cath attached the cartridge paper to the wall with drawing pins just above the table. She had decided to make a murder wall, like the ones she'd seen in the incident rooms on all the cop shows. A blank murder wall, for the moment, the way all murder walls must be in the beginning, before the opening credits started to roll.

Shirley would have loved this. She would have loved it more than anyone.

What exactly are we trying to prove here, detective?

I want to know why you died — simple as that.

OK, so let's play devil's advocate. Do you think Dad did it?

He must have done. No one's ever come up with any other suspects, not even wild cards. He has to be the killer.

That's you playing at being Sherlock again — eliminate all other possibilities and whichever possibility remains must be the solution. But what if the only reason there were no other suspects was because no one looked for them? And Dad were never a psycho. A crazy bastard, yes — he even punched me once. But with him it was always in the heat of the moment, off the cuff. He didn't brood and he didn't plan. If something were getting on his tits he'd either hit you or give you the silent treatment. Bury himself in his work. Find something to make or mend. He never liked people much, my dad. You'll think I'm an eejit for saying so but I think he was lonely.

Lots of people are lonely. They don't break people's wrists or get themselves thrown out of pubs for starting fights.

I'm not trying tae defend him, just putting the questions. That's what being a detective is mostly about, isn't it, asking questions?

What about this one, then? Was your mum having an affair?

Don't be daft. Mum wasnae like that. If Dad had found out he'd have killed her.

There you are, then. And that doesn't make sense.

What doesn't?

First you say she wasn't like that, then you say your dad would have killed her if he found out. Which one is it?

I just mean, if she had been having one. An affair.

So let's pretend she was. You say John Craigie would have killed her.

I didnae mean that literally — I meant he'd go nuts. People say those words all the time without meaning them – I'll kill ye if you tell her what I said, I'll kill ye if you break my iPhone, stuff like that. No one actually means they're gonnae go out and murder someone.

OK, but you have to admit it makes more sense for your dad to be the killer than anyone else. He finds out Susan is having an affair. He goes crazy in the heat of the moment and shoots everyone. Then he jumps in his pickup and drives off to kill the other guy as well, Susan's lover. That's why he was heading away from the ferry terminal. It explains everything.

It disnae explain the gun. This isnae Detroit you know. Even if someone down the Golfers gave him a name, Dad wouldae needed to go into Glasgow and he hated Glasgow. He'd have thought about it for five minutes then given up on the idea. Guns weren't Dad's style. If he wanted someone killed he'd have used his fists.

Did you know Finlay Matheson?

I've already told you I never laid eyes on the man. You're telling me he were sweet on Mum?

I'm not telling you anything. It's just a theory.

And your theory is, Mum were in love with this Matheson bloke, who tragically drowned like thirty year ago. Dad found out later and went psycho, blew us all away. Makes sense I suppose, if you're desperate enough and so long as you forget about where he got the gun from but you're forgetting something else. Dad wouldnae killed Sonny. He might have killed Mum for having the affair, he might even have killed me for giving him lip but he would rather have turned the gun on himself than shoot his precious Sonny. You know what the scene-of-crime report says? Sonny were in the living room, playing with his bleeding stickle bricks. Dad adored the wee maggot. Probably the only soul on this Earth he did love. He couldnae a' done it.

What about the other theory, then?

What other theory?

The one that was going around right after it happened. That your dad came home for lunch and found you all dead. That when his truck came off the road he was on his way to find the person who did it. That's why he was driving away from the ferry terminal — because he knew who the murderer was and meant to kill him.

That's cock though, isn't it? Who would have killed us in the first place? Who would have been bothered? We were no one.

What about Susan's lover? What if she'd dumped him and he wanted revenge?

You reckon that's the kind of guy Mum wouldae took up with?

She married John Craigie, didn't she?

Tou-bloody-ché. But you've got it wrong. I mean you're looking in the wrong place.

Where should I be looking, then?

That's for me to know and you to find out, detective.

I wish you were here, Shirl.

Me too an' all. We had a right laugh though, didn't we? Remember that time in Glasgow, when I nicked those earrings and then accidentally flushed them down the bog in that rat-pit burger bar?

Oh God, I'd forgotten about that place. We could have died of botulism.

We were a right pair.

Yes, we were.

Don't blame Dad too much, will ye? He were somewhere else when he did it. He were away with the fairies.

I still don't understand what you mean by that. Did John Craigie really believe in fairies? It doesn't seem possible.

It's like with that painter bloke you've been looking up. What goes on inside another person's head is hard to fathom sometimes. Some people see more than others, simple as that.

What they see isn't really there, though.

Who are we to know, when we don't see it?

CATH WROTE FINLAY MATHESON'S name on a Post-it note then stuck it to the murder wall next to John Craigie's, linking them with an arrow, like a married couple. Fast friends, Iris Docherty had called them. How come they'd ended up here, on the island? Not to make money – if they'd wanted to make money they'd have headed for Glasgow. Had they come separately, or together? Often, people who came to the island were running away from something.

PROBLEMS, Cath wrote, then underlined it. For one of them, anyway. Iris had liked Finlay Matheson – a lovely laddie, she'd called him. Finlay Matheson had friends, people he went fishing with, his death was a tragedy. A brother – Jimmy – had come to the island to collect his body. No one had come to collect John Craigie. No one ever had a decent word to say about him. Yet Finlay Matheson had liked him – he'd been best man at his wedding. Best man, fast friends. Then Finlay had died.

Cath began to understand why the concept of the murder wall had become ubiquitous. There was something addictive and satisfying about seeing your thoughts literally take shape, become quantifiable. Constructing a murder wall was important, Cath realised, because it forced her to separate her own memories from the facts of what had happened. She had started out believing they were one and the same, but as the web of Post-its and arrows expanded she was bound to concede they were not, or not necessarily. John Craigie's problems had started long before she encountered him, before his marriage even.

John Craigie must have been very young when he first came to the island. A young man a long way from home. A man whose only friend had died in a tragic accident. Might Shirley have a point after all – had John Craigie been lonely?

And didn't lonely men sometimes feel desperate? Or do desperate things?

You need to take a break. Remember that crazy journalist from out of Zodiac?

OK, you win.

Cath left everything where it was and locked up the flat. She was surprised to see it was getting on for eight o'clock. There were more tourists now the weather was improving and the Black Bull was packed. She went to Ghillies instead, ordered a toasted sandwich and checked her phone for messages. Nothing. She consumed one drink and then another. Finally, just before nine, she texted Alice: **hope you got in OK. I've been at the museum – some interesting stuff! Thinking of you xxxx** She quickly pressed send, before she could change her mind. She returned to the flat and put on the CD that had been delivered earlier in the day, while she was out, the disc of Bax tone poems she'd asked Steve to send her. Cath couldn't remember if she had actually listened to it before, though it was the kind of uncontroversial, interchangeably pleasant orchestral music she often played in the shop and then forgot about.

In the Faery Hills ran for about fifteen minutes. The opening was characterised by a repeated three-note motif on the clarinet – da-da-DAH! – falling and then rising, two fairy messengers, signalling to each other with their little trumpets across a wide valley. You would not see the fairies but you could hear their music, the calls increasing in strength and frequency before exploding into a rapid, triple-time rhythm involving the whole orchestra.

Fairy revellers, pouring out of the forest, whirling the observer away in a frenzied dance.

The central section was slower, like someone telling a story, a languid tale of magic and fairy abduction on Midsummer's Eve. Then as the strings reached a yearning crescendo the dance picked up again. The fairies scattered, leaving the mortal observer alone and confused in the heart of the forest. The CD's sleeve notes suggested that Bax had taken his inspiration from the legend of Osian the warrior. Osian had fallen in love with a fairy called Niamh. He stayed and lived with her in her kingdom for three blissful years. When he returned to the world of humans, Osian discovered that three hundred years had passed. His kinsfolk were dead. No one even remembered who he was.

And there it was again, the dangerous schism between our world and theirs. Seduction and abandonment, the lure of mystical power, catastrophic collapse. Richard Dadd had suffered a catastrophic collapse in his mental health and so had John Craigie. Could Craigie have been a schizophrenic, like Dadd? Their obsession with fairies was a classic indicator, along with hearing voices, seeing aliens, believing your father to be the emissary of the devil and Cath found it particularly interesting, the way they had both been fixated on detail to the point of neurosis, a kind of insane pride in their ability to render small.

Yet there had always been those who argued that the medics were wrong, that some forms of mental illness were themselves a symptom of preternatural sensitivity. A heightened awareness of psychic events and invisible beings, an ability to perceive parallel worlds, the lands of faerie so vividly described in their literature and art.

Like John Craigie's dolls' house, Cath found herself thinking, though she knew the dissenting voices were in a minority, and mostly cranks.

SHE WENT TO BED around midnight. Still nothing from Alice. As she turned out the light, an image came to her of the house on Westland Road, silent and unlit, with Shirley's dolls' house also silent and unlit on the table inside it. A house within a house, one world peculiarly nestled inside another. As the fairy world lay nestled within our world, as some still believed.

What happened inside a house when no one was watching? What lives did they lead, Cath wondered drowsily, all the silent objects, the moonlit shadows flitting like goblins through the empty rooms?

I 4 .

'THRIFTS FARM?'

'I was looking for James Matheson?'

'He's up in the top field. Who is this, please?' The slight trace of an accent. German, Cath thought, though she couldn't be sure.

'Mr Matheson won't know me personally. I'm trying to find out about a friend of his brother's – he died quite a long time ago. I was hoping Mr Matheson might be able to help me.'

'You're talking about Johnny Craigie.' The woman spoke it as a fact, not a question, the edge of anxiety in her voice replaced by a dull resentment. 'I don't want you speaking to my husband about Johnny Craigie.'

'I don't want to upset anyone. It's just a couple of questions. I'm not a journalist,' she added quickly. 'I wouldn't need to quote him or anything.'

'There's nothing more to be said about that man. He was worthless and a troublemaker and he was no good for Finlay. You have no idea how unhappy Jimmy was, after his brother died. He doesn't like to talk about those days.'

'John Craigie did grow up in Clovenfords, though?'

'He and his sister, yes. Ruth and Kenny are gone now. Ruth was a saint but you know what people say about holy fools.'

'Ruth? Was that John's sister?'

'I'd rather you didn't call back.'

'Could you just tell me——?' Cath said, but the line had gone dead. She stared stupidly at the screen, imagined Shirley flat on her stomach in a fit of the giggles. *Nice work detective. They don't call you the Limpet for nothing.*

Hey, come on, that's some quality info she gave me. Information Cath hadn't known before, at any rate. James Matheson was still alive, still lived at Thrifts Farm. John Craigie had grown up in Clovenfords, near Galashiels. He'd had a sister, possibly called Ruth or possibly not. Ruth and Kenny are gone, Matheson's wife had said – could they be John Craigie's parents? Why had Shirley never mentioned having an aunt?

Cath wrote the new names on Post-its and added them to the murder wall. At the top, Kenny and Ruth, each with a question mark – mother? father? – and then another, in capital letters – SISTER? – to the right of Johnny. Ruth was a saint, the wife had said, a holy fool. Did that mean someone who suffered in silence, or someone who——?

Was she as crazy as Dad, you mean? Don't ask me, I never met her. I never met any of them.

The sun was out and there were boats on the firth, more than ever since the beginning of April. The island felt different once the tourist season started, more open and less watchful, wreathed in pastel calmness. As Cath opened the door to go outside, her phone went off in her bag. She fumbled with the zip, certain that the caller would be Alice. When she finally retrieved the phone it was an unknown number. Cold caller, Cath thought, not recognising the voice, then realised with a jolt that it was Saheed.

'Is this Cath?'

'Are you OK?' Cath said, meaning Alice, is Alice OK. Her heart was racing. The relief of hearing his voice – a voice that had spoken to Alice, that knew where she was. He didn't answer at first. Cath could hear him breathing, like he was considering what he should tell her, wondering how much she knew.

'Is Alice there with you?' he said finally.

'What? She's supposed to be in London. She left here yesterday.'

'She was here. She's fine, I mean, we had a bit of an argument. She went off somewhere. Her phone's been switched off all day. I was just wondering if you – you know, if you'd heard from her.'

'What did you argue about?'

'Nothing. You know what it's like. She got upset and I had to go into work. I've been calling her every hour and I got off work early specially but there's no sign of her.'

He was worried, Cath realised. Worried as fuck. He wouldn't have called her unless he was desperate. He didn't even like her.

'Do you want me to go round to the house? See if she's there?'

'Would you do that?' He sounded relieved, like a weight had been lifted. Like they were friends. 'That would be awesome.'

'I'll call you back.' Cath ended the call and saved his number, wondered how Saheed came to have her number in the first place. From Alice, most likely, in case of emergencies. Had Alice known there was likely to be an emergency? She tried calling Alice, an action that seemed permissible suddenly, required. The call went straight to voicemail. Cath tried to imagine what Alice would do if her trip to London turned out to be a mistake, where she would go. The answer seemed obvious – she would return to the island. By the time she reached the house on Westland Road Cath had mostly persuaded herself she would find Alice there, that she had switched off her phone specifically to stop Saheed from reaching her.

She would be expecting Cath to turn up. She would be waiting for her.

The house stood still and silent. Alice's car was on the drive but from what Cath could tell it had not been moved since they'd driven to Scalpsie two days before. Cath opened the porch and pressed the doorbell. She heard it ring inside the hallway, then nothing. She waited a minute or so then tried again. She felt certain it was pointless but she had to do something. Cath wished she'd thought to ask Alice for a spare key – so she could keep an eye on the place while she was away, she could have said, though that might have sounded strange, intrusive even. She remembered how the Craigies always used to leave a spare key under a broken flower pot outside the porch. The flower pot had lain in the same place so long it had worn a groove in the soil. When you picked it up it came away smoothly, like the lid of a cooking pot. Cath knew the chances of the key still being there were next to nil, but she checked anyway.

The flowerpot was still in its place, the key beneath, gleaming against the dull earth, streaked with tarnish in places but intact.

The last person to touch it would have been Susan. Either Susan or Shirley. The wonder of this, the horror, caught Cath by surprise. The way old habits persisted, what they revealed. She reached for the key, then replaced the flowerpot in its groove and straightened up. She was going to try the key in the door, she knew she was. Because Saheed would want her to, she told herself. If he knew she had a key, he would insist upon it. What if Alice was trapped inside, injured, unable to reach the door? She called Alice's number again, just in case, but there was still no reply. Cath slid the key into the lock. It went in easily, as if it had been used only hours before. The years receded, scattering on the wind like confetti. Like the pages of a journal, opened and read and digested then thrown away.

'Alice?' Cath called out, just to make a noise, to announce herself. She knew the house was empty, but she felt the need to do this, nonetheless. She realised she had never once been alone inside the Craigie house. She was trespassing, which was a crime, though would it still count as a break-in if you used a key? She stepped fully into the hallway, closed the door behind her, called Alice's name again. There was a stillness, a quiescence, that confirmed her in her certainty that the house was empty, that Alice was not here, her presence so faint she might have been gone for weeks.

Cath went into each of the rooms in turn, searching for clues. There was no sign of anything untoward, no indication Alice had left in a hurry, even. In the kitchen, washed dishes were stacked neatly in the drainer. In Alice's bedroom the bed was made, the wardrobe closed, the only sign of disorder a pair of trainers kicked to one side beneath a chair. There was a book on the bedside table, a biography of the American chess prodigy Bobby Fischer. It seemed strange that Alice hadn't taken the book with her, but then again she probably read on her tablet when she was travelling, like everyone else.

Cath opened the top drawer of Alice's bedroom cabinet then quickly slid it closed. She was not going to spy.

You would if you were a cop, though. It's a missing person's enquiry, remember? You should go through her things, see what's what. A real detective would jump at the chance.

Alice is not a missing person and I'm not a cop.

It's not like she's ever going to know.

Cath opened the drawer again: the scent of Alice's toiletries, that musky green-tea smell, a jumble of cotton briefs and sports bras, dark colours, mostly – navy, grey and burgundy. Cath shoved the drawer closed and went back downstairs. The living-room door was slightly ajar. Cath could see the dolls' house on the dining table. Its first-floor windows seemed to stare at her, wide-eyed. Beside the dolls' house were some papers, sheets torn from an A4 block as well as printed-off articles downloaded from the internet. The one on top Cath had already read – 'Richard Dadd: madman, murderer, mystic.' Its author suggested that Dadd's doctors had provided him with opium in order to facilitate his visions of the fairy realm – rubbish, probably. More stuff on Dadd, including a muddy reproduction of *The Fairy Feller's Master Stroke*. The painting was really quite ugly, Cath thought. The more you looked at it, the uglier it got. A piece on Islamic art, a set of diagrams illustrating something called Penrose's infinite staircase. A much longer piece entitled 'Fairies in the Quantum Dimension: the cosmology of the impossible'. She skim-read the first few paragraphs, which talked about scientists who had shown how the movements of certain types of subatomic particles could be interpreted to suggest the existence of parallel universes. The author of the article was a Mabel Konig.

Cath made a note of the title, used her phone to take photographs of some of the other documents, then turned to leave. What did she think she was doing? She shouldn't even be here.

I've told you, she'll never know.

That's not the point.

On her way back down the hill she called Saheed. 'Alice isn't here,' she said. 'Her car's in the drive but there's no sign of her. The house is locked up.'

'Fuck.'

'I tried her phone again just now. Still nothing. What exactly happened?'

'I've been a complete and utter dick, that's what happened. She told me. Last night, about the baby, I mean, and I turned round and asked her if she thought this was really such a great time to get pregnant. I think I was in shock, you know? The look on her face, Jesus. I tried to explain, to say sorry, but it was too late by then, she phased me out completely. Never heard a word I said. I am just so frigging worried about her.'

He had assumed Cath knew about the baby, that Alice had told her. Either that or he was so deep in his own anxiety he hadn't considered the question either way.

'Might she be at her mum's, or something?'

'I seriously don't think so. Her mum's been on overdrive since Alice got ill and it drives Alice nuts. I don't want to call there unless I absolutely have to. Ally would kill me.' He laughed, a cold, joyless sound. 'I keep hoping she'll walk right through that door. I'm going crazy here.'

'Did she say anything before she left? Anything at all?'

'That she needed some air. But that was hours ago, this morning – she could be anywhere. You don't get it. When Ally was ill she was always wandering off like this. She used to go to shopping malls,

Burger Kings, places she wouldn't stand out or be noticed. She'd sit there for hours. Sometimes when I caught up with her she'd pretend not to know me. It was like she was someone else – a stranger wearing Ally's clothes. There were times when I was actually scared of her, you know? I'd get this chill on me.' Saheed sniffed, and Cath wondered if he was crying. 'Later when she was OK again she'd say she didn't remember any of it, but I know she did, she just didn't want to talk about it. Imagine if she's gone like that again. And she's pregnant. Jesus,' he repeated. Saheed had been an idiot but that didn't cancel out the fact that he was in a state. Cath felt a tremor of sympathy. She knew how he felt.

'She's been fine,' she said. 'I mean, really. She probably just needs some time by herself, time to think. If you've not heard from her by midnight call me again. I'll keep trying her phone.'

'You and me both.' He sounded embarrassed, finally, at having revealed himself so completely to someone he distrusted. The past hour should have drawn them closer together but Cath knew it hadn't, or not in any way that was likely to last. What was it about Saheed that made her hackles rise? The fact that he existed, or something more troubling? The fact that he reminded her – in the way he had of blotting her out, of making her not exist – of Johnny Craigie?

Not just the way he was with her, but the way he was with Alice. His need to be the only frigging person in her life. After ringing off from Saheed, Cath tried Alice's mobile again then made herself a sandwich. She was ravenous, she discovered. She wolfed it down then made another, ate that too. She poured a glass of Chianti. She had almost reached the bottom of it when her phone pinged. Cath made a lunge for the handset, almost knocking the wine glass off the table.

Tell Saheed I'm OK.

Moments later a second text arrived.

I really am. Back soon. Don't worry.

Cath stared at the display for perhaps thirty seconds then called Alice's number. Straight to voicemail.

She called Saheed.

'I've just heard from her,' she said, when he picked up. She read him the texts aloud over the phone. 'I think we have to trust her.'

'She's still pissed at me. Back where?'

London, or the island? There was no way of telling. 'It doesn't matter, does it?' Cath said. 'At least we know she's all right.'

'I guess she was scared I'd call the cops if I didn't hear from her.' He sounded less anxious, the relief finally hitting his system like a shot of morphine.

'I'll call again if I hear anything more.'

'Yeah, thanks.' Already he seemed absent, his thoughts elsewhere. Cath had served her purpose and now he could forget her, pretend their conversation had never happened. She said goodbye and rang off. She downed the dregs of her wine, then put her trainers back on and went outside. The light was beginning to fade, bands of pearl over dove-grey silk, stained with dollops of navy like Rorschach blots. Cath felt suddenly certain that if she were to go to the Craigie house now, Alice would be there. She set off up the hill, approaching with caution, as if the house itself might disappear if she made too much noise. Her heart leapt up, convinced for a second that she'd been right, that there was a light on in one of the upstairs windows. She realised more or less immediately she had been mistaken, that it was simply the glow from the deepening sunset, reflecting back off the glass.

She wondered where Alice was now. In a hotel room somewhere, probably. An image came to her of Richard Dadd, who had fled to France after killing his father, overwhelmed by his own obsessions, going slowly insane.

No use thinking like that. She pushed the thought aside. She kept her phone switched on all night but it didn't ring.

'WELL, SHE WAS LIKE a child really, Susan. Even with two bairns of her own there was something helpless about her. No, I don't mean helpless.' Iris sipped at her tea. 'Naive. As if she didn't understand the world she was living in. I don't mean she was stupid – not in the slightest. Too clever for her own good – that's what people say, isn't it? She was too clever for him, that's all I know. You can bet that animal never picked up a book in his entire life.'

Iris Docherty's sitting room overlooked Kames Bay, the wide sweep of water, busy with sailing boats, the wooded hills of the Cowal humped behind.

'There's a view I never get tired of,' Iris said, 'whatever the weather's doing.' The room itself was bright and cluttered. The ticking of clocks, the densely overlapping textures of assorted small objects, mementoes and keepsakes, chance acquisitions, the accumulated detritus of a long lifetime. A china owl, wearing schoolmaster specs and a tasselled mortarboard, an ancient Roberts radio, a Satsumaware bowl, overflowing with picture postcards and torn-off stamps. A watercolour landscape of mountains with a tiny white dot of a croft house nestled in the bottom right-hand corner. The painting looked as if it might be worth something, Cath thought, though she found herself more drawn to the family photographs, jostling for space on the mantelpiece and in the alcove shelves. Some of the people in the photos looked like Iris.

'My sister's children and grandchildren,' Iris said. 'I'm a great-aunt eight times over, last time I checked. Half of them live down south now but Ena's youngest, Valentine, is in Perth. She comes over to visit from time to time with little Angela.' Iris briefly touched one of the photographs, a dark-skinned child with bushy black braids that stuck out from her head at right angles. The girl looked rather like Alice, Cath realised, startled. Alice as she might have been at eight years old. 'Bright as a button, that one. I'm afraid for her sometimes, the world the way it is.'

'What did you mean about Susan being too clever for her own good?' Cath said. She liked Iris, she was beginning to realise. Despite the difference in their ages, they seemed like kindred spirits. They were both observers, rather than participants. Natural-born detectives.

'With some women, you know they'll just get on with things. No matter if the man she married turns out a rotten apple, she'll make her life in spite of him, if you see what I'm saying. Susan Craigie wasn't like that. Always looking for reasons, she was. Keep looking for reasons with a man like him and you'll wear out your sanity. I remember Susan once asked me if I believed a place could be haunted – not by ghosts, she said she didn't believe in ghosts, but by what had happened there in the past. Like how a person's memories might have an effect on the future. I told her the future was more often decided by what we chose to do about it, and she gave me this look, like I was speaking out of turn, which probably I was. Later on she was into geology – quartz and fossils and all that whatnot. She even brought in a find, for the museum – a prehistoric arrowhead she'd picked up on the beach at St Ninian's Point. Lived in a world of her own most of the time, that was her trouble. Couldn't see what was coming for her, or for those weans of hers. The lassie was different. Your friend, I mean. She was a tearaway but she was a survivor, you could see that right away. She had the island spirit.'

She replaced her cup in its saucer. 'You won't bring her back though, all this poking about. That was her mother's trouble.'

'I need to know why they died. For Shirley's sake. It feels important.' Because we were friends, Cath thought. Because I know she'd do the same for me if it were the other way around. Cath had no doubt Iris would do the same too, if it were Angela.

'I never lived with a man,' Iris said. 'I never found one that was worth the trouble.'

'What about Susan though? Do you think there is any chance she might have met someone – someone she was thinking of leaving her husband for?'

'Why do you ask that?'

'I can't help feeling there has to be something – a reason. People don't just get murdered,' Cath said. 'Or not usually.'

'You don't mean the archaeologist chappie?' Iris said. She seemed on guard suddenly. Like someone with a secret, Cath thought later. A suspicion she's kept to herself for many years.

'Fellow was from Glasgow,' Iris continued. 'He was doing up one of the wee cottages in Straad, down on the beach there. He used to give talks at the museum sometimes, for the island history society, about the Vikings and local history and suchlike. Not seen him in years. He'd be getting on a bit now, I suppose, but he would have been around forty then or thereabouts. I remember seeing him and Susan chatting together once or twice and thinking it was unusual because she wouldn't say boo to a goose normally. It's not much to go on I know but I did have a feeling about him. About them, I suppose.'

The folded-over timetable in Susan's journal, the programme of lectures. Cath experienced an eerie, stomach-dropping feeling of disjuncture, as if she'd turned over the whole house looking for something only to find it had been lying on the table in front of her all along. The lecturer from Glasgow University, who had spoken to her class about the Vikings. Could this have been him, the man Susan was seeing, the man at the museum? Cath tried desperately to recall his face, his voice, the way he was dressed even, but nothing came, just the memory of long-ago boredom, of feeling uncomfortable from sitting on the floor, of being distracted by Shirley fidgeting with the carpet.

Last night I saw upon the stair
A little man who wasn't there

And the dates fit too, didn't they? The dates bloody fit.

'Not that anyone ever said anything,' Iris was saying. She heaved herself up from her seat, grimacing slightly from the effort, moved towards the window and stood there, looking out across the water, hands on her hips. 'But the police made it clear at the inquiry, didn't they, that he was driving away from the ferry port. The monster, I mean. As if he were mad to get his hands on someone.' She paused.

'I'm not saying I know anything for sure, because I don't. Chances are you're right and she was seeing someone. Heaven knows she would have had her reasons. It's just a shame she didn't have the sense to get completely away.'

'It's not easy though, is it, not when you have children? Her whole life was here.'

'Anyone could see what was coming, with a man like that, see it a mile off. My granny believed we all of us could see into the future if we thought on it hard enough. Not clearly, like looking at a photograph, but we'd get an inkling. I've no time for that sort of nonsense myself but there you are. Eighteen eighty-eight, my granny was born. Makes you think, doesn't it? History isn't just what's in the history books, it's what you remember.'

They both fell silent. Cath thought about asking Iris if she'd heard of Richard Dadd but the moment passed. 'Thank you for talking to me,' she said instead. 'You've been so helpful. I hope you don't mind me asking you about these things.'

'I'm too old to mind,' she said. 'You'll come back and see me again, won't you?'

'I'd like that.'

'Mind how you go, then.'

'Do you happen to remember his name?' Cath asked as she was leaving. 'The archaeologist?'

'Livingstone. That I do know because people were always making jokes about it – Dr Livingstone I presume. His first name was Aaron, I think. Or was it Angus? They'd have it on file somewhere. The museum, I mean.'

'Thanks,' Cath said. She was conscious of the blood in her veins, its pulse insistent, like electrical current, like a strange machine. She walked away towards the bus stop, crossed the road by ear, without looking to see what was coming. A dangerous habit and later she would remind herself not to be so stupid but in those moments after Iris spoke Livingstone's name Cath was moving on autopilot.

As I was walking down the stair. She moved her lips silently, mouthing the words, grasping on to them as if to steady herself. I met a man who wasn't there.

Only he was there, wasn't he, slowcoach? He was there all the time.

THE BUS CAME TEN minutes later. It was beginning to get dark. The isle is full of noises, Cath thought. Which play was that from – *The Tempest*? She felt overwhelmed by the unlikeliness of it all. Angus Livingstone had been a key witness at the Fatal Accident Inquiry, the last person to see John Craigie alive. That this same Angus Livingstone had turned out to be the husband of Mary Chant, murdered twenty years later in Maryhill, was the kind of coincidence you only encounter in detective stories. That he might also have been the elusive lover of Susan Craigie – as coincidences went it was almost terrifying.

You're looking in the wrong place, Cath thought – words she had imagined being spoken by Shirley, fluttering about her head like moths at twilight, like a haunting.

A name is just a name. Ye've no proof yet. No proof, not even a photograph, just the blurred headshot from the university prospectus they'd used in the paper, which was proof of nothing. And there was still John Craigie. Iris had called Craigie a monster. Others – Johnny's neighbours – had described him as an accident waiting to happen. Calling a man a monster was an abdication – the kind of explanation people reached for when they ran out of ideas. It was rarely the whole truth though, and neither was Craigie. Johnny was one truth of many, one link in the chain.

She wished she could speak to Alice, or even just know for certain where Alice was. There was still no answer from her phone – Cath found she had almost stopped believing there ever would be. She spent half an hour wondering if she should email her again before finally sending her a one-liner – **hope you're OK, let me know where you are** – and then logging off for the night. That familiar creeping fear, that the slightest word or wrong action might bring an end to everything, whatever everything was. Cath had sworn she'd never let herself feel like this again about anyone and yet here she was, feeling it. She thought about ringing Steve, which was weird, because she never rang Steve unless it was work-related. It was almost eleven o'clock but she knew he'd be awake still – he rarely went to bed before one.

What would she say, though? I think I might be in love with someone but she's married, and pregnant? And PS, you know the guy who believes in fairies who committed the murders? My dead friend seems to be telling me he didn't do it.

Yeah right, Steve would say. All islanders are mad, I told you, alive or dead. When are you coming home?

In spite of her anxiety over Alice, Cath found herself smiling. She and Steve understood one another through osmosis, a set of rules that had not so much been laid down as evolved. They knew each other completely, and scarcely at all.

*

CATH SLEPT BADLY, CLAWING her way through dense banks of dreams that refused to subside. She was woken at eight thirty by the doorbell ringing. She pulled a sweatshirt on over her joggers, padded out into the hall. When she opened the street door, there was Alice.

'I caught the early ferry,' she said. 'I should have been back last night but the train was delayed and I ended up staying in Glasgow.'

They hugged. Alice dumped her bag in the hall – a different bag from the one she'd set out with, Cath thought, then remembered she couldn't know that, she'd not seen Alice leave. Cath made coffee and they sat together on the sofa with their feet drawn up under them. It was incredible, how instantly things felt all right again.

'Have you called Saheed yet?' Cath said. 'He's pretty worried.'

'I phoned him last night, from the hotel. Told him I was sorry for freaking out and that I was on my way back to the island. He's OK now – enough to stop him dashing up here on the train, anyway.' She leaned her head back against the sofa cushions. 'This is a weird flat.'

'Weird how?' It was the first time Alice had been to Argyle Terrace, Cath realised. She tried not to read too much into the fact that Alice had called Saheed first and not her. She would have to, Cath supposed. Saheed hadn't called Cath either but then he wouldn't.

'I don't know. I guess all rented places are weird.'

'Where were you? The night before last, I mean?'

'Carlisle. I knew it was too late for me to get back to the island so I booked a room over the internet and just got off the train. I had a meal in the hotel restaurant then went to see a film then wandered around, had a drink in a pub. It was strange, thinking how no one had a clue where I was. It was amazing, actually. I know I should have called but it was such a relief, not having to explain to anyone about anything.'

'I went up to the house. Saheed thought you'd come back here. He was scared shitless you were thinking he didn't want the baby.'

Now was the moment to tell her – about finding the key under the flowerpot, about going inside. Even as the knowledge came to her, Cath knew she'd bottle out. Alice was back, that was what mattered. Best not to complicate things.

'He said. Last night, I mean. I told him it was normal to react like he did, that everything was fine. I knew he didn't mean it.'

'How are you though, really?'

Alice glanced at her, quick as a bird, then looked down at her cup. Her hair was tied in a blue bandana, and Cath could smell her body odour, as if she'd left the hotel in Glasgow without bothering to shower.

'Saheed wants me to go back to London,' she said. 'Right now, for good, I mean. I don't know what I want.' She turned to look at the murder wall, seemed to register it for the first time. 'It looks like a cop show in here.'

'It works, though. I discovered it's the best way of laying out the evidence.'

'Evidence.' Alice closed her eyes. 'Knowing the facts doesn't always solve a problem. I hate that being true, but it is.' She seemed preoccupied, Cath realised, and very tired. 'I've been thinking about Ezra, the boy I was at maths camp with? I keep thinking about how vulnerable he was, how much he needed me. And I was so wrapped up in my own stuff I just abandoned him. I don't even know where he is now, if he's still alive even. He must have gone through hell.' She drew in her breath. 'What if I have another breakdown? It's not just about me now, is it? If I'm capable of doing that to Ezra, how am I supposed to cope with looking after a baby?'

'Ezra wasn't your responsibility, though,' Cath said. 'You were just a kid. It's like me and Shirley.' She took Alice's hand and squeezed it. Alice squeezed back, keeping hold of her fingers. Cath felt her heart expand inside her chest, the big red beat of it, opening and softly closing like a velvet glove. 'You're going to be fine. You need some time to yourself, that's all. You'll soon start feeling better now you're back on the island.'

'I know you're right.' Alice yawned. 'God, I'm knackered. I should be getting back.'

'Stay here if you like?'

Alice shook her head. 'I need to sort myself out. Have a shower and that. I'll call you later.'

When Cath offered to walk up the hill with her, Alice said there was no need. After Alice left, Cath found herself going back over their conversation, the comparison she had made between her own relationship with Shirley and the guilt Alice seemed to be feeling over Ezra.

We were just kids.

Yeah, we were. So what?

You're saying I could have done more? That I should have done more?

Cath listened for a reply but no words came, just a silent, unbending pressure inside her head, which was all the reply she needed, the only one possible. It was like Alice said: knowing the facts did not always help to solve a problem, just as knowing for sure who had killed Shirley could not cancel out the pain of missing her, of suspecting deep in her heart that she had let her friend down.

Knowledge was something, but it was not everything, and never could be.

MABEL KONIG

From Wikipedia, the free encyclopedia

Mabel Konig (12 April 1954 – 11 November 1989) was a British linguistician and philosopher. Originally trained as a journalist, Konig later became interested in the codified language systems she believed were embodied in Middle Eastern and Islamic architectural geometry such as girih tiles. After studying for a time under the mathematician Matthew Lord, she began to develop her own interpretation of Hugh Everett's Many Worlds theory of quantum physics, in which codified languages work as a method of exploring parallel states of reality. Her 1984 essay 'Fairies in the Quantum Dimension: the cosmology of the impossible' briefly enjoyed cult status among a younger generation of artists and linguistic theoreticians, although her work has largely been dismissed by physicists as philosophical rather than scientific.

Contents

Disappearance

Death

Legacy

Fairies in the Quantum Dimension

Early life and education

Konig was born in Croydon, Surrey. Her parents were Miriam Konig, a family doctor, and Frank Konig, a chartered accountant. Konig attended the local primary school and then the Addiscombe High School for Girls, where she showed an aptitude for languages and expressed interest in working for the United Nations. Konig completed her formal education at University College, London, earning an upper second-class degree in Politics and Philosophy, with additional modules in Arabic and Spanish.

In Egypt and Syria

Following her graduation from UCL, Konig secured a post as features writer for the English-language newspaper the *Egyptian Gazette*, based in Alexandria. It was while researching a story on the Persian mathematician Muhammad al-Kwarizmi and the roots of Arabic astronomy that she first became fascinated by the transition to symbolism within algebra and the concept of mathematics as a codified language. In a later essay about her time in the Middle East she wrote: These were concepts that were entirely new to me, and my progress was slow. As a student, I had displayed no more than average ability in mathematics, and would never have considered taking the subject at a higher level. I found huge satisfaction in the study of languages, the acquisition of new vocabularies, but it would never have occurred to me at the time that mathematics was itself a language, a language that could be learned and 'spoken' much as any other, that is, through the analysis and interpretation of codified symbols. The realisation was like a door opening. I came to understand that my study of modern languages had been merely a precursor to what would become the main passion of my life, the same way standing in a porch or anteroom might be related to entering the decorated banqueting hall of a great castle.[1]

The *Egyptian Gazette* funded a number of Konig's research trips, both within Egypt and further afield to other significant historical and cultural sites in Iran and Syria. It was Konig's visits to mosques in Cairo and Damascus in particular that ignited her interest in girih tiles, a preoccupation that laid the groundwork for the theories expressed in her series of essays on codified language. Girih design is a form of decorative strapwork which features extensively in Islamic art and architecture from the ninth to the sixteenth century. Later examples of girih patterning display levels of geometric complexity including multi-level and aperiodic designs created from girih tiles, a set of five polygonal tile shapes themselves subdivided by sets of straight-edge lines that link up to form still more elaborate patterning as the tiles are placed in position.

Late twentieth-century analysis has revealed the similarities and parallels between girih design and fractal algorithms and so-called quasi-crystals, whose structure is stable though lacking the uniform spacing of atoms that occurs in normal crystals. The chief characteristic of this advanced form of girih design is that, unlike standard geometric patterning, it does not achieve its effects through exact repetition. Konig found the inbuilt irregularities that are central to girih design philosophically exciting and profound, suggesting a knowledge of higher mathematics 'hardwired' as a universal into organic systems and existing beyond individual consciousness.

In 2007 Harvard physicist Peter Lu formally linked the non-repeating properties of girih design with the Penrose tiles developed by Roger Penrose in Oxford in the 1970s.[2] Lu's discovery was significant in identifying quasi-crystalline patterns created in the Middle East five hundred years before such structures had been recognised or understood in the West. Scholars of Konig's work insist her own discovery of the phenomenon pre-dates Lu's by two decades.[3] Such claims have been dismissed by the scientific community as unproven, owing to Konig's chaotic methodology and lack of peer review.[4]

Return to England

After five years touring the Middle East, Konig returned to England in 1976, where she took up residence in a studio flat in the basement of the family home. Her physical condition at the time appeared depleted, and her parents insisted that she see a doctor. She was diagnosed as suffering from exhaustion and advised to rest. The following months showed a significant improvement in her health, and by the spring of the following year she had declared her intention to give up journalism and return to further education. She enrolled on a postgraduate course in the philosophy of linguistics at Queen Mary College, London.

It was at this time that Konig began her correspondence with Matthew Lord, a Cambridge mathematician who had recently given a series of public lectures on geometry in nature and the golden ratio. Konig approached Lord after a lecture at the Renoir cinema in Bloomsbury. Lord was later to judge Konig as highly intelligent but with large gaps in her knowledge of mathematics. He found much to admire in her essays as written constructs, whilst remaining sceptical about much of their content.[5]

Disappearance

In the spring of 1980, Konig broke off her relationship with Lord. It was at this time that Miriam Konig began to notice substantive changes in her daughter's behaviour, describing 'a manic quality' in the way she spoke and acted.[6] Both parents suspected that the decision to break with Lord had not been mutual, as Konig claimed, and that Konig was finding difficulty in recovering from the termination of the affair.

In March 1981, Mabel Konig disappeared from her home for an unexplained period of three days. Konig's parents did not at first realise that she was missing – Mabel had told them she was staying overnight with a friend from university. It was only when she did not return, and when a phone call to the friend revealed that she had never been there, that they began to feel anxious. When a second night passed and Mabel had still not returned they called the police, citing Mabel's repeating pattern of mental health problems as grounds for concern. A full search had just got underway when Mabel returned, walking calmly up to the front door and letting herself into the house with her own key.

A medical examination revealed no signs of physical or sexual assault, and apart from minor dehydration Mabel was pronounced in good health. When questioned about her absence, she refused to answer.

Death

In the years following her disappearance, Konig retired almost entirely from social interaction, preferring to spend time alone in her apartment, reading or working. She suffered increasingly from what her father Frank referred to as blank spells – days at a time during which she did not speak or communicate, or even seem aware of the presence of other people.[7]

Mabel Konig died in November 1989 at the age of thirty-five. The cause of death was certified as anorexia nervosa, although this was later contested.[8] In

203

spite of the fact that there had been no verifiable decline in Konig's cognitive function, one doctor consulted about her case believed she had been suffering from a degenerative brain disease similar to CJD.[9]

Legacy

In the aftermath of Konig's death, hundreds of pages of manuscript were recovered from her room, including the full text of 'Fairies in the Quantum Dimension' and a substantial portion of draft copy for a work on the history and symbolism of girih tiles. A number of her friends and colleagues from Queen Mary College came together to raise funds for the publication of a book of her essays.[10] The edition quickly sold out, and the volume remained scarce until a later publication, in electronic format, made Konig's work more widely available.

Fairies in the Quantum Dimension

In her best-known essay, Mabel Konig posits that observable quotidian reality is only one possible variant of what she termed personally verifiable reality, and that some folkloric beliefs, for example a belief in supernatural beings such as elves and fairies, may be attributed to enhanced, synaesthetic or higher intellectual perception on the part of those who profess them. Konig cites the 'hardwiring' of advanced mathematical concepts into the material of the known universe as proof of the possibility of quantum realms, constituting every possible variant of empirical reality. Her argument, that the development of advanced fractal geometry in the Middle East, centuries before the same systems came to be understood in the West, points towards a 'wrong path' theory of cultural hegemony has been widely disputed.[11]

Mabel Konig wrote at some length in her essay about the nineteenth-century British artist and parricide Richard Dadd, who suffered a psychotic break while travelling in the Middle East and whose drawings and watercolours featuring fairies and other mythological beings, painted at Bethlem Hospital and later at Broadmoor, display an obsessive intricacy and a quality of intensity – what Konig refers to as singlemindedness of purpose – that is reminiscent of the codified language systems Konig purported to exist in girih design.

In his irregularly repeating and endless fascination with the realm of faerie, Dadd tugs at our sleeve, imploring us to acknowledge he is not mad, to see what is there in front of us if only we can bring ourselves to notice. As with the fractured planes and spaces of an Ishihara colour blindness test, observing an alternative reality might be a question of knowing not only where to look, but how. Might the imperceptions of today's majority be looked back on by future generations as a psychological analogue of colour blindness? Dadd's work seems to suggest this is entirely possible.[12]

After Konig's death, Miriam and Frank Konig donated funds to Queen Mary College for the foundation of a memorial bursary in their daughter's name. The Mabel Konig Prize is awarded annually to a student who demonstrates original or visionary thinking in the field of linguistics. Notable recipients to date include the cryptographer Mariya Okonkwo and the mathematician Ezra Goldacre.[13]

References

1. 'To See the World in a Grain of Sand' Mabel Konig c1986 collected in *Fairies in the Quantum Dimension and Other Essays*, Blueprint Press 1995.

2. 'Islamic Tiles Reveal Sophisticated Maths' Peter Ball, *Nature* Feb 2007.

3. 'The Tortoise and the Hare' Margarethe Geisler, *Die Schwelle* March 2009.

4. 'Not Proven' Paul Stack, Portal June 2011.

5. Chapter 3 Matthew Lord in *Music of the Primes: tomorrow's mathematicians today* edit. Julie Beynes, Backgammon Publishing 2004.

6. 'Tragic death of Croydon Sybil declared natural causes' *London Evening Standard* 14 December 1989 retrieved September 2011.

7. ibid.

8. 'Tragic mathematician "could have been CJD victim" claims doctor' *London Evening Standard* 20 March 1990 retrieved September 2011.

9. ibid.

10. *Fairies in the Quantum Dimension and Other Essays*, Mabel Konig with Valerie Josephs and Kaden Josephs (eds.) Blueprint Press 1995.

11. 'Suspicious Minds: a wrong road not taken' Melvyn Jacks in *How the West was Lost* ed. Piers Novotny, Far to Go Books 2011.

12. 'Fairies in the Quantum Dimension: the cosmology of the impossible' Mabel Konig in *Fairies* etc etc Blueprint Press 1995.

13. 'Check Mate: chess prodigy wins university prize' Evening Argus July 2009.

See also

Grand Design Theory

Outsider artists

Apocryphal Geometry

16.

MORE AND MORE, CATH had the sense that Shirley was trying to speak to her through her photographs.

It's all evidence. If you can't see what's in front of your face you're not looking at it right.

Her photographs of Mary Chant's house in Maryhill were all about absence, the bland grey light that creeps in when the meaning of an object or a place has been leached away. Was it Ronnie Mackintosh who was missing from the scene, or Angus Livingstone? The name, the absence of Angus – from the news coverage, from the photographic record – preyed on Cath's mind. Why was no one talking about him, when he seemed to be everywhere? The Fatal Accident Inquiry, the island, the city.

Wear the right clothes and you fit right in.

What's that supposed to mean?

Just that there's folk who have a knack for it. For being nobody.

The photographs she had taken since being back on the island were almost the opposite: dense with memory, with allegory, with presence. With what Adam Fairlie called context, a bollocks word perhaps but in this case, Cath was bound to admit, it felt like a true one.

Zavaroni's for example was Shirley standing at the counter with her back to the window, the pavement drenched with sunlight, the bright tap-tapping of high heels on the scorching asphalt. Cath photographed the ice-cream parlour every day for a week, at the same time and from the same angle. Like being on stakeout, she thought. Looking at something to know it, to know it so well that the moment anything changes you notice immediately.

Empty spaces, drawn shutters, chairs and tables set out on the pavement then taken inside. Cath remembered a conversation she'd had with Steve once in the pub after work. He'd told her about a time when he was a kid, when he'd gone to the park with his grandmother. How she'd suddenly taken him by the hand and marched him off to some beat-up district of Glasgow, pointing out streets and tenements and rows of shops that weren't even there.

'She kept saying she wanted me to remember,' Steve said. 'She couldn't walk long distances by then because of her arthritis, especially not uphill, and she was panting fit to burst. She was crying too, and Gran never cried, or at least she never had before in front of me. She told me they'd taken her world and bulldozed it under. Once we forget, it's gone for good, she said. They'll tell us we're crazy even to mention it. The thing is, a while ago I bought an old Glasgow A–Z online and I saw she was right, Gran was, those streets really had been there. I knew that already, or sort of, but seeing them on the map made everything real.'

*

'TELL ME ABOUT YOU and Shirley,' said Alice, later. 'I mean really. Did you love her?'

'We were fifteen,' Cath said. 'She was my best friend.'

CATH SPENT MOST OF a morning photographing the dolls' house.

'There's a room around the back that doesn't have an entrance,' Alice said. 'Did you know that?'

'What are you talking about?'

'Look, here.'

Alice pointed to the window on the first floor that looked in on the box room, a small, square chamber, unfurnished except for a blanket chest and an orphaned dining chair. The door to the room stood closed, a single wire coat hanger on the hook on the back.

'There's a door,' Cath said, peering in. 'It's always been there.'

'Yes, but look – the door doesn't open on to the landing. There's another room in front of it, one of the bedrooms. You can see through this window.'

She meant the window that stood at right angles to the box-room window, the window of the L-shaped bedroom with the rose wallpaper. There was a double wardrobe in the rose room. It stood in the alcove, directly in front of where the door into the box room should be.

Why had Cath never noticed? Why would anyone put a wardrobe in front of a door?

To keep someone shut in, why d'you think?

Had Shirley always known about the blocked-up box room? Cath supposed she must have done. The box room, which Cath had previously thought of as cosy, now seemed airless and sinister.

'There's other stuff like that,' Alice said. 'I've been checking it out. The back stairs come out in the wrong place, for a start. It's a deliberate error, like in a puzzle box. Saheed gave me a book on Chinese puzzle boxes for Christmas a couple of years ago. They have all kinds of deliberate errors – false walls and fake drawers, things like that. The more skilful the craftsman, the weirder the errors, the harder they are to find – kind of like the Easter eggs you get in video games and special program features. Some of the really elaborate boxes are considered to be priceless.'

'Why, though? Why put all that effort into creating something that might never be noticed?'

'Weird geometry,' Alice said. 'There's a whole category of apocryphal geometry concerned with how space can be forced to contain other spaces that aren't strictly possible – that don't exist, if you go by Euclidian geometry. It's not my thing really but it's what some of the puzzle box makers were into. I've been reading up on it. You know M. C. Escher?'

'The artist?'

Alice nodded. 'Escher was obsessed with impossible figures – geometric structures that can be represented as two-dimensional graphics but cannot actually exist in three dimensions. You remember his street scenes which are also still lifes? Or the steps that ascend and descend in a continuous loop. His key inspirations came from Islamic art, the patterns of tiles he saw at the Alhambra palace in Spain in the 1920s. Weird geometry is like Escher's lithographs, extrapolated into three-dimensional space – stuff that shouldn't exist yet somehow does. Like John Craigie's dolls' house. I wonder if he realised.'

'Like Penrose's staircase?' Cath said suddenly.

'That would be one example, yes.' She sounded surprised. 'You know about Penrose's steps?'

'Not really. I read about them somewhere, maybe in a magazine. I can't remember. Just that Escher and Penrose knew each other. That they collaborated.'

It was the diagram she was thinking of, the diagram she had seen with Mabel Konig's article the night she entered Alice's house with the hidden key. Not that she could admit such a thing to Alice. 'You don't think the errors in the dolls' house might just be mistakes?' she added, trying to play down her interest. There were subjects that lay beyond Cath's area of expertise – that's how Alice would see it, anyway. Roger Penrose and his infinite staircase was almost certainly one of them.

'You can't make something like that by mistake – too complicated. And nothing about this house was done by accident – I mean, look at it. It's like an ideal of a house, the kind of house a child might draw. The best of all possible houses, in the best of all possible worlds.' Alice laughed. 'Kind of creepy, actually. All perfect things are creepy. Think of *The Stepford Wives*.'

Abigail Mercer had mentioned *The Stepford Wives*, Cath remembered. A model village, populated by dolls. The next time Cath came round, she found Alice seated at the table in front of the dolls' house. The house was completely empty. All the furniture had been removed and placed to one side.

'What are you doing?' Cath said. The sight of the empty house made her feel queasy. It was as if the house had been attacked, ransacked by home invaders, like in a horror movie, the family that used to live there banished forever.

'Nothing. Just looking.' She showed Cath the inventory she had made, every accessory and item of furniture named and given a number in a spiral-bound notebook. With the furniture gone, you could begin to see how old the house was, how lived-in. How the wallpaper in the hall had been ripped at some point and stuck down again, how chipped the paintwork was, how the colours of the curtains were beginning to fade. Alice had removed the armoire from the rose room along with everything else, revealing how what looked like a door from inside the box room was really a fake – a flat piece of wood sanded and varnished to look like a door but made never to open. The box room door was a deliberate error, like Alice had said.

'Why would anyone do that?' Cath said, again. The whole idea still seemed bizarre to her. Alice rested her chin on her hands and pursed her lips. She seemed distracted, not quite there. A moment later she leapt to her feet and hugged Cath close.

'Let's go for a walk,' she said.

THE WESTLAND ROAD HOUSE was changing its nature, becoming Alice's. Her stuff was everywhere: books in little piles next to the sofa, items of clothing casually flung to one side across the back of a chair. A set of tea towels printed with mathematical equations drying on the stove rail, an untidy bunch of asters in a pottery jug on the kitchen table. Alice had been to the health centre, booked her twelve-week scan. She was beginning to talk about the baby as an established fact.

'Will Saheed be here for the scan?' Cath asked. She felt

uncharacteristically relieved when Alice said yes. 'You are eating properly, aren't you?' she added.

Alice laughed. When she got to her feet she staggered slightly, already heavier, though nothing was showing yet.

'Don't be an arse,' she said. 'I never stop.'

O N THE MURDER WALL, Cath drew a thick red circle around the name of Angus Livingstone, a confident swoop of marker pen that conveniently overlooked the absence of concrete proof. Still, she felt certain that Angus Livingstone was the missing puzzle piece — not only Susan's lover, but possibly her murderer, the man who had sent John Craigie over the edge. Angus Livingstone had been driving away from Straad on the day of the murders, Cath reasoned — it was because he'd been driving away from the village that he'd almost crashed into John Craigie's pickup, speeding towards him along the A844.

Cath had a new theory, a theory the police had never considered because why would they, when they knew nothing of Angus Livingstone's connection with Susan Craigie? So far as the cops were concerned, Livingstone was nobody, an innocent bystander. But what if Livingstone had committed the murders, then returned in haste to his cottage to clean himself up? He would have wanted to get away as quickly as possible after that, back to the mainland with no one on the island any the wiser.

That was why he had been driving towards the ferry terminal. Johnny had been coming in the other direction. Searching for Livingstone, Cath believed, she was almost certain. Had Johnny recognised him, lost concentration, run into the wall? She remembered her earlier theory, that Johnny had seen something out there on the road that had shocked him so much he'd lost control of his vehicle, that his death had been an accident after all. Forensic examination of the tyre tracks showed that Angus Livingstone's Granada had not come to a standstill until after it had passed the point where Craigie's pickup had come off the road. Livingstone had insisted there hadn't been time, a defence that had been accepted without qualification, though there were other explanations if you cared to look for them.

Cath wanted to go back to Straad, to see if she could find Livingstone's house mainly, but she was reluctant to ask Alice to drive her in case getting her involved with the search turned out to be a mistake. Alice seemed to have lost interest in renovating the Craigie house. Mostly she sat and read about dead mathematicians. Cath had called in one afternoon and found Alice asleep at the table. Cath called her name, softly at first and then more loudly, but she appeared deeply unconscious. When Cath shook her by the shoulder she came awake finally but seemed not to recognise her.

'You said you'd write to me,' she said. 'You promised.'

'Alice, it's Cath. What's going on?'

Alice gazed at her fixedly for a moment, her eyes wide. Then she seemed to relax, to come back to normal.

'God, I'm sorry. I get so tired these days. I can't seem to concentrate on anything for more than five minutes.'

'When is Saheed arriving?' Cath asked her, later. It was the weekend before Alice's twelve-week scan. Saheed had taken the Monday off from work so he could be there.

'I'm not sure. Tomorrow?'

'What do you mean, you're not sure?'

'No, I do mean tomorrow. Tomorrow's Friday.' Alice laughed. 'I lose track of the days.' A second later she was asking Cath about Susan's notebook, whether it had turned out to contain anything of interest.

'Lists, mainly,' Cath told her. 'Kings and queens, wildflowers. Like in a school exercise book.' She had already decided she would not tell Alice about the other things she had found hidden inside the notebook – the schedule of lectures, the strange little poem. Cath was concerned about Alice's state of mind, enough to make her feel it might be better to keep her away from certain subjects.

Like Richard Dadd, you mean?

Like what happened to him, more like.

'Why do you think she was doing that?'

'I'm not sure. To remind herself of things she was interested in? To bring some order into her life? I think I know who her lover was, though,' she added. 'Iris Docherty told me – the woman I met at the museum? She said there was a lecturer who used to come over from Glasgow University. He and Susan were often together, apparently.' She told Alice about Angus Livingstone, taking care not to mention the Fatal Accident Inquiry, her theories about Johnny's accident, Mary Chant. 'It has to be him, don't you think? The only problem is I can't seem to find out where he went after Susan died, what happened to him. There don't seem to be any photographs of him, either.'

'Have you tried contacting the university?'

'What?'

'Glasgow University. If he was a lecturer there they'd have records, even if he's retired. Even if he's dead.' She seemed much more alert suddenly, more like the old Alice. 'You could pretend to be one of his old students.'

'Make something up, you mean?'

Of course make something up. Why the scruples all of a sudden? Call yourself a detective.

Alice made a face, turning down the corners of her mouth in a mock grimace. 'I don't like your methods, Morse.'

'Fuck, that's scary.'

They both started laughing. Then Alice leaned forward suddenly and kissed the corner of Cath's mouth. A sister's kiss, Cath thought, though her heart was racing. She closed her eyes, wondering what would happen if she put her hands on either side of Alice's face and kissed her for real.

'I'm OK,' Alice said, drawing away. 'Really. You don't need to worry.'

'I know you are,' Cath said, and in that moment she even believed it. The old thoughts crowded into her mind again, that they could be together on the island, raise the baby, that things would work out. She was planning to spend the weekend not going out, editing photos and pretending that Saheed Rahman did not exist. She did not want to see Alice with him, she realised, did not know if she could bear it.

When the doorbell went at around five o'clock on the Sunday afternoon, Cath was curled up in an armchair, watching a holiday programme and trying not to think about what might be happening at Westland Road. She muted the TV and went to answer the bell. The person on the doorstep was Saheed.

'What the hell is wrong with her?' Saheed threw out his hands then leaned his forehead against the door jamb. The aggression seemed to drain from his face and it was clear to Cath that if Saheed had come intending to accuse her of driving Alice crazy, then that intention had evaporated the moment he saw her. When he remembered she was just Alice's friend, after all – Alice's weird clingy friend, boring and a bit of a misfit with the mind of a child. Cath saw all this in his expression, that defeated look – that he'd forgotten in his fury to get here that if anything she was crazier than Alice was.

'Do you want to come in?' Cath said. Saheed followed her into the living room, shoulders slouched, bunched together the same as Alice's when she was trying to get a handle on something. Cath saw him take in the murder wall, though they both seemed to come to a silent agreement not to mention it. Saheed seated himself on the sofa, elbows on knees.

'Can I get you a coffee? A beer?'

'Coffee's fine, thanks.' He kept glancing around the room. 'Alice doesn't know I'm here, in case you're wondering. I said I was going for a walk. What the hell is wrong with her?' he repeated, once she'd brought the coffee.

'Nothing,' Cath said. 'She needs some time to adjust, that's all, with the baby and everything. She told me she wants to stay here, on the island, but she knows you want her to go back to London. She's obviously feeling under pressure.'

Plus he more or less told her he didn't want the baby. He said he didn't mean it, but he still said it. Work it out, sunshine.

'I'm not talking about the baby. I'm talking about her not saying a word to me for hours while she scrolls through fucking acres of online bullshit looking for God knows what. I'm talking about her passing out in the middle of a sentence, dead to the world. This is how she was before, when she was ill. I want to know what's going on. She wasn't like this when she came down to London the other week. I even wondered – you know – if she might be using.'

'You think she's on drugs?'

Saheed shrugged. He looked uncomfortable suddenly. 'I don't mean smack, I mean uppers. Speed, or coke or something. There are guys in the office who use that shit when they've got some big deal going down. They say it helps them keep awake, stay on top of the detail. They get manic, exactly like Alice is now. I asked a mate once how it felt and he said it was like you could see every molecule in a shot of vodka, every individual transaction in a column of figures. Winking like diamonds, he said, like your brain was an electron microscope set to zoom. And then afterwards you'd just crash. Nothing would wake you, not till you'd rebooted. World War Three could break out and you'd sleep right through it. That's what Alice was like last night. It was fucking scary.'

'Alice wouldn't take drugs. Not with the baby.'

'How do you explain it, then?'

'She's getting back into her work maybe and it's taking it out of her? That might be a good thing. She applied for that chess course, did she tell you?'

'The one in Toledo?'

Cath nodded. 'She seems really keen to go.'

'I guess that's something.' He seemed almost convinced, seduced by the worldview Cath was offering. Alice was not deteriorating, she was improving, getting back on her personal track, working to get her life sorted before the baby came. 'She needs to leave the island, though,' he added.

'Why should she?'

'Because it's crazy, her being all the way up here while I'm down there. I can't keep hiking five hundred miles at the drop of a hat, it's frigging knackering. I want her with me, she's my wife. Why do you think?'

'What if London's not good for her?'

'Why shouldn't it be? It's where her friends are, where her life is. It's her home.'

Talking about her as if she didn't have a voice of her own. As if she were a murder victim.

'I think you should be discussing this with Alice, not me,' Cath said.

Yeah, like you haven't been dying to have it out with him all along.

'She's still angry with me,' Saheed said, the fight gone out of him suddenly. He was just a man at sea, Cath realised. Confused about his wife's motives, like a character in one of those bittersweet American romcoms about messy divorces. 'I know you guys are close. I'm trying to make sure she gets what she needs. If anything happened to her, or the baby . . .'

'Nothing can happen to her here. This is a safe place.'

Saheed glanced across at the murder wall. 'Nowhere is safe,' he said. 'Not always. Not completely.'

'Don't you think it should be up to Alice, where she gets to live?' Cath could feel her anger mounting, taste it in the back of her throat like gone-off milk. Saheed believed he was protecting Alice – the same way you might protect a beautiful pair of shoes or an expensive briefcase. The same way John Craigie had probably believed he was protecting Susan and Shirley. Saheed wasn't like John Craigie of course but here it was, all the same, that sense of entitlement. Men came with it fitted internally, a bonus special feature they didn't even know they had. 'She hates the people you work with, did you know that?'

'That's all old shit, she's out of there. She doesn't expect me to give up the job though, so shoot me. I guess everyone needs their own brand of crazy. Just ask Alice.'

'What makes you so in love with those trading rooms? Is it the money?'

Saheed curled his lip. 'People always assume it's about the money and that pisses me off. Like they think we're not being paid *for* something. What I love is the absolute present tense of it, like driving in a Formula One car, like listening to music. You're not thinking about the money when you get that rush. The money's what keeps you grounded, stops you burning your brain out. I guess that's why we use a lot of it.' He laughed, coldly. 'You think you love her, but I have loved her forever and if you try to take her away from me I will fight you.'

'I care about her, that's all.'

'You call it what you want. Whatever makes you feel better about yourself. I know what I see.' He drew in his breath. 'You hardly know her. You don't know me either. You think you do, but you don't. You need to butt out.'

His voice was toneless, as if he had lost interest in the argument, saw no further point in trying to prove himself, least of all to Cath. His abrupt change in direction had caught her off guard. Saheed was right, Cath realised. She barely knew him.

'I should be getting back to her,' Saheed was saying. 'I'm sorry if I said some things. I didn't sleep well last night. That train journey wrecks my head.'

'It's fine,' Cath said. 'Tell Alice I said hi.'

He left, and Cath found herself wondering what he would say to Alice when he got back, whether he'd tell her the truth about where he'd been or make something up. If he made something up, he would run the risk of being found out later but perhaps he didn't care. Perhaps he would tell a second lie to back up the first.

You're right, he's a dick. Quite fanciable though, isn't he?

Trust you to see the up side.

Cath smiled, not because she found Saheed attractive but because even after all these years she could still conjure up the sound of Shirley's laugh, that particular back-of-throat chuckle that meant she was interested in someone but didn't want to admit it.

Shirley had never had a proper boyfriend. She had slept with boys of course, plenty of times, but she'd never really gone out with any of them. Said she was sick of the lot of them and maybe that was true but then again maybe it had more to do with having a father who would threaten to kill any lad who dared come within a mile of her.

Already at the age of fifteen Shirley Craigie had seen enough of men to last her a lifetime.

*

CATH DIDN'T HEAR FROM Alice that evening, but she didn't expect to, not while Saheed was still there. She watched some more TV then went to bed. The following morning she woke up feeling certain that Alice would call, before remembering that Saheed would not be leaving the island until first thing Tuesday. On the Tuesday morning Cath woke early. She sat in the window drinking tea and watching the first ferry of the day chug out of the harbour and begin its journey across the bay. Saheed was probably on it. By lunchtime he'd be back in London.

Cath showered and dressed and ate breakfast. At around half past nine she found she could stand it no longer and hurried over to Westland Road. The Yaris was not on the drive, and no one came to the door when she rang the bell. Cath went away again, telling herself that Saheed must be catching a later boat, that Alice was probably out giving him a lift to the ferry terminal. She came back after lunch and then again at five o'clock but the car was still gone. Cath did not dare to use her spare key but she did, at this point, call Alice's mobile. It went straight to voicemail. After half an hour of agonising she tried Saheed's phone as well. It rang a couple of times, then went to voicemail also.

He's screening his calls.

The thought of Saheed glancing down at his screen, seeing her number and thumbing the off key made Cath feel queasy with panic. Had he known, even while he was round at her flat on the Sunday that he was planning to take Alice away from the island the instant she could be persuaded? Had he forced her, or had she gone willingly? There was no way of knowing – of knowing anything. They had cut her out.

Love fucks you up.

Something Shirley had said once, or a line from a soap opera? Either way it was true.

CATH HELD OFF FROM using the key until the Friday. She told herself she was only doing what Alice would have wanted – keeping an eye on the place, making sure there were no appliances left running, no dripping taps, no spoiled food in the fridge. Who wants to come home to milk that has turned to yoghurt? If she had known she was going to be away, Cath reasoned, Alice would most likely have given her a key herself.

She wondered if any of her self-justifications would stand up in court. Probably not, probably the prosecution would make mincemeat of her.

Did Mrs Rahman, at any time, ask you to assume caretaking duties for her place of residence on Westland Road?

No she did not.

Did Mrs Rahman personally give you the key that granted you access to her property?

No she did not.

Was Mrs Rahman aware that you possessed such a key?

No she was not.

Did you make use of this key on previous occasions without the knowledge or consent of Mrs Rahman?

Yes. Yes I did.

They'd make her out to be a stalker, an obsessive, like in *Single White Female*. The idea was appalling and yet at the same time Cath discovered she did not care, or at least not as much as she needed to see inside the house, to make herself believe that Alice was gone.

And there was always the chance that Alice had left her a message, if not a written explanation then a clue only Cath would recognise, something that was meant for her to find. She approached the house in what she hoped was a confident manner, the stride of someone who was supposed to be there, who had been invited.

My friend's away in London for a couple of days. I'm watering the plants.

There was junk mail on the mat but nothing more: an advertising circular, the latest Betterware catalogue, the previous day's edition of the local paper. Either no post had arrived, or Alice had already arranged for it to be redirected. In the hall, an empty coffee mug on the telephone table, Alice's red trainers, tossed to one side at the foot of the stairs. To Cath, it looked like the opening scene from a cop show. She just popped out for a moment, never came back.

We're going to miss the ferry, Ally – just leave it.

I don't want to be in London, Alice had said. I want to have the baby here on the island, Alice had said. Either Saheed had bullied her into leaving, or Alice had fallen ill, or one or both of them had been lying all along. In the living room the dolls' house stood on the table with its front latched closed, and Cath found herself thinking once again of Emmy, the doll Shirley used to bring to school inside her pencil case. What had happened to her, and to the rest of the dolls? How come they had disappeared when their house was still here?

Cath went slowly upstairs, walking on tiptoe to stop the floorboards from creaking and making them creak worse. In Alice's bedroom there were similar signs of minor disorder as there had been downstairs: the duvet pulled up crookedly to cover the pillows, a pair of balled-up socks on the bedside table. The wardrobe stood open and partially emptied. Cath stared at what was left – a couple of shirts, Alice's green anorak, a pair of gold sandals. The sandals especially seemed to belong to another life.

A corner of the bedroom rug was flipped back. Cath stooped to lift it aside, imagining an envelope with her name on it or – preposterously – the outline of a trapdoor. Nothing. Nothing in the guest room either, just the same half-emptied storage boxes.

The cupboard at the end of the landing stood firmly closed.

I need to leave, right now. Cath felt overwhelmed with panic suddenly, terrified at the possibility that she might be discovered.

Fuck it, you were only looking. Shirley would be pissed off by her timidity, her willingness to be defeated almost from the outset. She was right – what kind of a detective did she think she was? This was Shirley's place, after all, or had Cath forgotten that? This was the crime scene.

She remembered what Iris had told her, about Susan asking if Iris believed that places could be haunted, not by ghosts but by memories. But what if ghosts *are* memories, memories ghosts?

Then every house would be fucking haunted, wouldn't it? Now shut up and listen.

I COME IN FROM the garden to get a drink and Mum's there, she's lying face down on the kitchen floor and all I can think is that she looks like one of those diagrams on TV, when the scene-of-crime guys draw an outline around the body. I don't have time to scream or even think about it. Mostly I'm curious — what the fuck happened? — but then I hear a noise inside the house and I just run. I run out the back, which is stupid because there's nowhere to go from there and I know it, and even as I'm dashing for the hedge I'm thinking I'm not going to make it, not in time, I'll no' get through there. I'm thinking mistake mistake mistake you stupid bitch, should've run round the front, like a rat in a trap now aren't ye but that's what they all do when the killer's after them or there wouldn't be a story. Those eejits didnae have a choice because it's in the script but you did, you did only you blew it and oh fuck like my chest is killing me and I don't know if that's the first bullet or if I've just got a stitch. And it's easy you know, once it happens. The last thing I feel is the earth under my nails. Here's the clincher though and ye's gonnae kill me but I never even got to see his face.

CATH IS CRYING, WEEPING like a banshee there on the landing. It isn't the last time she'll be inside the Craigie house, not quite, but suddenly she knows with utter certainty that she will never see Alice again and the knowledge of their parting burns like a wound.

18.

ALICE FINALLY CALLED HER the following Wednesday. Cath had sent several emails, a one-liner simply asking if she was OK, another apologising for not having said anything about Saheed's visit to Argyle Terrace and one last, much longer letter in which she told Alice she was sorry if she'd done anything to upset her and that whatever happened next she was glad they had met. Cath cried a lot while writing that email. Afterwards she lay awake half the night wishing she hadn't sent it, convinced she'd made things worse than they already were.

How can someone just disappear? Cath thought on repeat. It's not right.

Alice did not reply to any of the messages. Cath felt convinced Saheed must be intercepting her emails. She replayed their last meeting endlessly inside her head, Cath asking when Saheed was arriving and then telling Alice what she'd discovered about Angus Livingstone. They had joked around, made faces. Alice had kissed her. It felt like years ago that these things had happened, useless to keep going over it. For whatever reason, Alice was gone. Thinking about her was like feeling tremendously hungry and having nothing to eat. Better not to think, to imagine yourself into a world where being hungry – the hollow gut, the sense of weightlessness, the complete dissociation from the passage of time – was the natural order of being.

The one high point in all those days: seeing an email from Adam in her inbox and deleting it unopened, sight unseen.

HEARING ALICE'S VOICE ON the phone was like being given a glimpse of the world before. Like the lights coming back on after a power cut. When exactly had things got so shit?

'I shouldn't be calling,' Alice said. 'Not really. Saheed's at work though, so.' She spoke in a rush, as if she felt guilty, as if she was afraid someone might be listening in. Afraid Saheed might return unexpectedly and catch her out. It was eleven o'clock in the morning. 'I'm sorry if you've been worried.'

'Don't apologise,' Cath said. She felt sick with relief. She had to get this right, she thought. Get this right or you've lost her for good.

You've lost her already, can't you feel it? This is goodbye. You're lucky to get that, to know she's still out there. There are plenty of times when people just – go.

A lump formed in her throat, and Cath wondered what it was exactly that produced that sensation, what physically happened. A constriction of the muscles, she supposed. Something involuntary, anyway. A thing we do without knowing how it is done.

'Are you all right?' Cath said. 'Did you get my emails?'

'I got them. I'm fine.'

'Are you back in London?'

'I'm at home, yeah,' Alice said, then silence, austere and grey as the passage of many years. 'I'm not coming back, Cath,' she said, finally. 'It's not anything you've done, honestly. It's just that everything is different now, because of the baby. I have to put the baby first, you do get that, don't you? I need to be in London. For the foreseeable future, anyway.'

'Was this Saheed's idea, or yours?' Alice was silent. Cath could hear her breathing, in and out. 'What about the house?' she added, quickly. What else was left?

'I don't know at the moment. Saheed wants me to sell it, but we'll see. I don't feel like deciding that yet.'

'Alice—'

'Don't say anything. Let's leave it like this, can we? Like it's all still happening. Everything was real.'

The line went dead. As if the wire had been cut, Cath thought, which was stupid, they were both on mobiles. Landlines were as good as extinct now, like the telegraph. Like the gramophone. Like the ZX Spectrum. Cath went to call back, then didn't. Calling back would cancel out everything. It would be awful.

She stood holding the phone. She felt a tightness in her chest, a shortness of breath. When her mobile started ringing again her hand jumped so violently she almost dropped the handset. Her immediate, euphoric assumption was that it was Alice – Alice calling back, saying sorry about before, she didn't know what she'd been thinking, of course she would return to the island, she was packing now. Saying she had to hear Cath's voice, one last time. But of course it was not Alice. The caller was Norah.

Cath stared blankly at the display then picked up the call.

'Hey,' she said.

'Hey,' Norah said. 'Are you OK? You sound a bit freaked.'

'The phone made me jump, that's all. I was on the computer.'

'I won't disturb you for long, but I wanted to tell you. You know you were asking me about Angus Livingstone? I found out he's dead. I heard it from this girl I know in English,' she continued. Cath felt dazed. Dr Livingstone I presume, she thought stupidly. The conversation seemed to be happening out of sequence somehow, like an outtake, a deleted scene. 'Her girlfriend's doing History and Archaeology and she told me Angus Livingstone was killed in a climbing accident just after Christmas. The whole department's been in a state about it. Some of his colleagues thought it might have been suicide, you know, because of what happened to his wife. He was a nice guy, apparently. People liked him.'

'Oh my God,' Cath said. A stock phrase, a placeholder, a synonym for shock, though she realised she did not feel shocked by what Norah was telling her, not even remotely. Cath's first thought was that Angus Livingstone falling from a mountain felt strangely appropriate. Up the airy mountain, down the rushy glen, we dare not go a-hunting for fear of little men.

She felt the laughter build up inside her, then quickly repressed it. Livingstone had succeeded though, he'd escaped. Now no one would ever realise the harm he'd caused. Angus Livingstone was a nice guy, people had liked him. He had been married to an English lecturer named Mary, and his wife had been tragically killed. At another time, in another place, he'd loved a woman named Susan who had a no-good husband called Johnny who everyone despised.

When Johnny went crazy and killed his family everyone seemed to think they'd seen it coming.

The real Angus Livingstone was a phantom, the man who wasn't there. And now he was gone, too.

YOU STILL DON'T know it all though, you still need proof.

How do you prove a negative?

Look where no one else has. Then you'll see.

Fairies black, grey, green and white, you moonshine revellers, and shades of night

W HERE DID YOU GET your tunes, son? Johnny's father slurred in his cups. You can be certain it's no' from oor side of the family.

WHEN JOHNNY FIRST HEARD Shirl singing, her voice stole the wind from him. He remembered what Granny Lin had said to him when he was eight, that his own voice was surely a miracle, a proof of their regard.

No such thing as something for nothing, lad. They'll be returning to claim their debt one o' these fair days.

What will they want, Granny?

He strained to keep the fear out of his question. Debt was a word Johnny knew and so was payback.

Granny Lin laughed and ruffled his hair. Nothing, most like, she said, like her thoughts had already moved on, like she'd been jesting with him. There are times when they'll grant a wish just for the fun of it, to keep the rest of us guessing and marvelling. It's your gift to keep.

GRANNY LIN HAD BEEN wrong though or else hid the truth to spare him. This school play or concert Shirl was in and Susan insisting he had to be there, though she knew fine well how it preyed on his mind, those jumped-up teachers and the way they mocked him, his daughter's work on those coloured placards lining the corridors. What could it mean to him except she'd written it, his fingers out-stretched for a trembling second to touch Shirl's marks. A skill he'd never learned nor cared to master, those rounded letters with their pigs' tails and uprights, inscrutable as code.

But she's singing a solo, Susan said. You can't not go. And had his heart flinched, even then, at the thought of her singing? He did not believe so. Rather he was stupefied with rage at the thought of the school. Even as Shirl came out on the stage, her mouse-nest hair perked up with glitter like a fairies' crown, her skinny-malinky frame swamped in red velvet, there was not one part of him that suspected the truth of it, the worst of all possible paybacks, that the tunes the good neighbours had spiked his tongue with had passed from him to her.

BALOO MY BOY LIE *still and sleep, it grieves my heart to hear thee weep*. Hardly a song for a child to ken, and with the great hall still as a stanchion, all the puppets lost in thrall to thrill at the sound of her. *O'er thee I keep my lonely watch, intent thy slightest breath to catch,* and watched he had, too, when she was a chick at least. Afraid, he supposed now, that they'd decide to take her back, though he'd never admitted to such a fear until this moment. He'd not dared believe she was his and so it had proved. The sound she made, though – could the others in the hall not hear how unnatural it was, her a twelve-year-old lassie with no thoughts in her head save what idiocy she meant to watch on TV the second his back were turned? That she should be folding her hands and arching her neck for all the world as if she got the gist of what she were singing about, when the song in her mouth told the tale of a cursed child and a whore of a woman, a dead ghost soldier who'd given his life yet had been forgot most like, the instant he took hisself out of her bed and marched away.

I dreamed a dream but yesternight, thy father slain in foreign fight. Johnny felt his own hands tighten to fists. An old song, Granny Lin had taught it him, telling of the pity of war and the babes left father-less in its wake. And Johnny had asked her what if the soldier's away for a year and a day, fighting in Queen Mab's army, not dead but in the realm? What if his kin forget him as they forgot Osian the poet?

Granny Lin had smiled and looked away. Johnny had never known his granddad, he realised. Never seen him once, not even in a photo.

AFTER THE CONCERT THE music teacher, Miss Anderson, had come up to speak to them.

I've been hoping to catch you, Mr Craigie. We've been thinking that Shirley could really benefit from extra music lessons. There's a teacher from Glasgow comes down to the school in Gourock once a week. One of our classroom assistants has volunteered to go with Shirley on the ferry. The school would like to sponsor her, pay her fees.

No, he'd said at once, the word coarse and bold and shocking in the air of that place, like they'd never once heard of a man who knew how to speak his mind. There's no sense in it, giving a wee lassie like ours ideas above her station. Who's this singing teacher anyway, some kind of pervert?

Susan's face grey and stodgy as day-old porridge. Like she'd had her brain removed, what there was of it, and all at once Johnny was wondering if she'd been conniving with these teachers beforehand, if that was why she'd insisted on him coming here, to make him look like a fool in front of the lot o' them.

As if they didn't see the wrongness in it, what they were doing with her. The wrongness in her.

We're going, he said. Susan not speaking a word the whole way home and Shirl with that look on her, that blank-faced look she always got when she was working against him. Johnny staring at the back of her head, the stupid red dress Susan had wasted his money on and the cobweb hair and thinking there was no way that aching, powerful sound couldae come oot o' her – her, skinny and pathetic enough to be snapped like a twig if he'd a mind to. That song were like a message from another world. A missive, Granny Lin wouldae called it, and Shirley were but its conduit, a skinny-malinky length o' human pipework.

What right did she ever have to sound like that? Back at home he'd had to lock her into her room, just to think on things, to remove her from his sight for half an hour.

*

236

HEARTSICK, JOHNNY WAS, AND filled with rage.

Fucking Susie so hard in the darkness he were afraid something might have come adrift in the back of his head.

The next morning were a Sunday. Black bruises, like iron manacles on her upper arms. Susie made breakfast for the three of them the same as always, then Johnny went out to the car port to cut some wood. Sweet oak, sweet as roses, golden as corn. Johnny sawing to the rhythm, the rhythm of a song he had believed forgotten. Thinking on his Mab, how he'd done her in the cornfield and then again beneath the hedgerow, bramble cuffs about his wrists, black earth beneath his nails, hot seed in the dirt. The way things used to be, used to be and fuck, who had he become and where was he going?

Since Finlay Matheson drowned, Johnny's mind had become untethered, like a rotting barge. His little family, so timid and fragile he had nightmares of crushing them to dust beneath his claggy workboots. Finlay Matheson, Granny Lin, that bossy cow Denise – all those who had truly known him, dead and gone.

THE ISLE WAS FULL of noises. More and more Johnny was afraid he would be swallowed by them. Finn had been his anchor, his compass, more even than Susan for what could Susan know of where he had come from and all he had seen? He remembered what Finn said when Johnny first told him he and Susie were to be married. She's just a person, Johnny, she cannae fix everything an' specially not you. He'd felt like punching Finn right there but managed not to. Wasn't Finn's fault he didn't have a clue about him and Susie.

How could Finn have a clue, him shagging a different bird every week and each and every one of them rough as dogs.

More and more though he'd come to realise that Finn had been right, Susan McClellan were just a person, just a straight wee lassie, and what if he'd traded one for the other, Susie for Finn? He knew he'd not made such a bargain willingly, wouldnae allow such a thought inside his head even, but it wouldnae be the first time the good neighbours had gotten the best of him. Finlay's absence feeding his anger, rising like steam from the cleft in his mind, that blue-black abyss. Where Susie was, the anger was too. Because he knew with a blackness of heart that Susie like Finlay's mother Julie would have loved Denise. Because his anger at himself were bigger'n both o' them. Because it drove him almost to madness that she always forgave him. Because he did not know in his heart of hearts if he would trade her back again.

AND WORK, THE SAVING grace of him. Because he was good at what he did and liked it, preferred to work when other men preferred to be down the pub or on the frigging golf course. Johnny found peace with his hands on the wood as he always had done, one week's end to the next and those hands never idle. Except there were rules and men and alliances he could not fathom. Step here and you tread on toes, step there and you end up brawling, say nothing and the buggers are laughing behind your back.

Brian McKeith, giving Susan the eye across the supermarket car park. Johnny seeing red, grabbing the rat by his collar and knocking him down in the frigging dirt where the rat belonged. Next thing he's lost the Smale contract and who knows what else besides. No one crosses Brian because his uncle's a Mason. No one crosses Pete or Mack or Ted-the-Ned because they're mates wi' Brian. So much simpler in your home place, where you know fine well who's off limits unless youse asking for it. Who you can thump and dump and get away with, who holds the cards.

Saying sorry dinnae come easy to Johnny but he'll suck the cunt's dick if he has to, buy the whole sorry lot o' them a round in the Golfers if that's what it takes. Brian's uncle claps him on the back and says they're fine, why not play a round with him and Brian one o' these fine days, we're all friends now and men will be men, after all, boys will be boys. Like he gave a shit. Pete did offer him a discount on the oak planks though, which he didnae have to, the oak Johnny needed to make the chairs for that Laura McKinty down by Loch Fad. It had been Pete who'd scored him the job in fact. Woman wants something fancy, he'd said. Think you're up to it?

Brian McKeith had sniggered and them two arselickers with him but even so when Johnny called the number Pete gave him there was a job right enough, set of eight dining chairs, and could he call at the house as soon as possible to take a look at the drawings?

THE HOUSE, AT THE end of a long dirt road, mile or so from the loch. When Laura McKinty came to answer the door her feet were bare, long and bony and grubby along the margins. From where she'd been walking outside, Johnny supposed, in the dirt and leaves. Nor did she paint her toenails the way some women did. Her hair was long and straight and deathly fair, swaying like a satin curtain as she moved about. Not ugly and not pretty, except for the hair. Stern, Johnny thought. Pale eyes narrowed to slits, like a barn owl, watching. Older than Johnny maybe though not by much.

You're the carpenter? she said, and the hairs on Johnny's arms all stood on end. Sounded English and later she told him yes she were born in England though she didnae look it, she looked like that German woman Jimbo Matheson had married, that witch Ulla. Laura McKinty showed him drawings she'd made herself, sketches in pencil of the chairs the way she saw them. Not like a pro's but they were fine for him to work with and when she asked if he could do ornamental work – she meant carving – Johnny said yes to that too. Carving was what you might call his special skill, though there weren't much call for it on the island, never had been. Laura McKinty laughed in a way that made him feel uncomfortable though he could not have said why, then opened up a book she had ready, an album filled with photographs of different kinds of furniture.

Johnny's pulse started racing immediately but it was all right, she didn't want him to read, just to look at the pictures. Art Nouveau, she said, whatever that was, wood worn smooth as wax from use and with carving so true to life it made him shiver. Flowers and acorns and bees and here nestled in the chair's curved arm rest a tiny harvest mouse. Something like this? said Laura McKinty, and Johnny nodded, mind racing from the thrill of what he might make, but when he'd brought a sample to show her the following week it was another woman, not Laura McKinty, who opened the door to him. A weasely, weather-beaten crone with thin grey plaits hanging down over her shoulders and cracked leather boots covering her feet. Same pale eyes though, same voice too if you cared to think about it, which Johnny did not. When he asked for Laura McKinty the crone said not to worry, she would pass on his message, tell Laura what needed telling, he could be sure of it.

He offered her the sample, a foot-length of oak, carved with a design of blackberries and waxed to a shine. The woman rubbed the glowing wood between her hands and there was something in the way she did it that made Johnny hard. A tremor passed through him. His teeth snapped shut with a clunk, almost catching his tongue. The woman laughed and Johnny found himself wanting to run, to course like a hare down the mile-long driveway and never return.

Will it do? he said, instead. He drew himself up, forced himself to look at her, to admit the truth he'd known from the moment he arrived – that the crone was Laura McKinty in another guise. Still he stared, and the crone stared back, understanding passing between them like a sinew of lightning.

He followed her inside, through the living room he'd already seen and into a smaller room leading off from it, doors open to the lawns and gardens at the back of the house. In all the days and years that followed Johnny would not be able to tell himself who he had joined with, who he had fucked on the flowered chaise longue there – Laura McKinty, or the grey-haired crone, which one of them had sat herself on the gold-fringed cushions and opened her thighs. Just that 'twere like all those times before, out on the hillside. Mab, so close to mad, shouting both names in the teeth of a gale and you'd no' hear the difference. Had she taken off her boots? He strained to remember, but could not. Boots or bare feet? his mind kept roaring. As if it mattered.

He woke slumped at the kitchen table, a mug of tea at his elbow, almost cold. This will be perfect, she was saying. She rubbed the stick of wood between her hands. The isle is full of noises, Johnny thought. Words he'd heard from Granny Lin a lifetime ago. He wondered if he might be losing his mind, the way Denise had when she realised she was pregnant.

His thoughts would not lie quiet. It was not just the sounds in the woods that disturbed him but other things, too. Susan's notebook for instance, the one she kept hidden, its pages dense with her script that might as well have been a foreign language for all the sense it made. He had enrolled in the classes as Susie had wanted, had urged him for years. Finally he'd done it, bitten the bullet as Finn might have said and Johnny could not deny the swooning relief he felt, the triumph to be had in the simplest act of deciphering. How the world and Pete McKeith would shit their pants laughing if they knew the excitement that leapt in his heart with each new word. Yet still he could not read Susan's maddening sentences, opaque as the scratching of insects, just scrawls on the page.

And maybe he was still stupid after all if she could escape him this way, like a spider weaving her trapdoor, pulling shut the hatch. What was she thinking and what was she writing? What had changed?

Johnny thought of challenging her over the notebook, demanding to know what was in it, yet this also would yield her the advantage of knowing that he had found it. Worse, she would know the depths of his continuing shame, might discuss it with Shirl even, when he was out. The two of them, heads together, thick as thieves. The lass barely into double figures but see how canny she was, so heedless of his authority, so like Denise. Susie in his presence seemed made of fear, made to torment him as it tormented him simply to wonder how she had become like this, so like a whipped dog that if he marched in and told her now the things he had done with Laura McKinty she would just stare at him wide-eyed, like the deer he'd knocked down near Ettrick Bay that time, then turn back towards the sink, scrawny shoulders hunched together like the wings of a bird. So fucking whipped it made him want to hit her, made his fists ache.

When Dorothy McAslan found out what her Willie had got up to that night in Glasgow she'd come down the Golfers and dragged him out by the hair, cheeks on fire with rage and the whole bar cheering.

Best night ever, Willie had told them two evenings later. Best fucking night of my life. Clearly I need to be fucking more hair-dressers.

How they'd bellowed with laughter then, like stags in rut. Johnny thought of Susan, turning back towards the sink, her skinny frame and doe's eyes. The torment of it, like a hole shot through his heart, knowing that something had changed and not knowing what.

WORKING ON THE DOLLS' house took his mind away from everything, even Finn's drowning. He built a room inside the house, a room for Denise. Patchwork counterpane on the bed, a trunk for all her treasures, all her secret letters from Iain the cunt. Johnny wondered if Iain Fletcher was still alive, and if he were alive what he were doing now. He'd like to hunt him down and kill him, for real this time, no matter if he'd banged his sister up or no. Johnny's mouth filled up with saliva at the thought of it, of landing that first blow, the same way it would fill up with saliva at the scent of roasting chicken, or the heady golden beer smell that came wafting out of the Golfers at the close of day.

AND THEN HE WERE damned if the good neighbours weren't listening in on him, granting him his wish the way they did most times – giving you what you asked for only never in such a way as you might have wished for out loud. He'd be damned for saying so perhaps but the guy was haunting him, frigging Iain Fletcher whose life wouldae been over if Johnny'd had his say on it and yet here he was again, or at least his shade, the skinny shadow of him, or so he'd hae sworn first time he clapped eyes on the fellow although he were bound to admit that so far as actual likeness went, the actual look of him, there was little to bind the two. Iain Fletcher were a skinny runt – still was, most like – all pipecleaner arms and knock knees and those *ethereal* flaxen curls of that poofter fair hair.

This other – the university man – was taller and with dark hair and though he were skinny there was some muscle behind it. Not the kind of muscle and bulk you'd get from grafting – him with his fucking onyx fountain pen, his fucking leather satchel and waterproof notebook – but from running track maybe, or lifting the odd rack of weights if he could fucking be arsed.

Poofter. Nae, it wasnae his looks that made him the ghost of Iain Fletcher, it were the feel of him, the smell that came off him: booklearning stirred in wi' contempt, that snarky way of spinning his words which posh folk called irony but that were really just sarcasm dressed up in silk brocade, and didnae Granny Lin always say that sarcasm was the lowest form of wit and the highest form of vulgarity? Don't you be mocking folk, Johnny lad, it disnae become ye. And it's true that all his life he's hated talk with a twist in it, he a plain-speaking man himself and like his father before him. Better silence than the spoutings of a fool was what Kenny Craigie used to say, and Johnny never had cause to find fault with such a saying, if anything the opposite, only that didnae mean he couldnae recognise sarcasm when he heard it, its jabbing snake's tongue, the whisperings of the devil in impressionable ears, the rumours put about by fools in the butcher's shop the moment he pulled the door to on his way out, the jingling bell to cover their tittle-tattle, pring pring pring.

Susie, helping to set up refreshments for the talk in the museum.

Susie, asking Johnny if he'll no' go with her to hear the lecturer from the University o' fecking Glasgow ramble on about the Vikings.

Some fellow spinning his tongue for two hours and them turning their noses up soon as Johnny appears, the rest o' them, like there's a dog in the room? There's nothing there for me and you knows so, so why's youse asking?

That look of pain, then the look of relief. Quickly hidden because she is quick, his Susie, but he sees it all the same, just as he hears the voices whispering from the bushes and still he keeps his peace.

OISIN. OISIN THE POET and Niamh his fairy bride. The university man, the man of words and his Susie so fond of writing in that notebook of hers it's like she's caught a disease off him. And she's different. Different how? he can hear Finn asking. You sure it's not you who's different, Johnny? Different on account o' imagining

245

what's not there is there, the way you've had a fancy to dream up visions of treachery the whole of your life?

Never, or not this time. Susie with that calm on her – not the mouselike quiet of always and everyday but a peace that fills her up and makes her great with it, radiant, is what Granny Lin would say and although that's not a word Johnny would use as a rule he hears it shining and pringing inside his head like the ring o' the feckin' butcher's bell, like the roar of the sun.

He's not seen them together, not even once – as if she would dare! – still there's a picture inside his head that won't ever leave.

Fletcher and Denise, their bodies entwined on the hillside and drowsy with heather, not fucking or not in his sight anyways and by his queen he'd done all in his power to keep hisself hidden while he searched them out. But with their fingers touching, just so, tip to tip, as if they'd be forever reaching one for the other, even in sleep.

Even in death, or so the whisper comes to him and he asks hisself which would be the more unbearable: to know that Susie had lingered that way with the university man – to know for certain – or to carry on until the day he passed and never knowing for sure.

For his Susie to be safely dead or freely living.

For the booklearned fellow with the black hair and hooded eyes – Lucifer! – to take his Susan from him or for Johnny to take his Susan from this life before he'd let that happen.

Their hours in the realm one blue-mauve swathe of heather summer with no return to Earth.

Susie, Denise, Denise, Susie. 'Twas the old witch talking of killing, that Laura McKinty. There'll be no killing, son – Jimbo's words, Jimbo Matheson who saved Johnny's soul the one time and here he was again.

Susie was Sonny's mother, which made her queen of this world and the next across every account.

Devil take the hindmost, he was done with thinking.

As the days grow longer and hotter here's Johnny nailed to the post of his own lack of knowing and his soul on fire.

My lady, let me be.

My lady, let me rest, lest I expire.

'T HRIFTS FARM?'
　　'Mr Matheson?'
'That's me.'

'My name's Cath Naylor. I was a friend of Shirley Craigie's. I hope you can help me.'

Jim Matheson sounded different from his wife – open, relaxed, friendly. He said he'd be happy to talk to Cath about his brother Finlay only it would probably be better if she didn't come to the farm. 'Ulla won't like it,' he said. 'The past upsets her. The Clovenfords Hotel is good though,' he added. 'Used to be called the Whytbank. Walter Scott liked to stay there, you know. Pub's our main claim to fame.'

TO EDINBURGH BY TRAIN, then the X62 bus to Clovenfords. Dramatic glimpses of the Border hills from the A72, a left turn then a roundabout and there it was: a small and ancient farming community and not much expanded, though you could see where the road into the village had been widened to allow for heavier vehicles.

The Clovenfords Hotel advertised itself as an ancient coaching inn on the main route from Melrose to Edinburgh. Cath had arranged to meet James Matheson – Jimmy – in the restaurant at four o'clock. She checked into her room and put her phone on to charge then went back down to the bar, an attractive, wood-panelled room that looked newly refurbished. Cath tried to imagine what the place might have looked like in John Craigie's day: the hiss and pop of the fire, the smell of wet anoraks and beer, carpet worn to a sliver and chipped, dull paintwork. A billiard table, a darts board. And cigarette smoke of course, the air would have been thick with it. Cath had brought her camera – the pocket Nikon – though she could see now there wasn't much point in photographing anything, not here anyway. The Clovenfords was a gastropub now, with a whisky menu on deckle-edged cardboard and a star-rated chef. Johnny Craigie wouldn't be seen dead here. The timeline was closed.

She took a couple of shots out of habit then began studying a leaflet on Walter Scott. She looked up to see James Matheson coming towards her. Cath was always nervous of meeting up with people in a crowded place in case she didn't see them or didn't recognise them. Usually she got around this by arriving early and finding a seat as she had done this afternoon, busying herself with something to read then listening and waiting until they found her. As it turned out she recognised James Matheson immediately. Even from a distance, his likeness to his younger brother was clear for her to see. The same square shoulders and fair complexion, the same open face.

'You're Cathy.' He put out his hand. 'I'm Jim.'

'Cath.' The skin of his palm was dry and heavily callused. 'It's good to meet you. Can I buy you a drink?'

'I'll get them. What with you dragging out all this way and all. I'm sorry we couldn't put you up at the farm. It's Ulla, you see, I don't like to worry her. I hope you're comfortable here?'

'Very, thank you.' Cath said she'd have a beer, whatever was local. When Matheson returned with the drinks, she asked him why his wife didn't like him to talk about his brother. She wondered if she should mention her previous phone call to the farm, when Ulla had asked her not to call again, but decided not to.

'Och, it's not Finn so much as the past in general. When Ulla first came to live here, things were hard. People were like to make fun of you just for having a German accent. I used to tell her folk meant nothing by it but it still made her nervous. Ulla couldn't abide the Craigies – Johnny and Kenny, I mean. She got on with Ruth all right but she wouldn't go near their place, not after Denise died. She's still convinced it was all Kenny's fault. It wasn't, of course, but you see how things are.'

'Denise was Johnny's sister?'

'Aye. Two years younger than him, she was, though the way Johnny ran wild sometimes you'd have reckoned it was the other way around.'

You're going too fast, Cath thought, and how extraordinary it was, that this man Jim Matheson had known Johnny Craigie when he was a child, when he was a teenager, moody and disconsolate. Kicking a stone against the side of the bus shelter and swearing under his breath at every passer-by.

'What was he like?' she said. 'Johnny?'

'Well, Ma was never particularly keen on Finn knocking around with Johnny as much as he did but Dad knew Ken from way back, said it was just his manner. There's no point telling kids who they can and can't be mates with, any road – only makes them fall in with the other all the more. Romeo and Juliet, Ma used to call them, Johnny and Finn. They were inseparable.' Matheson chuckled, gulped at his beer. 'Johnny Craigie was sharp as a needle but he hated school. Finn swore blind I should never tell anyone, but Johnny couldn't read. Well, he could make out the letters all right but if you asked him a question he couldn't answer he'd sweat like a pig. He needed help, that boy, but things were different back then. You answered yes sir no sir or you got the belt. Most times, Johnny got the belt. He couldn't get shot of the place fast enough. But the talent he had as a joiner was remarkable. Kenny was always good with his hands but Johnny was something special. It's a sad business. Things weren't easy for him.'

'What made Johnny move away then, do you know?'

Matheson sighed. 'Sometimes I think Ulla's right. All this harping on the past – what good does it do? Kenny's mother Helen was the one with the stories, Johnny's grandmother. Ken used to say it was his ma who got Johnny the way he was, all those silly fairy tales she put in his head, but Johnny loved her. He loved his sister too. He took it hard when she died. You're sure you're interested in this?'

'Yes, very.'

'Well, Denise was a clever lass. Always with her nose in a book. She was sweet on the minister's son, Iain Fletcher, and he was sweet on her. Folk say they were planning to marry, soon as they left school. Before that could happen though, Denise fell pregnant. Swore the baby wasn't Iain's but wouldn't say who the father was. Denise hanged herself in the barn and it was Johnny who found her. Johnny beat up Iain Fletcher, broke his skull. Lad landed up in hospital for more than a month. Young Iain's a minister himself now, would you believe, three bairns of his own. There were people around, afterwards,' said Matheson, 'who swore the baby was Ken's, said that was why Denise killed herself. I've never believed that myself, not for a second. Kenny was a hard man right enough but he was never like that. He didn't care about women, not really. He'd have slit his own throat rather than lay a finger on his daughter and I mean that literally.'

'Was Johnny's father a violent man?'

'I don't know about that. I dare say he gave Johnny a thick ear now and then but that's fathers and sons for you.'

'Did your father hit you?'

'Dad wouldn't hit a nail too hard in case he bent it. I saw him crying once, after he sent a batch of steers off to the abattoir. Wiped his eyes on his sleeve soon enough but I saw and he knew I saw and we were always all right. Dad adored my brother Finn. When we told him about the accident, it was like a light had gone out. Ten years older in a single moment, just like that.'

JIM MATHESON EXCUSED HIMSELF soon after six. 'Time I was going,' he said. 'I don't want Ulla fretting. There'll be no end to it.'

Cath ordered a meal at the bar – locally caught salmon with wild rice and ratatouille. The food was excellent and she was hungry. She took out her notebook and put it away again. She'd had enough of text. She thought it was interesting, that Jim Matheson had been adamant Kenny Craigie was not the father of Denise's baby. Just as Shirley would have sworn blind Johnny couldn't be the killer because he'd never shoot Sonny. The red lines people drew often said more about them than about where the lines happened to fall. She wished she'd thought to ask Jim if he had any photos – photos of Finn and Johnny, Ken and Denise. Denise had been Shirley's second name, Cath remembered. She wondered if Susan had known what that meant even, how much Johnny had told her about his life before he knew her.

You know what Dad was like when it came to words. You can bet your cotton socks he never said a thing.

She let the noise of the pub wash over her, the light dimming beyond the windows as the sun went down. She longed to text Alice, but didn't. She texted Steve instead, a photo of the Clovenfords whisky menu, **just in case I go missing**. Steve texted her back immediately with two emojis, a magnifying glass and a handgun. Cath smiled into her phone, felt better at once. Still, none of this made sense. If you set aside the Richard Dadd stuff, what was left? Johnny Craigie had been a troubled teen with a sister who killed herself, Kenny Craigie yet another bully who lashed out with his fists. Did these facts add up to anything, or were they just more facts?

Cath ordered herself a whisky. Thank God for Glenfiddich. In her mind's eye she saw the long, ropy figure of Shirley, rushing out the kitchen door of Westland Road and towards the back hedge. Her hair was bunched together with sweat, a halo of curls, bright white against the sun. Panting like a dog because it was too hot to run really, who could be arsed to run in weather like this? *You fucking psycho, don't you frigging touch me.* Full tilt into the brambles. A shot rang out.

Cath woke several times during the night, her mouth dry from too much alcohol, mind racing with contradictions and unanswered questions. If John Craigie was not the killer then why had she come all this way in search of him? Cath lay awake in the half light, remembering how Shirley's father had seemed to her back then, her tense dislike of him. The way he cast a shadow over a room simply by being there, his dumb adherence to routine, the limited and boring way he seemed to see the world. None of these things made him a killer though, or not necessarily, that was the bummer, so why was she here?

He's the red herring, isn't he? Every detective story has to have a red herring – that's the rule. Cannae have people knowing who the killer is in Chapter One.

Shirley, grinning up at her and laughing. Her dirty-Martini laugh, Cath used to call it. *Dirty Martini and her cunning sidekick, Cinzano Bianco.*

THE CRAIGIES' OLD HOUSE was gone. Kenny Craigie died of a heart attack two decades ago, not long before the murders, Jim had told her. Ruthie Craigie sold up and moved away – Jim didn't know where she was now, if she was even alive still. The Craigies' cottage was purchased by someone in Edinburgh who never lived in it. The place had been in a right state, and then the pigeons got in. Eventually the land was bought up by a developer, the cottage demolished.

'They put these flats in,' Matheson said. 'Some folk objected but it's better than seeing a building go to ruin. Ken's mother's place is still there, though, just a mite out of town on the Bowland Road. A woman and a half, was Helen, had a doctorate from the university. Came marching into the village one day with young Kenny in tow, so my dad said. She used to have Connie Danby fetch Kenny from school and take him up to hers to play with her Michael until she got home from work. Ken was apprenticed to Dickie Stevenson when he was fifteen and never looked back. Johnny, though, right from when he could walk he was always up at his gran's. It was Helen who taught Johnny his love of the hills, I reckon. Certainly didn't come from his father. Kenny was either at work or down the Whytbank.'

OPEN FIELDS BEHIND, ROUND-SHOULDERED hills beyond. The house was set back from the road and looked well cared for. Russet paintwork and granite walls, a ceramic plaque with the name 'Grey Cottage' screwed into the gatepost. No one about, no car on the drive. Whoever lived there must commute into Edinburgh or one of the Border towns. Cath photographed the house straight on, flattening the perspective as she had done with Mary Chant's house in Maryhill, though Helen Craigie's house was not a murder house, or a fairy palace, somehow you could tell. Just a place where people had lived, and continued to do so.

Had Helen Craigie believed in the old ways, like Alice's grandmother? Or had she simply wanted to give Johnny something wonderful, to present him with a vision of the world that was different from the harsh reality he saw at home? His mother's fear, his father's fists. His sister, stolen by redcaps, or so it seemed to him.

Come unto these yellow sands
And then take hands.

On the bus journey back to Edinburgh Cath read a play she'd downloaded, the text of a radio drama by Angela Carter about the life and death and obsessions of Richard Dadd. She'd found out about it by chance – a reference from a reference – and knew little about Angela Carter as a writer. Carter's theory seemed to be that Richard Dadd's art could be read as a metaphor for Victorian hypocrisy. Before his breakdown, Dadd's paintings of fairyland were idealised fantasies of paradise, like those of his colleagues. The works he painted after murdering his father revealed a twisted, feverish other-land, frozen in time and populated by demons.

Like the woods after dark? Like Susan's marriage, the fake Susan and the real Susan? Like my whole fucking life?

The play was odd, not a drama at all so much as a mosaic, a put-together sequence of scenes featuring characters from Richard Dadd's life and from his paintings. The language Carter used, though. Not like text at all but like liquid reason. Colours and splashes of words, fused together to form a picture like the myriad marks and streaks and impressions made upon the canvas by Richard Dadd.

Language as painting. Could you even have that, was it possible? Reading Angela Carter, Cath felt that it was. Adam would tell her she had it wrong, most likely, that there was much more to it, but Cath didn't care.

The words sucked her in, bright jewels. She was there with Dadd, looking and listening. Like when she put on that tone poem by Bax, she heard the music of the fae.

Titania, Oberon, Sir Thomas Phillips, a stall holder in an Egyptian bazaar, the fairy feller himself. Parading in front of the microphone as if they were giving evidence at a Fatal Accident Inquiry. Their voices ran into each other, like voices in a dream or in a crowd, sharply in focus one minute then receding, as if, as if. This should have been confusing but it wasn't. This is how stories should be told because this is how they are, Cath thought. Like scraps of memories scribbled down on to paper before they disappear.

Or like photographs, maybe. A bunch of old snapshots found in a drawer. Like on your murder wall.

William Frith, a friend of Dadd's who had trained with him at the Royal Academy, insisted that the man who returned from Cairo was not the same man who had left London the year before. Dadd wrote to Frith frequently while he was travelling and in one of his letters he described an incident he witnessed in the crowded side streets of Damascus. A camel had collapsed beneath its load and broken its leg. When beating and cursing failed to get it up again, furious traders began hacking off its limbs to allow traffic to pass. When the animal still refused to die they cut its throat.

Cath felt stiff with horror. She tried to tell herself the incident might not be real, that Carter might have invented it, or lifted it from another source to inject more drama. Yet the further she read the more she felt convinced that the words were Dadd's own. Their knowledge of his condition seemed so acute, the visions they conveyed as suffused with dissolution and danger as the paintings he made from them.

Intolerable marvels, Dadd called these scenes. The vast pitiless antique land welcomed me as if I was its son.

No wonder he went crazy, seeing those things.

Like Johnny seeing his sister strung up in the barn?

Cath arrived back on the island just before eight. She felt exhausted, almost too tired to eat. She placed two pita bread under the grill, switched on the TV. She barely registered what was on, though the sound of human voices was reassuring.

There was a watercolour by Dadd, called *Dead Camel*, she remembered later, she had read about it, though when she checked online she discovered the painting was lost, that it had gone missing after being lent by its owner, a lawyer from Preston, to an exhibition in Manchester.

The painting that had been lent with it, *Halt in the Desert*, had also gone missing, though unlike *Dead Camel* it had turned up again a century later, famously rediscovered by Peter Nahum on the BBC *Antiques Roadshow* in the Devon town of Barnstaple.

The year had been 1986, the year Shirley was born. One hundred years exactly after Richard Dadd's death.

20.

'Have you managed to find out anything more, dear?' Iris said.

'Some,' said Cath. 'The story keeps changing, though. I'm not sure what to think.'

Because all the people who had been part of it were dead. They had taken their knowledge with them. There was no one left alive who knew the whole truth. Cath had spent a lot of the morning looking up the most recent details of the Mary Chant murder. The case against Ronnie Mackintosh had collapsed for lack of evidence – no forensics to place him at the scene, no blood on his clothing or in his van, no weapon. Ronnie was back managing the betting shop. Cath wondered if he was missing Mary, or if he felt secretly relieved. If the relationship had been a mistake, now at least he was free.

A short paragraph at the end of the *Herald* article stressed that enquiries into the murder were still ongoing.

Cath moved Angus Livingstone's name to the top of the murder wall, next to John Craigie's. Even if Angus Livingstone was not the murderer, even if he had not killed so much as a fly in his entire life, he was still a part of this story because of Susan. Clearly he had known her – Iris had confirmed as much – but had he killed her?

What if he were just what he claimed to be – an innocent bystander? They do exist, you know.

I don't believe that. It doesn't fit. There was a side to Angus Livingstone that no one saw.

So this Livingstone bloke must be the killer, even after everything the cops said, even though everyone on the island thought it were Johnny. That's what you're thinking, isn't it, detective? That he was really more like my dad than anyone would realise, him and his fine way of talking and his bloody degree and his love for museums? He liked to be in control and he tended to lose his rag if he thought he was being made a fool of. When Mum gave him the boot he couldn't accept it and so he killed her. He killed Sonny because he could, to punish Mum. He killed me because I bust in on them – if I'd been left alive to talk he'd have gone down for life.

What about the gun, though? University lecturers don't carry guns. Not in this country, anyway.

Who cares about the frigging gun, or how he got hold of it? All I know is, he'd have found a way. Angus Livingstone was a planner, unlike Dad. He would have known people – lawyers, even cops, maybe. He couldae spun it as a joke, like one of those party games folk wind up playing when everyone's drunk – if you had to kill someone, how would you do it, rubbish like that. If the likes of my dad or Ronnie Mackintosh says the word gun, folk go diving under the table and calling the cops. With the likes of our Angus, everyone laughs and takes his word that it's only a parlour game. A thought experiment, he'd call it, like he were frigging Wittgenstein or something. You know it's true.

Since when have you been into Wittgenstein?

There's loads of stuff about me you don't know.

I love it that I don't know, Cath thought. She saw it clearly, the photograph she would take of Shirley now, if she could: looking into Zavaroni's from the street, the cool shadows of the interior contrasting with the bright white light of the pavement outside, Shirley up at the counter with her back to the door, yellow T-shirt and red purse, her head bent in concentration as she counted out coins.

A moment later she would come out on to the street and hand Cath an ice cream.

Hurry up and eat this. I want to get to the pub.

Cath drew a question mark on Livingstone's Post-it. She thought about returning to Glasgow, tracking down some of his colleagues from the university, trying to find out more about how he met Mary and why she left him. She really would be back at square one then. None of the Glasgow people would know about Susan Craigie, either, Cath felt sure of it. Whatever had happened afterwards, Angus Livingstone's time with Susan on the island was another life.

She was my mum. She could be a real pain in the arse but she was different from what people thought. She wasn't stupid and she wasn't a pushover but she did love my dad. She never did stop loving him, and that's why whatever was going on with this Livingstone bloke, she'd have put a stop to it. In the end she would have, because she knew it wouldae killed him. My dad, I mean. Dad couldnae live without her and she loved him. She loved me, too. She was scared for me, all the time. It used to drive me mad.

*

'WAS SHE YOUR GIRLFRIEND, love, this Alice?'

'I don't really know.' Cath wanted to cry then, to cry properly, but the tears wouldn't come.

'That's the way it is sometimes, isn't it?' Iris said. 'I had someone once and she didn't know, either. She was a teacher, from Iceland. Came over on an exchange programme with the Academy. She told me she was staying and we had a flat worked out for us and everything. Then the summer ended and she was gone. Didn't say a word, nothing. I was out of my mind with worry about what might have happened to her. Then a postcard arrived. Sorry, it said, with a picture of Reykjavik. I've still got it somewhere.'

'How awful.'

'I dream of her sometimes. It used to hurt but not any more. I'm glad to see her face.'

CATH PHOTOGRAPHED THE OBJECTS on Iris's mantelpiece, the china owl and the Murano glass tiger, the porcelain jug with the enamelled outline of Tenerife. She photographed the photographs – Ena and Valentine and Angela, focusing on the gilded edges of the photograph frames, their curlicued outlines clipped and stark against the painted wall, the faces of the sitters slightly blurred, like the photograph of Angus Livingstone had been in the *Herald*. She thought about how the photos would look once they'd been edited and enlarged and printed – like posters for a film, she thought, one of those Russian epics where everyone winds up dead or living in exile. Steve liked Russian films. Cath couldn't remember how she knew that, but she did.

Iris sat in her armchair by the window, watching her work. Cath felt aware of her but not distracted. It was almost as if they were making the images together.

'What will you do with these pictures?' Iris asked.

'I'd like them to be part of the project, if that's all right with you.'

'Does that mean they'll be exhibited?'

'I hope so, yes.'

'But they don't have anything to do with the rest of it – why you came here.'

'They do, though. You were here when it happened. You were Susan's friend.'

'I wish I'd been a better one. A better neighbour.' Iris crossed and uncrossed her hands. 'Who do you think killed them?'

'I can't be certain, but I think it was Angus Livingstone.'

'The archaeologist? That's not possible, surely.'

'I think it is. I don't have any proof, but I believe he did it. His wife was murdered too, you know. Last year.'

'Wife? I didn't know he had a wife. Whenever he came to the island he was always alone.'

'I think she was later. She was a lecturer at the university. Do you think you could come out to Straad with me?' Cath added. 'I'd like to have a look at his cottage, the one he was renovating. Can you remember where it was?'

'I expect so. I would once I got out there, I'm sure. Jessie will take us. If you wait here a moment I'll ask her. Do you want to go now?'

JESSIE MORECAMBE WAS IRIS'S neighbour from across the close, a part-time plumber and a full-time artist. Her blue Ford van had a deep scratch across the passenger door from where she'd miscalculated a turning into someone's driveway. She was somewhere in her thirties, Cath guessed. Hair cropped short, large hands roughened from constant immersion in turpentine and water.

'I'm from Liverpool originally. Been on the island ten years now. Wouldn't change a thing.'

Cath climbed into the van's narrow back seat. The vinyl upholstery was ripped in numerous places. Yellow foam stuffing poked out through the holes. 'Thanks for doing this,' she said. She felt overwhelmed, self-conscious. Two people she barely knew were altering their plans for her, just like that. They would look back on this afternoon as one they had shared.

'Don't worry about it. I love driving out to Straad. The beach is great for driftwood.' Jessie seemed curious about what Cath was doing but not intrusively so. It occurred to her that if she were to remain on the island permanently, she and Jessie might become friends.

Iris Docherty already was a friend, she realised. In that curious way that sometimes happens, they had fallen into close familiarity without ever meaning to.

The van bumped along the road, the same route she had taken with Alice. Jessie parked outside the village hall and they all got out.

'The cottage was on the beach road,' Iris said. 'Right at the end.'

'I can take the van all the way down, if you want.'

'I'm sure I can manage,' Iris said. 'It's easy going.'

Straad was really more of a hamlet than a village, a loose agglomeration of houses and farms. Water, water everywhere, the humped brown stripe of Inchmarnock Island, slumped in the firth. Steel-blue wavelets lapping at the heels of Kintyre and the Isle of Arran. They walked slowly along the foreshore, Jessie slightly in front. Iris moved with caution, leaning heavily on her cane. The loose gravel and dirt of the unmade road crunched beneath their feet.

'What was he like?' Cath asked. 'Livingstone?'

'Quiet. Softly spoken. But he could be talkative, you know, if you got him on to a subject that interested him. He loved the Stone Age artefacts in the museum. Said he never got tired of looking at them, the way they could magically transport you to another time. Those were the words he used – magically transport you. I can't say I warmed to him, if I'm honest. There was something distant about him. He was always polite though. What you might call a gentleman.'

To be in this place where Angus Livingstone had walked along the shoreline. Susan too, most likely, the two of them together. Had they stood and looked out at the water, hand in hand? Searched for fossils and prehistoric relics among the pebbles?

She imagined Susan laughing aloud, happy and in love. Cath had never once heard Susan laugh, she realised, not even in her head. The Susan she remembered was mouse-like and downtrodden, her thoughts concealed behind bland pleasantries and small talk.

From the way Iris talked about him, it seemed that Angus Livingstone hadn't gone in much for small talk. Was that why she hadn't taken to him – him and his Neolithic artefacts? Iris hadn't exactly called him sinister, yet the word seemed to fit.

'This is the one,' Iris said suddenly. She came to a halt. 'Look at the state it's in.'

They were standing in front of a terrace of three cottages. Two of them were pristine, well maintained. The third – the one on the right – looked badly neglected. Yellow knee-high grass sprouted behind the granite retaining wall, the windows of the lower storey opaque with dust. The place was unlived in, that was obvious, left to its own devices years ago. From the day of the murders? Possibly. What if Livingstone was inside, his mummified body withered to a bloodless husk? Cath pushed the thought away. She already knew how Livingstone had died. He hadn't even been on the island. Jessie Morecambe stood with her arms folded. She seemed totally unfazed and Cath liked her all the more for it. Iris was breathing hard. The walk had exhausted her.

'I'll go back and bring the van down,' Jessie said.

'There's no need,' said Iris.

Jessie stuck up two fingers and began walking back along the stony path towards the village hall. Iris raised her eyebrows and Cath smiled. The easy relationship between the two neighbours, the older woman and the younger, was unexpected, like so much else on the island. Perhaps Jessie reminded Iris of one of her nieces.

'This house was standing empty for a long time before he took it on,' Iris said. 'It's gone downhill since then, that's for sure. Shame when you think of the work he put in. Strange that he would abandon the place but there's no accounting for folk, as Ena would say.'

'He's dead,' Cath said. 'He died in a climbing accident. A friend of mine told me.'

The house gave her the willies. The house on Westland Road had managed to survive in spite of what happened there. Like Shirley, Cath thought. She'll no' go doon without a fight. Angus Livingstone's cottage was different. It had given up the ghost.

'I did wonder,' Iris said quietly. 'And with no kin to claim the place?'

'Not that I know of.'

If that were so then the house might stand empty until it fell down, until the end of time. Cath lifted the latch on the iron gate. The short brick pathway up to the door was obscured by weeds, and when Cath pressed her face to the glass of the filthy downstairs window she could see almost nothing. The outline of something large and dark against the opposite wall – a sideboard? – and to its right the shape of a fireplace, the mantelpiece cluttered with books and what looked like greetings cards.

One of the cards had been sent by Susan Craigie. There was no way Cath could know this, yet she felt certain of it, so certain it made her gut ache. The card would prove what Susan's notebook and the stack of old Christmas cards and Angus Livingstone's testimony at the FAI had refused to disclose – that Susan Craigie and Angus Livingstone had been lovers.

Cath reached out a hand and twisted the doorknob. The door was locked.

'You'll not get in,' Iris said. 'Not unless you're thinking of smashing a window.'

Take a rock from the beach and lob it through, claim it was an accident. Brandish the greetings card at the sheriff like a weapon.

This proves it, my lord. The man was a monster.

And what would it prove, exactly, even supposing Cath was right and the card was in there? That Susan Craigie had been in love with Angus Livingstone – bully for her. That hardly made him her killer. If anything it proved Johnny's motive, not Livingstone's guilt.

'You'd not do a silly thing like that, would you?' Iris said.

Cath shook her head. 'It's probably nothing.'

She could hear the sound of Jessie's van, jouncing along the uneven road towards them. There would be tools in the back, possibly glass-cutting equipment. Cath entertained a brief fantasy of herself and Jessie, returning to the cottage at sundown, removing the glass from one of the windows and climbing inside. Jessie looked like she'd be up for it, if Cath told her what they were looking for, what was at stake.

Youse got to be joking me. The moment a neighbour switches a light on you'd be running like rabbits.

The way Shirley used to cover her mouth just before she laughed. She was right though. Cath sighed. She knew she was not cut out for housebreaking, not the right stuff.

Where do you find a criminal when you need one?

It's just a card. You don't need it, trust me. Go home.

And where is home?

That's up to you, hen. You've no' so far to go though, I can smell it. Like a river coming down from the mountains. You're almost there.

2 I .

*YOU RETURNED TO THE island to take some photos, detective.
End of story.*

IF EVERYONE INVOLVED WITH the case was dead, Cath thought,
does it even matter now, who the killer was? John Craigie had
not been a good man, still less an innocent one. He had been
controlling and coercive and violent. He had made Susan's life a
misery, Shirley's too. If people thought of him as a murderer, was
that not justice, of a kind? Assuming justice was even possible
after so many years.

She used the Minolta to take some shots of the murder wall,
positioning herself carefully to highlight the alternating bars of
sunshine and shadow – like the bars of a prison cell – unfurling in
fuzzy stripes across the arrows and Post-its. She wanted the photographs to resemble a series of stills from a slightly old-fashioned
police procedural, one with a bad-tempered maverick detective and
a garrulous boss. Spoof photos, only looking like the real thing. She

examined the results on the viewing screen then began to dismantle the murder wall. There was nothing more to add.

Where would I hide the gun though? Cath asked herself again, later that night. She couldn't sleep. She had once been told that the best way to tackle insomnia was to do muscle relaxation exercises. Sometimes they worked and sometimes they didn't. Cath often found more relief in concentrating her mind upon something definite but abstract, like a word puzzle, or a memory game, or what she would do with the gun if she were Angus Livingstone.

Could you think logically about something like that if you'd just shot three people? Cath had read that this was why most murderers were caught — they hadn't reckoned with the aftermath of the act, the sense of disbelief and horror that inevitably sets in. They made stupid mistakes.

But what if you were a psychopath? Psychopaths thrived on the extraordinary because for them it was not extraordinary, just things going to plan.

Someone who planned would have worn gloves, or used a hand-kerchief to wipe the weapon clean of fingerprints. He could then dispose of the gun at his leisure, or even leave it behind at the scene of the crime. He could have taken it back to his cottage, hidden it there, though if the police had chosen to question him further then having the gun so close at hand would prove a terrible risk. Leaving it behind might actually be safer — less chance of being caught trying to get rid of it, less chance of stumbling over a tree root and muddying your clothes. Leaving it behind might also discourage the police from searching further afield. Why waste time chasing red herrings when all the evidence they needed to close the case lay right in front of them?

Three murdered bodies and a suicide husband – what more proof did you need?

The police searched the house though. Dusted it for fingerprints, used that stuff that shows up bloodstains under ultraviolet light. Still no sign of the gun.

There were things they didn't find though, we know that already. Boris the bastard, Mum's notebook – the cops never noticed them. If they had they would have been impounded. The cops fucked up, and if they missed the stuff in the cupboard who knows what else they missed.

Do you have to think of everything?

Why break a lifetime's habit?

You were always the better detective. I was only the sidekick.

Och, bollocks.

Bollocks yourself.

We gonnae have a look then, or what?

Tomorrow, Cath mumbled. She felt unbearably sleepy all of a sudden. Soon as it gets light.

SHE REALLY WASN'T MUCH of a detective, Cath thought afterwards. If she had been, she would have noticed the shoes in the porch the moment she arrived. Black trainers with an orange trim. Saheed's. As it happened, she saw them only in retrospect, after she had used her key to enter the house, after she had stepped into the hallway and closed the front door, after Saheed appeared in the kitchen doorway and asked her what the hell – no, what the fuck – she thought she was doing there. A kind of trace memory, a phantom rewind: the trainers, yes of course, why didn't I clock them? Saheed was wearing grey plimsolls, simple and stylish and perfect for indoors, much more suitable than the muddy Nikes next to the doormat.

Cath held out the key.

'I found this,' she said, lamely. Look up 'red-handed' in a picture dictionary and the way she appeared at that moment would make a good illustration.

'The heck you did. How long have you been sneaking in here?'

'Only the once, I promise. The night you called to say Alice had gone missing. You wanted me to come over and see if she was here, remember?' She told him about the flowerpot, about finding the key. 'I was worried. That she'd done something stupid. I came inside to check.'

The truth, or very nearly, although it didn't sound like it. It sounded deeply dodgy, the kind of excuse the prime suspect in a TV cop show might blurt out just before the detective sergeant slaps on the handcuffs.

'So why are you here now, then? To search through her stuff? I'll take that, thanks.' He snatched the key from her hand. They glared at each other, a standoff. 'No wonder she was going crazy out here.'

'Is Alice all right?'

'She's a hell of a lot better for getting far away from you.'

'Saheed, I didn't mean—'

'I could call the cops, you know that? Breaking and entering.'

'I didn't break in. I didn't break anything.'

'You know what, I don't care any more. I'm here to pack up Ally's things and then we're selling this place. She's not coming back here, ever. She deleted your number. And before you go accusing me of anything, no, I didn't tell her to, she just did it. Told me she was sorry and the whole thing with moving to the island had been a mistake. She said she blocked your email as well so if you were thinking of trying to screw her up again, forget it.'

Like her own explanation for entering the house, it sounded like a lie. Cath knew it was the truth, though. That leaden feeling in her stomach. She'd known it since Alice's last phone call. Whatever connection had existed between them had been broken.

'Can we talk?' she said. 'I mean, properly. I'll go afterwards, I promise. I really am sorry about everything.'

'Why would you know what she needs, what's right for her?' He still sounded furious. 'She was getting better before she came here.'

'Why did she come here in the first place, if she was so OK with everything?' Cath couldn't help herself. The grief she felt, a sharpness, like flowers of ice were sprouting inside her lungs. At least with Adam she had the explanation she needed – he was a dick. With Alice, nothing was settled, it was all loose ends. Alice had been scared. What kind of pressure had she been put under, to return to London?

Did Saheed not have a point, though? Cath had known Alice less than three months. How could she be so certain of what was good for her?

People are cunts, as Steve would say. Don't blame yourself for that.

'Listen,' Cath said. 'This isn't about Alice. I didn't come over here today because of Alice. This is about the house, about what happened here before.'

'More of this murder bullshit?' Saheed threw up his hands. 'Fuck that too. I don't want to know.'

But even as he spoke the words, Cath could see he had decided to hear her out. There was a part of Saheed that did want to know, Cath realised, that was as compelled by the story as she was. Hadn't Alice once told her he was addicted to cop shows? He had asked for Cath's help the night of the phone call and she had given it. Maybe this was Saheed's way of repaying that debt. Maybe he was just relieved he would soon be leaving.

'Stay if you want,' he said. 'I was making coffee anyway.'

THIS WOULD BE HER last time inside the Craigie house. Whatever happened next, this would be final. Cath glanced sideways towards Alice's bedroom. The door was ajar. Something of Saheed's – a black T-shirt, or sweatshirt – lay adrift on the floor. She spotted the corner of a wheelie bag with the zip half open.

Alice's presence seemed obliterated, gone.

'I've already checked,' Saheed was saying. 'There's nothing to find.'

The door to the cupboard at the end of the landing was standing wide open. It had always been closed before, Cath thought. Always. Even after Alice had put a new lock on, she had kept the door closed. Cath felt a sense of disquiet, dismay almost. She knelt on the floor and peered inside. The cupboard's interior was bare, a triangular void. Cath ran her hands over the tongue-and-groove panels, wondered why anyone would bother to lavish such attention upon a cupboard that was so seldom used. The workmanship was beautifully exact, the ends of the boards that lined the walls rising up to meet the boards that covered the cupboard's sloping ceiling in a perfect herringbone.

Patterning so exquisite and so harmonious it made you feel calmer just to look at it, yet its creator had been a misfit and a misanthrope, the kind of throwback who seemed to belong to an earlier age. Cath closed her eyes, imagining John Craigie in the smock and leather trews of a ship's carpenter, eleven months at sea and the twelfth at home, drunk. Sparring and fighting with the other sailors, his wife on shore a distant memory, an irrelevant daydream.

Cath's searching fingers noted an irregularity in the wood of the left-hand wall, a deeper groove, cutting across the upright divisions between the boards. She shifted her body to let in more light, but it was still hard to see. Not just a groove, but a rectangular outline, some two feet by three. Was it some kind of hatchway? She traced her fingers around its perimeter – as so often when the light was inadequate, Cath relied on touch as well as sight to gain a sense of what was there. Four retaining screws, one in each corner. A door in the wall.

Cath leaned back on her haunches, feeling dizzy. The police couldn't have missed this, surely? There was something here.

'What?' said Saheed. He leaned forward, pressing a hand against her shoulder, straining to see.

'Don't, you're blocking the light.'

'Looks like a safe to me, some sort of stash. I'll fetch a screw-driver.'

He disappeared downstairs, plimsolled feet thumping on the bare treads. Cath listened to the sound of his footfalls, heavy and light at the same time, bomp bomp bomp. She ran her fingers over the panelling once again, testing the sharp division where the boards had been cut. The four screws were positioned exactly, their heads neatly recessed. John Craigie had created this hidey hole, but what had been its purpose? Somewhere to secrete money, or maybe drugs? Stolen jewellery? What?

The realisation stole over her then, like a stray piece of darkness, a shadow emanating directly from behind the panel: this must be where the gun was, where it had been all along. They were about to find the murder weapon.

Cath's hands felt cold, and her teeth were chattering. This was not at all the way she had imagined it would be.

'Hey,' Saheed said. He was back, with the promised screwdriver. Red handle, black stripe, a Phillips. It looked brand new. 'Shift over a bit.'

Cath moved back from the cupboard's entrance, allowing him access. 'Be careful,' she said.

Saheed glanced at her over his shoulder. 'I'm not going to find anything dead in here, am I?'

'I don't think so.' Her lips felt numb. 'How should I know?'

'I guess we'll find out together, then.'

He began to remove the screws, laying them carefully to one side on the floor as they came free. As the final screw began to loosen, Saheed pressed his left hand against the panel to prevent it from falling outwards. He placed the screwdriver on the ground between his knees, levered the hatch from its moorings and propped it upright against the wall.

'It's empty,' he said. He sounded rattled. 'I think it is, anyway. I can't really see.' He shoved his head partway inside the hole, and Cath found she had to resist the urge to tell him not to do that, that he should be careful, that there might be something down there. Something dangerous.

'Let me have a look,' she said instead. She had imagined it so clearly – the boarded-out cubby hole, the weapon wrapped in a greasy rag or blood-spattered T-shirt. She felt starkly disappointed, yet the gun's apparent absence emboldened her, too. The hole was nothing, after all, just a weird little empty space at the heart of the house. Like the blocked-off room inside Shirley's dolls' house, with no reason for existing other than that it was there. Stuffed with porn magazines, probably – John Craigie's secret stash. No wonder he'd kept the cupboard locked. Now everything made sense.

'Be my guest.' Saheed moved aside and as Cath slid over towards the hole their bodies briefly touched. Cath caught a wisp of his odour – acrid and masculine – and it made her think of Alice. She peered blindly into the hole, then put in her hand. The space went back a long way, much further than she would have guessed. Her fingers brushed against stone, dry and gritty with a coating of mud, or maybe brick dust. She felt around, parsing the space, which seemed roughly box-shaped, only the box had no bottom. Below the lower edge of the gap in the wall, the hole went straight down. Further than she could feel anyway, even with her arm inserted all the way to the elbow.

'We need a torch,' she said. Her teeth were still chattering.

'Yeah, sure.' Saheed went back downstairs. Cath withdrew her arm from the hole. There was dust on her sleeve and on her fingertips, otherwise nothing. Saheed came back with the torch, a black rubber camping light. 'I bought this for Alice,' he said. 'In case there was a power cut.'

The torch's switch was stiff to operate but it made a good light. Cath shone the beam into the hole, swinging it back and forth like a searchlight. She peered inside again, expecting more nothingness, the remains of a blocked-up chimney most likely, they should have thought of that earlier.

She glimpsed the diagonal stripe of a stair-tread, below it another and another after that. A miniature staircase, leading downwards into the dark. Bare wood, worn smooth with time, the steps decreasing gradually in width as they went down. Too small for a child, too large for a dolls' house. The whole structure was ludicrous, impossible, and yet how could it be impossible when she was looking right at it?

Cath rocked back on her heels. She brushed a hand across her face.

'What's down there?' said Saheed. 'Shove over, will you.' He grabbed the torch from her hand, sent the beam skittering back and forth, like the light from a swinging bulb in a darkened hallway. He shone the light into the hole. Cath stared at the back of his head, haloed in yellow. She felt sticky with dread.

'What,' Saheed said quietly, 'the actual fuck?'

Cath was silent. His incredulity was reassuring, she realised, the calmness overtaking her nerves like an injection of sedative. He saw what she saw, so it must be real. The miniature staircase seemed the embodiment of a delusion, a construction so miraculous it veered towards the insane. She pictured John Craigie as she had so often seen him: slumped in front of the television, chugging a bottle of beer and saying nothing to no one. A genius, Alice had said. A madman, said Richard Dadd's doctors. Cath found she was with Saheed: what the actual fuck.

'I think we should leave it,' she said at last. 'Put everything back how it was.'

'Did you know this was here?'

'Of course not. The cupboard was always closed before. Shirley said the door used to swing open. People kept banging into it in the night, so they kept it locked.'

'You wouldn't though, would you?'

'Wouldn't what?'

'Bang into it. You can get past easily, even with the cupboard door wide open.'

'Maybe not in the dark.'

'Maybe not.' Saheed turned to look at her. 'This is weird shit though. Why would you build a staircase inside a cupboard?'

So our good neighbours could come and go as they pleased. So she could come and go, more like, that filthy-minded queen of his. He believed he were in love with her and could be he was. Stranger things have happened. Ask Bridget Cleary.

What are you talking about?

'I see Queen Mab hath been with you. She is the fairies' midwife, and she comes in shape no bigger than an agate stone.' Shakespeare, that is. Romeo and Juliet. We did it with Mrs Mackenzie, don't you remember? That Richard Dadd bloke you're always on about who murdered his father – he painted Mab's portrait.

Cath shrugged. 'To prove that it could be done? To test his skill? John Craigie made all kinds of things. He made that dolls' house downstairs, did Alice tell you?'

'She told me to sell it, give it to house clearance, whatever. Just so long as I got rid of it.' Saheed turned back towards the cupboard, put his arm down inside the hole. 'Jesus. How far do you think it goes down?'

Cath remembered Alice telling her about weird geometry, the

article she'd seen when she went through Alice's papers, the infinite staircase. Penrose's Steps could not be constructed, only drawn, yet the diagrams had clearly shown how the staircase would look. How could something that did not exist, still exist? Was the angle between reality and illusion really so small?

'I don't know,' Cath said. 'I think he was mentally ill. John Craigie. I believe he heard voices.'

'Voices? The guy gunned down three people. He was out of his tree.'

'We don't know it was him. Not for sure. He was—'

Lonely, Cath thought. Like a fish out of water. Ensnared by his own wild imaginings, like Richard Dadd. And it was Dadd the staircase in the cupboard brought most clearly to mind. The obsessive, intricate neatness of it, the inherent darkness, thickly clotted as the overworked background of Dadd's unfinished masterpiece, *The Fairy Feller's Master Stroke*.

The sense that it had been thought about, and thought about, and thought about until the balance of the maker's mind had become disturbed.

'Like I said, out of his tree,' Saheed said. He sounded irritated, one step from losing it. Then he drew in his breath. 'There's something down here, I can feel it.' His cheek was pressed to the wooden panelling, his arm thrust inside the hole all the way to his shoulder. He grunted. 'Fuck. Got it.' A moment later his arm reappeared. He was holding something, Cath saw, a whitish bundle. Dirty cloth, with a faint blue stripe. Looked like an old tea towel.

'It's heavy.' Saheed backed out of the cupboard, dumped the bundle on the floor. He poked at it with his forefinger. 'Feels like metal.'

'We shouldn't touch it,' Cath said. 'We should call the police.'

'What if it's an old mouth organ? The haunted harmonica. They'd think we were total plonkers and they'd be right.'

The corner of his mouth twitched. He had cobweb stuck to his forehead, a great grey rag of it. Suddenly they were both laughing. The laughter tore at Cath's heart like tears.

'I think this is it,' she said. 'This is what we've been looking for.'

'Hang on,' said Saheed. He went into Alice's bedroom and Cath could hear him unzipping the wheelie bag. He came back with a pen, a blue Bic biro, which he used to flip back a corner of the grubby material.

They glimpsed the dull gleam of metal. Cath had never seen a gun before, not in real life, but she knew that was what they were looking at. Even before they had fully unwrapped it, it was obvious. Cath stared down at the weapon, thinking how there was nothing that could have prepared her for how sinister a gun is really, how naked its purpose. Almost as if it had been lying in wait for them, watching for its chance, driven newly insane through its internment of twenty years.

'There's something in with it, look,' said Saheed. He seemed as overwhelmed as she did, like someone who had sobered up suddenly after an all-night drinking binge, and yes he was right, Cath saw, there was something wrapped around the gun besides the stained tea towel, a crumpled piece of paper. Saheed hunkered down, used the Bic again to draw the paper forward without touching the gun. He didn't want to get his fingerprints on it, Cath supposed. She felt a grudging admiration, that Saheed could retain his capacity for logic even in the shock of this moment. Yet at the same time she recognised – she knew for certain – there was more than just logic here, that his reticence was born of an instinct Saheed might not even be aware of: the desire not to be contaminated, not to acknowledge that such a thing as the gun even existed.

'We shouldn't touch it,' Cath said, again.

'I'm not. I thought you'd want to see what this is though – before we let the cops get their hands on it, I mean.'

A piece of notepaper, yellow with age. It looked like it had been screwed into a ball and then flattened out again, though you could see from the deeper marks crossing it at right angles how it had been folded neatly in four before that, to fit inside an envelope maybe, or simply to hide its contents from curious eyes. The note was handwritten, the same writing, Cath could see that at once, that had filled the pages of the notebook found in the Persil box. **Dear Angus**, read the first line, **I am sorry but I cannot see a way through this. The thought of hurting you kills me but this has to end.** There was more, but Cath found herself reluctant to read any further. The words were so naked, so private. The proof Cath had been searching for, that she had sensed from the beginning was here to be found.

She did not know which was stronger – the sorrow or the relief.

'The man who wasn't there,' she said, quietly. Her throat felt tight with tears. 'Only he was.'

'What are you on about?'

'The guy Susan Craigie was writing to. It's what we used to call him.'

'You and Alice, you mean?'

Cath shook her head. 'Doesn't matter.'

Not Alice, not this time. Me and Shirley, she wanted to say, I'm talking about Shirley. There was no way to explain.

Saheed was silent for a moment. Cath could feel his discomfort – with the situation, with her obvious distress. Good, she thought, serves him right, though there was little anger left in her. That part seemed to be over.

'This proves it though, doesn't it?' Saheed said at last. 'That Craigie bloke must have found this note she'd written, realised his wife was having an affair. The note was his trigger.'

'I don't think so,' Cath said. Her thoughts flew in an avalanche, faster than light, yet her words sounded slow in her own ears, deliberate, like she was walking along a clifftop and afraid of falling. 'If he'd only just found the note he wouldn't have had a gun. And if he found the note earlier – long enough before the murders to think how he might get a gun – he wouldn't have waited that long to act on it. It's like Shirley said,' she added. 'John Craigie wasn't a planner. If he'd wanted someone killing he'd have used his fists.'

'What do you mean, like Shirley said? She's dead, isn't she?'

'Yes, she's dead, but that isn't the point.' Cath felt on the verge of laughter, high on revelation. 'I think Angus Livingstone – Susan's lover – came here intending to confront her with the note, to throw it back in her face. It was Angus who killed them. Then when John Craigie came home and discovered his family murdered, he found the note, too. That's how he knew who the killer was – either that, or he suspected beforehand and the note confirmed it. That's why the gun and the note are together – they're the proof of what happened.'

'Why not take the gun with him, though? If he meant to kill this other guy, I mean?'

Cath shook her head. 'Perhaps he didn't mean to kill him. Or even if he did, he knew that using the gun himself would contaminate the evidence.'

'So you reckon he hid them inside the cupboard for safekeeping? That's mad – why didn't he just call the police?'

'Maybe he would have done – after.'

After he found Angus Livingstone and beat the living shit out of him. After he wore out his grief with his rage. The way he did with Iain Fletcher, only this time with no Jimmy Matheson to keep him from—

From the singing in his ears. From her song, Mab's song. That, and his own bleak madness.

She was mine and youse fucking stole her. Now you'll pay.

Only the gun and the note remained.

He left them with her and she kept them safe for him. All these years.

Her? Do you mean Queen Mab?

No, I mean the wind in the willows. Who d'ye think I mean?

'WHAT DO WE SAY, though?' Saheed said, later. 'If we show the police where we found the gun, we'll never hear the end of it. The place'll be swarming with TV cameras and shit. They might even stop me putting the house on the market. I don't want Alice hearing about that staircase – it would make her freak out again.'

'We can say we found the gun in the bureau, in Sonny's old room. You've been cleaning the place out, remember? You were checking inside the drawers and it was just – there.'

'Yeah, but what were you doing here? I mean, how come you happened to be here when I found it?'

'That's easy — I came over to return the spare key.'

They exchanged glances, then cautious half-smiles. Saheed nodded.

'OK then but you'll have to call them. I don't trust cops. One look at me and they'll say the gun's mine. Give them half a chance and they'll be claiming I'm the killer.'

'It happened twenty years ago. You were in primary school.'

'Like I said, you don't know cops.'

Told you he was dishy. Too bad he's married, though.

He's still an arsehole. Cath felt in her backpack for her phone. *Why do you always go for arseholes?*

You can talk. Shirley turned her head in that way she had, the ends of her hair flashing silver in the light from the window. *Anyway, arseholes are better-looking, or haven't you heard?*

2 2 .

NORAH FINALLY CAME THROUGH on her promise. On a warm day in early July, Cath travelled across to the mainland for a meeting and lunch at Margo Kasabian's studio in Milngavie. Margo Kasabian came to the door in black jeans and with her hair pulled back from her face in a long brown ponytail. She spoke with a soft Eastern European accent. From her work – intense, pin-sharp street scenes, often shot at night and technically superb – Cath had imagined she would be aloof and reticent and probably intimidating. In fact she was warm and energetic and tactile, a darting, wiry woman with expressive hand gestures.

'I like these, these are good,' she said, once they'd had coffee. She laid out Cath's prints in sequence on a long white trestle table. She seemed especially taken with the Maryhill photographs, Mary Chant's house, the shot of the woman coming out of the betting shop, and it was these she kept returning to, moving them from one juxtaposition to another and back again. Then she said she would be keen to use some of them in a group exhibition she was curating for a gallery in Manchester the following spring. 'You have captured,

I don't know, something disturbing and yet so normal at the same time. The way we all see these sights and then move on down the street. A person could be anything, and we'll never know. Is that what you meant with these?'

'You put it so beautifully,' Cath said. 'I'm not good with context.' She laughed. Margo had not so much as mentioned Adam Fairlie and Cath was relieved.

'Text is not your job. These are your job.' Margo lifted one of the photos – the one of Mary Chant's empty wheelie bins – into the light from the Velux window that ran the length of the studio. 'This was a horrible thing, with Mary. I met her only once or twice, when she was still with Angus, I mean, but everybody liked her.'

'You knew Mary's husband?'

'Angus was in History and Archaeology so I didn't see him at work all that often but I knew him from the university gun club. We became good friends, actually. We were all devastated when he had his accident. So soon after Mary, too. I think it had been preying on his mind.' She paused. Cath stared at her. That stomach-lurching feeling again, as if a thing she'd been searching for forever now lay plainly in sight.

'People always look like that when I tell them I'm in a gun club,' Margo added. 'I think I enjoy it because it is so opposite from my normal work. A different kind of shooting.' She smiled. 'It is perfectly safe, you know. We are only permitted to use the guns on the club premises. No one would ever dream of taking them outside.'

23.

'SO WHAT'S THE LATEST?' said Steve. They were sitting on a bench in the Winter Gardens, eating fish and chips. Cath had dropped in at the shop the week before, on the way back from her meeting with Margo. She had told Steve about finding the gun and for a wonder Steve had seemed interested. He'd also said he was thinking about coming across to the island one weekend.

'If the mountain won't come to Mohammed,' he added. He shrugged, smiled in a sheepish way that wasn't like him. Cath privately thought there was no way the visit would happen but here it was, happening.

It was good to see him.

'It's definitely the murder weapon,' Cath said. 'Or rather, it's the same kind of gun as the gun that fired the bullets that killed the Craigies. The forensic traces on the weapon itself are very faint now though, apparently. They'll take some time to verify. There was stronger DNA on the tea towel – some skin flakes and a couple of hairs. The hairs are John Craigie's – they know that for certain. They haven't identified the skin or the traces on the gun yet. The police are trying to track down Angus Livingstone's brother, to see if there's a match – Susan's note convinced them, I think. And this is important for Mary's case, too. The brothers were out of touch for decades, apparently. They assure me they'll find him, though.'

'It's strange he didn't take the note away with him. This Livingstone bloke, I mean. After he shot them.'

'I've been wondering about that, too. But I think it was just a mistake he made. Not the only one, either. If the police had had reason to link Angus with Susan – if they'd known about their affair – they'd have been all over him in five minutes. But they never did.'

'And no one thought to take any DNA samples from Livingstone at the time of the murders?'

'He was never a suspect. A witness to Johnny's death, but nothing more. So far as the police were concerned, he was nobody.'

I met a man who wasn't there.

You and me both.

'Well, they'll be kicking themselves now for sure, the useless wallies.' He ate another chip. 'Do you know when you're coming back yet?'

'I'm thinking of staying, actually. On the island.'

Steve gave her a look. 'You're not serious?'

'I don't mean I'd leave the shop. I thought Norah and I could split the hours – she could do four days and I'd do three. I can easily commute. Catch the seven o'clock ferry and I'm in by nine. Loads of people manage it. If I sell the Partick flat I could buy something outright, dump the mortgage. Mildred has said she'll take my stuff on a regular basis. You know, at the gallery. That means I'll be part of her stable – I'll get more exposure. More freelance work too, hopefully.'

'You've already spoken to her?'

'We had a conversation, yes. I'm not committed to anything yet but the option is there.'

Steve coughed and wiped his nose on his sleeve, something he always did when he was nervous.

Bet he doesn't know he does that. If he wasn't so cute it would be disgusting.

Cute? Steve? You are joking.

Don't tell me you haven't noticed because I'll know you're fibbing.

Steve was sane, Cath realised. Sane in a mad way of course, but completely solid. Cath doubted he'd ever knowingly told a lie.

'What about the other guy believing in fairies?' Steve said. He was trying to change the subject, Cath could tell, another thing he always did when he was nervous. 'Did that all turn out to be bullshit or what?'

'A red herring, I think,' Cath said. She smiled. Every detective story has to have a red herring, that's the rule. 'From what James Matheson said, John Craigie had a difficult childhood. The one person who made him feel safe was his grandmother. He loved her and he loved the stories she told. For his grandmother they were just stories, the kind you make up to keep your grandchildren entertained, only Johnny took them seriously. They gave him somewhere to escape to, probably. I don't know.'

I don't know either an' I were stuck with having him as a father. Just because you can't see something disnae mean it's no' there – ask any physicist. Why does anyone believe in anything?

290

'Did I ever tell you my dad was an astronomer?' Steve said suddenly.

'I don't think so.' From what Cath could remember, Steve had never mentioned his father to her at all. She knew his mother lived up in the Highlands somewhere – Oban, she thought – though Steve had grown up in Glasgow. If anything, Cath had always assumed Steve's dad must have walked out when Steve was a child. She'd never asked.

'I don't mean as a job. He worked for British Telecom. But he kept up with all the latest. Used to go on field trips with this club he was in. Even wrote articles for some of the magazines. He absolutely believed we'd make contact with aliens one day. He used to talk to me about it when I was a kid, said that in the future people would look back on the world today as if it were the Stone Age. Used to scare me shitless. I was convinced aliens were coming to get us. I never told Dad to shut up though. There was something about him when he got started, a look in his eyes, like the thought of speaking with aliens was all he was living for.

'Dad used to suffer from depression,' Steve added. 'For ages he'd be all right, then something would happen and he'd be back down again. Just tiny things could set it off, stuff most folk wouldn't take account of, but Dad was Dad. You'll never guess what did for him?' He smiled and tried to laugh, didn't quite make it. 'That mad cow thing. You remember how everyone was convinced thousands of people were going to die from eating hamburgers? Dad couldn't stop worrying about it. I don't mean just normal worrying, it was all he thought about. He started doing these memory tests, and every time his score went down a point he thought that was proof. Mum convinced him to see a doctor at one point. They ran a load of tests, told him he was fine, that he had nothing to worry about and for a while he was OK. It all started up again, though. I even wrote a letter to the BBC, telling them they should take mad cow disease off the news because they were frightening my dad. Bet someone had a right laugh over that. Anyway, in the end Dad couldn't stand it any more. He killed himself by touching a live wire. It happened at work. The health and safety wrote it off as an accident but Mum and I both knew.'

'God, Steve, I'm sorry.'

'Don't worry about it. It was twenty years ago. If there was one thing Dad taught me it was not to worry, because worrying can kill you, literally. He was an amazing bloke though, my dad. Kindest guy you'd ever meet. Anyway, the reason I'm telling you all this is that if there was one person in the world who would have believed in all that fairy shit it was my dad. Give him half an hour after work for a cup of tea and he'd have been down on his knees in the bushes, searching for them. There were people who said Dad had a screw loose but they didn't really know him. When he was low the world terrified him but he never stopped seeing the wonder in it, either. Most people stop seeing the wonder before they're even half grown.'

'What was his name?'

'Gordon. Gordon Fraser.'

'I wish I'd met him.'

'Aye, well.' Steve wiped his nose on his sleeve again, looked about himself. 'It's all right here, isn't it? Can't think why I've never been over before.'

'You'll have an excuse to visit more often now, won't you? Now that I'm staying, I mean.'

'Only if you promise to shoot me if I start going native.'

He had accepted her decision, Cath realised. No tantrums and no pressure, no trying to talk her out of it or telling her she was crazy. Adam would have told her she was making a mistake, a big one, shutting herself off out here, all that guff. Not because he cared what became of her, but because it might turn out to be less convenient for him. What Adam thought didn't matter though, not any more. He was a leftover, a blast from the past, a face she had glimpsed once in a crowd and then forgotten.

'Steve,' Cath said. 'What's the most personal question you've ever been asked?'

'I don't know. Are you gay, I guess. I told him we could find out, if he wanted, which was a stupid idea because I knew the guy was mental and he'd fuck up my life. Why?'

'I once asked Shirley if she'd ever thought of running away from the island – just packing a bag and leaving – and she said all the time. I've never forgotten that. I should have tried to help her.'

'Don't be daft. All kids say things like that. You could never have known.'

The sky was bright and clear, almost colourless. The last ferry of the day hove into view, gliding across the bay towards the harbour. Steve screwed up the paper with the remains of his chips and got to his feet.

'Best get going, I suppose. Don't want to miss the boat.'

They walked back along the promenade to the ferry terminal. Steve bent quickly to kiss her, then disappeared inside.

ACKNOWLEDGEMENTS

The Good Neighbours passed through many stages of evolution in its passage from my hard drive to the printed page, not least a five-hundred-mile relocation. I would like to thank all those who have travelled alongside me on this journey – the camaraderie and supportiveness of my writing family have been and remain boons beyond price.

The life and works of Richard Dadd have haunted my imagination for decades, and I can only hope that the creative fruits of that possession are to some small extent worthy of their inspiration. I would also like to make mention of John Cornwell's 1984 book *Earth to Earth*, in which he chronicles his quest to uncover the mystery surrounding the tragic and untimely deaths of three last surviving members of a Devon family. Cornwell's search for answers, together with my own memories of what I learned about the case while living in Exeter, provided the initial stimulus for *The Good Neighbours*. Though its strands are now well hidden, the Luxtons' sad story remains inextricably woven into my novel's DNA.

In addition, I would like especially to thank my agent, Anna

Webber, for her steadfast support and insight, as well as my editor Jon Riley and the entire team at riverrun for their enthusiasm and continuing commitment to my work. Thanks to my amazing mother, Monica Allan, for the hours of laughter and soul-searching, and to my partner, Chris Priest, for being exceptional in every way.